THE BODY AT CARNIVAL BRIDGE

AN IRIS WOODMORE MYSTERY

MICHELLE SALTER

Boldwood

First published in Great Britain in 2023 by Boldwood Books Ltd.

Copyright © Michelle Salter, 2023

Cover Design by Lawston Design

Cover Photography: Lawston Design

A CIP catalogue record for this book is available from the British Library.

Paperback ISBN 978-1-83751-057-3

Large Print ISBN 978-1-83751-059-7

Hardback ISBN 978-1-83751-058-0

Ebook ISBN 978-1-83751-060-3

Kindle ISBN 978-1-83751-061-0

Audio CD ISBN 978-1-83751-052-8

MP3 CD ISBN 978-1-83751-053-5

Digital audio download ISBN 978-1-83751-054-2

Boldwood Books Ltd
23 Bowerdean Street
London SW6 3TN
www.boldwoodbooks.com

For Mum & Dad

1

DEPTFORD, LONDON

September 1922

'Iris Woodmore. Journalist.' This was a lie. Unemployed was a more accurate description of my current status.

The young woman ran a pen down a list of names until she came to mine. 'Thank you, Miss Woodmore. Please go through.'

A police constable opened the gates of Timpson Foods. Newspaper articles had branded Constance Timpson a dangerous socialist, but I hadn't expected this level of security.

From the outside, the factory appeared to be a single grey-stone building. Once inside the gates, I could see it was a series of separate buildings. A makeshift stage was surrounded on three sides by the factory – it faced outwards, separated from the grimy streets of Deptford by a tall iron gate and railings.

PC Ben Gilbert was standing by the stage. I started to walk towards him, then realised that Percy Baverstock was by his side. I pulled my straw hat down over my eyes and moved sideways to hide among a throng of people. Ben hadn't said anything about Percy being there. He'd probably kept it from me on purpose in case it stopped me from attending. I'd been away for nearly a year and had only told my close family I was back in England.

Constance Timpson wafted into view, and I saw Percy's eyes light up. He looked like his old self, laughing and pushing his mop of unruly hair back over his eyes. Although Ben was smiling too, he didn't share Percy's carefree manner. In matters of the heart, things hadn't worked out for either of them. Nor had they for me, for that matter. But Percy and I would recover. I wasn't so sure about Ben.

I watched Percy and Constance walk away and waited until they were out of view before going over to Ben. I knew I was being silly. There was no point in being there if I wasn't going to talk to Constance. I just hadn't counted on Percy's presence.

'You came.' Ben's tone suggested he knew I would. When he'd handed me the invitation, I'd been annoyed with him for telling Constance I was back. At first, I'd said I couldn't attend, then curiosity had got the better of me. And I had another motive. Constance was keen to generate more favourable press coverage than she was currently receiving. It occurred to me that if I wrote an article about her work, I could use it to approach a few editors.

'I didn't expect to see so many police here.' Another police constable, a female one, to my surprise, was standing on the other side of the stage.

Ben pulled me closer and lowered his voice. 'Constance found a threatening letter on her desk this morning.'

'And she still decided to go ahead with this?' The forecourt was filling up with workers from the factory.

'She couldn't be persuaded to cancel. She said it's too important.'

Constance Timpson had taken full control of the Timpson

Foods empire earlier that year after the death of her mother, Lady Delphina Timpson (née Hinchcliffe). Lady Timpson had inherited Hinchcliffe Holdings from her father, and apart from renaming it, she'd run his food production company in exactly the same manner that he had.

Constance, on the other hand, had made radical changes since taking over. She'd removed all child workers from the company's factories and female employees now received the same salaries as their male counterparts. This made her extremely unpopular with trade unions and fellow business owners.

Today's announcement was going to do nothing to improve her popularity. Constance had to explain why she was closing the Basingstoke Canal, the navigation that linked the factory in Deptford with the Tolfree & Timpson biscuit plant in Walden. The Deptford barge workers had been offered alternative jobs in Timpson factories, but the closure of the navigation would have wider implications for the biscuit factory and other manufacturers in Walden who used the canal to transport their goods.

Constance had picked a Friday afternoon to make her speech and had closed both factories early, transporting the Tolfree & Timpson workers up to Deptford by charabanc so they could listen. Refreshments would be provided afterwards, then her staff would be free to start their weekends early.

A sudden influx of employees arriving from the Walden factory caused the forecourt to fill up. It was a sultry September afternoon and the treacly scent coming from the factory's chimneys merged with the clammy odour of a crush of bodies.

Ben called over to the female police constable. 'WPC Jones, the staff from Tolfree & Timpson have arrived. Once they're all inside, can you make sure the gate is closed.'

The blonde WPC nodded and strode towards the woman at the entrance who was still checking names off her list.

Ben turned back to me. 'Percy's here.'

'I saw him.'

'He's appointed himself Constance's protector. I think he'd like to be her knight in shining armour.'

This was typical of Percy. After everything that had happened, I was pleased that he was still enamoured of Constance. 'How is he?'

Ben smiled. 'His old self.'

'Still dancing?'

'Oh, yes. He goes to the Foxtrot Club every Friday night. He'll probably try to persuade Constance to go with him tonight, but I don't think it's her style.'

'Have you been there?' I didn't think dancing was Ben's style either. Then again, I'd never have imagined him policing the streets of London. In truth, I didn't like city police officers much; I remembered their treatment of the suffragettes. But things seemed to have worked out for Ben. Not least, the cosy domestic arrangement he had with my gran and aunt.

While I'd been away on my travels, my father's housekeeper, Lizzy, had written to tell me Ben had decided to leave Walden and join the Metropolitan Police. Like me, he'd found the confines of the small market town we'd grown up in too suffocating after the loss of our close childhood friend. Thanks to Lizzy's powers of persuasion, he was now lodging with my grandmother and Aunt Maud in Hither Green.

When I'd shown up at Gran's door, it had soon become apparent that Ben had usurped my position in the household. I hadn't expected to receive a prodigal's welcome, neither had I expected to feel like a cuckoo in the nest. Gran and Aunt Maud doted on Ben and I had to play second fiddle.

'Percy dragged me to the club once. I ended up having to escort him back to his flat after "a few too many lemonades", as he put it.'

Ben glanced over my shoulder. 'Brace yourself. Here he comes with Constance.'

'Iris. How lovely to see you again.' Constance Timpson was as elegant and poised as ever in a silk navy suit. 'I'm so glad you could come.'

'It was kind of you to invite me.' I smiled at her and Percy, but he stared down at his shoes.

'I'm about to make my speech. Let's chat afterwards,' she said in her silvery voice.

Ben took Constance's arm. 'I'll be to the left of the stage and WPC Jones will be to the right.' They walked away, leaving me with Percy and an awkward silence.

'It's good to see you again,' I ventured.

He turned to face the stage. 'Are you still with that chap? I forget his name.'

Although I knew he remembered George's name, I supplied it anyway. 'George Hale. He's still travelling. I decided to come back.'

'Didn't live up to your expectations?' He glanced sideways at me.

I didn't ask if he meant George or my travels. I'd left without a word and I didn't blame him for feeling hurt. But I'd expected him to understand my reasons for going.

'It was wonderful.' This wasn't entirely true. 'I came back to see my family.'

'Really?' I could tell he didn't believe me.

I wanted to change the subject. 'How are you? Still at the museum?' He worked at the Natural History Museum and was a member of the Society for the Promotion of Nature Reserves.

He nodded.

'Ben said you still go to the Foxtrot Club. Do you remember my hopeless dancing?' I was desperate to try to rekindle some of our old comradery.

'I still go there. I haven't changed.' The implication was clear. He obviously felt I'd changed. And maybe too much for us to be friends again.

I gave up and turned my attention to the stage. All I wanted was some normality, for things to go back to how they were. Evidently, I wasn't going to be forgiven that easily.

Constance stood at the centre of the stage and gazed down at the mass of upturned expectant faces. Emblazoned behind her on a large display board were the words *A fairer future for all*. She made a slight gesture with her hand and the crowd was silent. She'd lost none of her easy authority.

She cleared her throat. 'Thank you all for coming. I—'

A loud cracking noise ripped through the air. The audience recoiled in unison at the strange sound. Constance appeared momentarily startled and then slumped forwards onto the wooden boards of the stage.

2

An eery silence was followed by screaming. The crowd ran for cover, realising a shot had been fired. Would there be more?

Ignoring the chaos around us, Percy rushed toward the stage. I followed him, aware we'd be in the line of fire but not sure where else to go.

Ben got to Constance first. He was shielding her with his body. 'Are you hurt?'

'No. I don't think so.' Constance's face was white and she seemed unable to move.

Percy crouched down on the other side of her.

'Get her off the stage,' Ben ordered.

Between them, Percy and Ben hauled Constance to her feet. We all stumbled towards the back of the platform to the *A fairer future for all* display board. I gasped when I saw the bullet hole. It was perfectly positioned in the centre of the letter 'o' of the word 'for'. Constance saw it too. She seemed mesmerised by the sinister gash in the wood.

I gripped her hand and dragged her down the wobbly steps at

the back of the stage. Ben and Percy jumped down beside us. We crouched low and came face to face with a young woman hiding under the makeshift wooden structure.

'Rosie,' Constance exclaimed. 'Are you alright?'

'Some bastard shot at you.' Rosie's large blue eyes were more indignant than afraid.

I nearly laughed at this crude but accurate summing up of the situation.

One of the doors to the factory opened a fraction and WPC Jones waved at us from inside.

Ben pointed to Rosie and me. 'You two go first. We'll follow with Constance.'

I held out my hand to the girl. She crawled out from under the stage and nimbly got to her feet. Hand in hand, we dashed over to WPC Jones, who ushered us inside.

'I saw Dr Mathers helping a woman who'd fallen,' WPC Jones said to Rosie. 'I think he was taking her to the sickroom. See if you can find him and tell him Miss Timpson needs attention.'

Rosie nodded and scampered away as Ben and Percy burst through the door with Constance propped up between them.

Ben pulled me towards him and shifted Constance's weight from his shoulder onto mine. 'Take her to her office and stay there,' he commanded. 'WPC Jones, we need to make sure everyone's inside.'

'Be careful,' I called as they headed out.

Percy and I supported Constance up a flight of stairs and along a green-tiled corridor. We stumbled across a mezzanine that overlooked the factory floor and through a heavy wooden door which displayed Constance's name on a brass plate.

We gently lowered Constance into the chair behind her rosewood desk. I spotted a jug of water on a matching rosewood cabinet and poured her a glass. Her hand shook as she took a sip.

Percy delved around inside the cabinet and retrieved a crystal decanter of brandy. He didn't bother taking out the delicate crystal glasses and poured a slug into another water glass. Constance took it gratefully and, pushing away the glass I'd given her, took a large gulp.

Percy poured another shot for me and one for himself. We sipped in silence until Constance whispered, 'Why?'

I exchanged a glance with Percy, not knowing how to answer. Constance wasn't popular in certain quarters. But I'd never expected anything like this. And evidently, neither had she.

Percy pushed his wavy hair back over his brow. 'Whoever fired that gun knew what they were doing. If they'd meant to hit you, I think they would have. They're trying to scare you.'

'They're doing a good job.' Constance's coiffured hair was coming loose, and her usually elegant white hands were grazed and dirty.

'Percy's right,' I said. 'Ben told me you'd received a threatening letter. Someone serious about killing you wouldn't have done that. It's more likely they're trying to frighten you.'

She stared unseeingly for a few moments, then nodded. 'You're probably right. In which case, I shall do the opposite of what they want.'

Percy frowned with concern. 'You have to take this seriously. Perhaps let someone else take over here for a while.'

'No.' Constance's mouth was set in a hard line. 'The newspapers are responsible for this. They've been stirring up trouble for me. And now they're turning on Mrs Siddons because she supports me. I want someone to write an article explaining what we're trying to achieve.' She sipped her drink and stared at me. 'When Ben told me you were back, I thought you might be able to help.'

'I'm, er, well, I don't have a position at present. I mean, I'm not with any particular newspaper.' I felt like I was there under false pretences.

In 1920, Mrs Siddons had stood as the Liberal candidate in the Aldershot by-election, and I'd helped her campaign. I'd worked for *The Walden Herald* at the time, and with the newspaper's support, she'd won the election and become only the third female MP to take a seat in the House of Commons. A general election was only months away, and I wanted to ensure she kept that seat. The only problem was, I no longer worked for a newspaper.

But I did want to help. I'd seen the snide comments in the press, implying that by supporting Constance, Mrs Siddons was sacrificing the livelihoods of disabled ex-servicemen in favour of a female-dominated workforce.

'You've come back to resume your career?' Constance queried.

'Yes,' I said with as much conviction as I could muster. I'd come back because I'd run out of money, and George and I had been arguing on a daily basis. But I wasn't going to admit that. Not in front of Percy.

'When you were at *The Walden Herald*, Mr Whittle sometimes sold your articles to other newspapers, didn't he?' Constance was thoughtful. 'Quite a few of the London papers reprinted the one you wrote about Mother.'

Lady Timpson had given me an exclusive interview when she was involved in a national scandal. It had received widespread attention, though I can't say it was because of any skill on my part as a writer; I was the only one who'd had access to the story. Constance knew that as well as I did, but I guessed few journalists would be willing to side with her right now. Most newspaper proprietors were closely associated with the business owners that opposed Constance's reforms. The wealthy male elite stuck together.

'Why don't you ask Mr Whittle for your old job back?' she suggested.

I struggled to find an appropriate response. I did plan to go and see Elijah Whittle, my old boss at *The Walden Herald*. But first, I needed to pay a visit to my father. And that was something I'd been putting off since my return to England two weeks ago.

Fortunately, the door opened at that moment, and Rosie appeared with a tall gentleman in a smart tweed jacket. He had grey hair and a neatly trimmed grey beard.

'Miss Timpson. How are you feeling?' He hurried over to Constance and took her wrist, feeling for her pulse. 'Dreadful, simply dreadful. I can't believe someone would do such a thing.'

'I'm perfectly well, Dr Mathers.' She allowed him to keep hold of her wrist for a few minutes until he was satisfied she wasn't about to keel over.

'Would you like me to prescribe you a sedative?' He released her hand and peered at her over the top of his wire-rimmed spectacles. 'You'll be feeling distressed, I've no doubt.'

'My distress has passed. I feel quite well.' Constance tucked loose strands of hair behind her ears as she spoke.

The doctor looked astonished. 'I admire your resilience.' He turned to me. 'And may I enquire if you're suffering any ill effects, Miss, er...'

'Iris Woodmore,' I replied. 'I'm perfectly well, thank you.'

Rosie, on the other hand, was beginning to look queasy.

'Would you like to sit down?' I stood up and gestured to the seat.

'I'm fine, Miss,' she replied but flopped into the empty chair.

Dr Mathers put his hand on her forehead. 'You feel rather clammy.'

'It's nothing, really.' Rosie seemed to squirm with embarrassment at being the centre of attention.

Percy poured a small brandy and handed it to her. She eyed it uncertainly and sipped the liquid as if it were a foul-tasting medicine. She coughed and then her eyes widened in panic. She lurched forward and was sick in the wastepaper basket.

'Perhaps water would have been better.' Percy hastily retrieved the glass from Rosie's hand before it fell to the floor.

She slumped into the chair and wiped her mouth with the back of her hand. I gave her my handkerchief, noticing to my mortification that it was one that my grandmother had embroidered with my initials. Rosie took it gratefully and coughed into it.

'If you don't require me, Miss Timpson, I'll take Miss Robson to the sickroom.' Dr Mathers smiled down at Rosie. 'She came up with the others from Walden in a charabanc. It would be advisable to get her well again before she attempts the journey home.' He paused. 'Or are you wearing that pretty frock because you have a date in town with young Mr Denton?'

Rosie's cheeks turned as pink as her dress. I knew the doctor was only trying to be fatherly, but I felt if she vomited over him, it would serve him right for embarrassing her.

'That would be for the best. Thank you, Dr Mathers.' Constance had assumed her usual air of authority, although I noticed a slight tremor as she drank the remains of her brandy.

The doctor helped Rosie to her feet and she sheepishly offered me my soiled handkerchief back.

'Why don't you keep it,' I suggested.

She gave an impish grin. 'Thank you, Miss.'

They left the room, and to my dismay, Constance picked up the conversation where she'd left off. 'We were discussing your return to *The Walden Herald*?' She said this as though the matter had been decided rather than suggested.

I could feel Percy's eyes on me. Constance was waiting for an answer, so I muttered, 'I'm planning to go and see Elijah.'

'Good. Once it's sorted, we can meet at the Tolfree & Timpson factory, and I'll show you the set-up there. In the meantime, let's discuss the best approach to take with your first article.'

Constance seemed to take it for granted I'd get my old job back. Didn't she know I'd spent eleven months travelling through Europe with a man I wasn't married to? Percy certainly did. My return to Walden would be met with raised eyebrows and muttered comments. And that was just from my father. The smell from the wastepaper basket filled my nostrils and a wave of nausea washed over me.

* * *

It was some hours before we were allowed to leave Timpson Foods. Police had searched the area, and there was no sign of the shooter.

The Tolfree & Timpson workers had departed on the charabanc and Percy had insisted on driving Constance back to her ancestral home of Crookham Hall in his new Ford Model T Roadster. He'd obviously wanted to show it off. Constance had smiled politely, even though I was sure she'd have preferred the comfort of her chauffeur-driven Daimler.

WPC Jones was by the factory gates, stopping reporters from entering. As I left, several tried to talk to me, but I ignored them. If anyone was going to write up my eyewitness account of the afternoon's events, it would be me.

I paused outside the gate. It was difficult to judge where the shot had come from. I guessed it must have been fired from a height. The sniper might have been on the roof of one of the factory buildings, but the angle of the shot suggested it had come from the front. The only building tall enough to overlook the factory was the church opposite. It had a cylindrical tower with a steeple on top. A perfect vantage point. Could someone have got up there? The police obviously thought so as there was a Black Maria parked outside. More reporters hovered nearby.

I spotted Ben on the steps of the church. Standing next to him was a man who immediately caught my attention. He was around six feet tall with the physique of a soldier. There was something animal-like about his narrow, intense eyes and sculpted jaw. He was talking to Ben and gesturing up at the tower.

Intrigued, I crossed the road and tried to catch Ben's attention.

'Can I help you, sir? Do you—' The man turned to look at me and stopped mid-sentence. He must have glimpsed the outline of someone wearing trousers and assumed I was a man.

'I was...' I began, then stopped. He was wearing a white collar. Despite the fact that he was standing on the steps of the church, I hadn't considered for one moment that he could be a vicar. He looked more like the brutish but handsome villain in a Mary Pickford motion picture.

'My apologies, Miss...' His eyes flickered with amusement. He seemed to be enjoying our mutual confusion at each other's clothing.

'Iris, why are you still here?' Ben dragged his attention away from the church tower to glare at me.

I tried to regain my composure. 'Is this where the shot was fired from? Has someone gone up there?' I gazed up at the steeple.

'Reverend Powell has kindly allowed Detective Inspector Yates and his sergeant to search the church.' He nodded towards the vicar. 'Merely as a precaution.'

'You do think that's where it came from?' I persisted.

'I think you should go home,' Ben growled. 'And don't speak to any reporters. I'll see you back at your gran's later.'

I blushed, annoyed with him for making me appear like a child in front of this strange man. The slight curl of Reverend Powell's lips suggested he knew what I was feeling. His piercing green eyes locked with mine and there was a lazy sexuality in them that was completely at odds with his clerical garb.

'A pleasure to meet you, Iris,' he said with a slight drawl.

3

It was ten-thirty before Ben trundled up the path of my gran's house. I watched him go through the back gate to the garden shed where he kept his bicycle locked up overnight.

In the kitchen, I heated the soup Aunt Maud had left on the stove and placed the ham sandwich she'd made on the table. He opened the back door quietly.

'They've gone to bed.' I poured us both a glass of beer.

He looked relieved. I imagined being fussed over by Aunt Maud and Gran each evening must get quite tiring. He went over to the sink to wash his hands and then joined me at the kitchen table.

'What happened after I left?' I asked.

He took a gulp of beer. 'We searched the tower of St Mary's Church and found a shell casing.'

'I thought it must overlook the stage.' I scribbled a few sentences in my notebook.

'Don't write that down. We don't want anyone knowing yet.' He bit into the sandwich.

'I won't put it in my article. I'm writing about why Constance has become the target for this type of attack.'

'Most newspaper proprietors are against her. They're unlikely to publish anything that supports her.'

'I'm thinking of asking Elijah for my old job back.' I got up and poured the soup into a bowl and put it in front of him. 'Constance is blaming the press coverage she gets for inciting what happened today. She wants someone to tell her side of the story.'

He looked at me quizzically. 'You're going back to Walden?'

'Maybe. Depends on the reception I get from Elijah.'

He smiled. 'He'll be pleased to see you, though he won't admit it.'

'Do you think so?' I wasn't sure how Elijah would respond. As editor, he may welcome my return to the paper. But Horace Laffaye, owner of *The Walden Herald*, would have the final say. The two men had a close personal relationship and I didn't want to be the cause of a row between them.

I'd missed Elijah, although I hadn't let myself think about him too much before now. When I was away, part of me had felt homesick for my old life in Walden. I wanted some normality back. A routine to my life. The thought of sitting in Elijah's smoke-filled den, arguing over what to put in the next edition, was oddly comforting.

Ben finished his supper and went over to the sink to wash the dishes.

'What about you?' I picked up the tea towel to dry. 'Do you think you'll ever go back to Walden?'

'I enjoy the work here.'

It wasn't an answer, but I knew not to question him further. We both felt the same sense of loss for the past, and there was no point in discussing it.

'Are you still in touch with George?' he asked.

I shook my head. We finished the washing up and sat back at the table. The kitchen felt cosy with its smell of soup and bread and the occasional whiff of my gran's gardenia scent emanating from the cushion on her high-backed chair. I poured the remaining beer into our glasses.

'Where did you go when you left Walden?' he asked.

'France. We crossed the channel and headed to Paris. We stayed there for a while and then travelled south to Dijon.' I smiled. 'Every day seemed to be sunshine and blue skies. We went to Lyon, then followed the Rhone through Montelimar, Orange and Avignon to Marseille. We stopped in Nice for some weeks.'

'Lizzy said in one of her letters that you met up with your father when you were in Paris?'

'Briefly.' The least said about that, the better. 'After Nice, we went along the coast into Italy. We travelled around a bit, Genoa, Milan and east to Verona. We stayed at Lake Garda for about a month. It was beautiful.'

'Did you find Reg's grave?'

George's cousin, Reg, had been killed in one of the last battles of the war at the River Piave a week before the armistice was announced. George had promised his aunt he'd find Reg's final resting place.

I nodded. 'It was in a field in a village high up in the hills. The views all around were stunning. We'd gone to Treviso and headed east to cross the River Piave at Ponte di Piave and go north to Tezze. The villagers had marked the graves of overseas soldiers with temporary markers. The bodies are going to be recovered and reburied by the Commonwealth War Graves Commission. They're building a British Cemetery in Tezze. Reg will have a headstone there.'

It had given George some comfort to know Reg would be honoured. The pair had been more like brothers than cousins, brought up on the same street in Basingstoke. They'd joined up on the same day, looking forward to escaping their small town and seeing the world. I could still hear George's bitter laugh as he said, 'war wasn't what we'd expected'. He felt guilty that he'd survived and Reg hadn't.

'I'm glad for George. I know how important it was to him to find it.' Ben drank the last of his beer. 'Where did you go after that?'

'Back to Treviso, then on to Venice. We decided to go south to Padua, Bologna and Florence. Then down to Rome. We finished up at Naples so we could see Mount Vesuvius erupting.'

'Perhaps that's what I should have done. Got away from everything and everyone for a while.' He stared into his empty glass. 'It sounds incredible.'

'It was. To begin with.'

I'd been in raptures over every place we'd visited in those first months. But our journey seemed to lose its purpose after we found Reg's grave. We became restless, travelling aimlessly and growing more distant. Our relationship began to flounder. To run away with George had been an impulsive act on my part, doing what Ben had said, getting away from everybody and everything. I'd wanted to leave my grief behind and be with strangers.

Ben was watching me. 'Why did you come back?'

I shrugged. 'We started to argue, bickering about where we should go and what we should do. We were running out of money, and it was difficult to find work. I sold a few travel articles – not as many as I'd hoped. The adventure was wearing thin, I suppose.'

After a particularly heated row, I'd left George in Naples and headed back to England alone.

I picked up my pen, wanting to change the subject. 'Who has access to St Mary's Church?'

'Pretty much anyone. It's not locked. Next door to the church is

Creek House, a charity funded by the Timpsons. It offers a temporary home to unemployed and often disabled ex-servicemen.
Archie helps them to find work and a permanent place to live.'

'Archie?'

'Reverend Powell, the chap you saw me speaking to earlier. He
and Daniel Timpson became friends during the war. The reverend
was a chaplain and served in France and Belgium. Daniel told me
Archie had once saved his life.'

Daniel Timpson was Constance's older brother. He spent most
of his time at Crookham Hall, managing the farm and estate while
Constance took care of the family business.

From what I'd learnt, Constance's philanthropic activities
focused mainly on her support of equal rights for women. It would
help to write about her other charitable work. It would also give
me an excuse to go and speak to Reverend Powell. I pushed the
image of his amused green eyes from my mind and dragged my
thoughts back to the afternoon's events.

'What about the bullet?'

'WPC Jones found it behind the stage. It's gone to a ballistics
expert. The shell we found in the tower appears to have come from
a standard issue rifle. Since the war, there are far too many in
civilian hands. Most of whom don't have permits.'

'Kept by ex-serviceman?'

'In a lot of cases. But there are other sources. I don't think the
type of rifle used is going to help us narrow things down.'

'Why target Constance?'

'The changes she's made since her mother died have been too
fast and too radical for certain businessmen. She's unpopular with
the trade unions because she trains women for higher positions.
And she doesn't make them leave her employ when they marry.
Men feel those jobs should be theirs. Other factory owners don't
like her because she pays male and female employees the same

wage for doing the same job. They think that's destabilising.' He watched as I scribbled in my notepad. 'What are you intending to do with this article?'

'Present it to Elijah as part of my eyewitness account of what happened this afternoon with explanations for why Constance was targeted. See if I can persuade him to employ me again.'

'Do not mention the church. Detective Inspector Yates doesn't want to upset the clergy at this stage by suggesting one of their premises was used.'

'What's Yates like?'

'I've only met him a couple of times. It's difficult to tell what he's thinking. I always knew where I stood with Superintendent Cobbe, but Yates doesn't give much away.' He yawned. 'For the time being, I've been ordered to keep an eye on the factory and stay close to Constance when she's there.'

'Does he think the sniper will try again?'

'Possibly. It depends on how Constance reacts. This time it was done to scare her. They shot above her head. Next time...'

'They might hit their target?'

He nodded.

4

I lay in my narrow bed, listening to sparrows chirping in the hedge in the back garden. In Walden, I'd wake to the noise of wood pigeons in the chestnut trees on the road outside. I thought of Italy. Of the sound of doves on the tiled roof. Of the heat, the smells. And the feeling of George's body next to mine. For a moment, I wished I was back with him.

I'd have to get up soon, or Gran would be shouting up the stairs. I couldn't stay in bed forever. Nor could I remain in Hither Green for much longer, as much as Aunt Maud would like me to. So far, no one had mentioned my returning to Walden. But I knew it wouldn't be long.

I was right.

'I think you should go home to your father.' I hadn't even sat down at the breakfast table before Gran made this statement.

Ben hastily got to his feet and headed out of the back door, saying he was late for work.

'No.' Aunt Maud interjected before Gran could say any more. 'She can stay here for as long as she likes.'

'This is my house, not yours,' Gran said in a superior tone.

'Then I'll leave too,' Aunt Maud threatened. This was stale-mate. Gran couldn't manage without my aunt to look after her.

I sat down and poured tea. 'I was planning to go and see Father today. And Elijah. I'm going to try to get my old job back.'

'You'll need to do something to support yourself.' Gran sniffed. 'No man will marry you after what you've done.'

I gave my aunt a small smile. There were some advantages to being considered a fallen woman. Gran would no longer attempt to persuade me to make a suitable match. Although to be fair to her, she'd pretty much given up on that notion before I'd abandoned all sense of decency and gone away on my travels with George.

* * *

I stood on Queens Road, looking up at the windows of *The Walden Herald*. The newspaper's headquarters consisted of two rooms on the first floor above Laffaye Printworks. My desk had been in the main office, while the smaller room was Elijah's den. The window of the main office was open, so someone must be up there.

I'd planned to call at Elijah's cottage on Church Road, then decided to stop by the office first, knowing he often worked on a Saturday.

The doors to *The Walden Herald* and the printworks had been freshly painted bright green. I thought back to when George would lurk by the entrance of the printworks, waiting for me to finish work. In those days, the doors had been a dull brown colour. I wondered what else had changed in my absence.

Climbing the steep stairs, I rehearsed in my mind what I'd say to Elijah. The bannister and door at the top had been decorated in the same vivid green and the smell of paint hung in the air. I paused, swallowing my nerves, then pushed open the door.

'May I help you?' A tall woman of about fifty years old was sitting at my desk. I hadn't been prepared for that.

'I came to see Elijah, er, Mr Whittle,' I stammered.

'Do you have an appointment?' She lifted her reading glasses and balanced them on her neatly waved brown hair.

'No.' I turned to see Elijah sitting behind his desk, cigarette in hand. He had a wry smile on his face.

'It's alright, Miss Vale,' he called. 'This is Miss Woodmore, my former assistant.'

'Oh-ah.' I guessed by the way Miss Vale dragged out this syllable my reputation preceded me.

I felt myself redden. Feeling peeved, I strode past her desk and into Elijah's den, firmly closing the door behind me.

'Come in, why don't you.' He smirked. 'How kind of you to remember me. I expected you, oh, about eleven months ago, but your timekeeping was always erratic.'

'Sorry,' I muttered.

He contemplated me as he puffed on his cigarette. As usual, the den was filled with smoke and the window closed. I regretted shutting the door.

'Have you seen your father?' His familiar grey eyes looked bloodshot, and his hair was thinner than it had been the last time I saw him.

'Not yet. I came here first.'

'I'm honoured. Why?'

'Can I have my old job back?' I blurted out. This interview wasn't going the way I'd anticipated.

He snorted. 'Of course. Walk out without a word, and we'll keep your job available for you should you choose to show up again a year later.'

'I'm sorry for leaving like that. I thought if I told you what I planned, you'd try to stop me.'

'Stop you from going abroad with a man who'd already lied to you? Why would I do that?' He waved his cigarette in the air.

'I admit George and I didn't have the most conventional courtship.'

He snorted again. 'Courtship? That would imply there was some intention of it leading to marriage. I seem to recall you saying that you would never wed. And I'm damn sure he wasn't fool enough to want to marry you.'

'That's true,' I said with a grin.

He tried to suppress a smile. 'And now I'm supposed to welcome you back with open arms?'

'I've got a story.'

'That makes all the difference.' His sarcasm made me squirm. 'Did you notice the lady you passed on your way in? Sitting at your old desk?'

'She doesn't look like a journalist to me.'

'Because she's a woman?' I knew he was trying to goad me. 'How close-minded of you.'

I tried to think of a retort but failed. I stood up, hoping to call his bluff. 'Sorry.' I lowered my head and walked to the door.

'Sit down. I haven't finished with you yet.'

I hesitated for effect, then turned and sat down again.

'When are you going to see your father?' he demanded.

'I'm going there next.'

'Shouldn't he have been your first port of call?'

I didn't reply. He was right; I should have gone there first.

He sighed and stubbed out his cigarette. 'What's this story then?'

'I was at the Timpson Foods factory in Deptford yesterday when a sniper fired at Constance Timpson. I can give you a first-hand account.'

His eyes narrowed. 'I heard about that. What were you doing there?'

'I've been staying with Gran and Aunt Maud. Constance invited me to the speech she was giving about why she's closing the Basingstoke Canal.'

'Was it an assassination attempt?'

'More likely trying to scare her. Ben told me she'd received a threatening letter that morning.'

'Ben Gilbert?' He perked up at this.

'Yes.'

'How is he?'

'He says he's fine.' I paused. 'He seems sad and lonely.'

'I was sorry he left Walden. But I could understand why he wanted to leave.' Elijah folded his arms in front of him. 'And why you left too.'

I nodded. I didn't want to talk about the summer of 1921 and the events that had caused such heartache for Ben and me.

'Go on, write this piece. I'll pay you for it. I'll have to talk to Horace before I can consider taking you on permanently. And find out what Constance Timpson plans to do with the canal. Locals are concerned.'

Horace Laffaye wasn't just Elijah's boss. During the time I'd spent working at *The Walden Herald*, I'd grown to realise the two men shared a love for each other that could never be made public. If Elijah wanted me back, I hoped Horace would indulge him.

'What about Miss Vale?' I asked.

'She isn't a journalist. She does my typing and handles the admin for the newspaper and printworks.'

This sounded promising. Elijah was probably relying on free-lancers. I knew Horace would prefer him to have at least one permanent reporter. Whether that was me or not depended on how disreputable Horace considered me to be.

I left the office, bestowing a warm smile upon Miss Vale. She tried to smile back but failed.

* * *

I took my time sauntering around Waldenmere. Being by the lake used to have a calming effect on me. But after the loss of my dearest friend, I'd needed to escape from all the memories it held.

I'd spent my childhood in Walden until I was thirteen, when my mother had decided we should relocate to London. She'd died a year later. I'd spent much of the turbulent war years working in a Voluntary Aid Detachment in Lewisham Military Hospital. During that time, I'd longed for the comfort and tranquillity of Waldenmere, and in 1919, my father had decided we should return.

A few residential roads led away from the eastern side of the lake, and reluctantly I left the footpath and turned onto Chestnut Avenue. I wasn't in a hurry to see my father again, but it had to be done.

I opened the front door to 9 Chestnut Avenue and heard Father's voice in the drawing room. 'I've ordered those curtains you liked.'

I smiled. Lizzy must have finally persuaded him to smarten up the house a bit. I nervously made my way into the room, uncertain of the welcome I'd receive.

I stopped on the threshold. A smartly dressed lady was sitting in the high-backed leather armchair that I used to occupy. For the second time that day, I had the sensation of my place being taken by someone else.

'Iris.' My father rose from his chair and hurried over to me. The strength of his embrace told me he was genuinely pleased to see me and I felt relieved.

When he drew back, he turned to face the woman. 'You remember Mrs Keats?'

'Yes.' I remembered Mrs Keats, who was viewing me apprehensively.

George and I had been in Paris when Lizzy had written to say that my father was there too, staying with a friend. She'd given me the address of his apartment and I'd felt obliged to pay him a visit. George had wisely decided not to accompany me.

I hadn't written to tell Father I was coming and when I'd knocked at the door of the apartment, it had been opened by an attractive woman of about forty.

'I'm Iris Woodmore. I'm looking for my father?'

Her embarrassment told me everything I needed to know.

'Thomas isn't here right now. Would you like to come in and wait?'

I'd wanted to leave there and then. Instead, I'd followed her into a spacious sitting room. While she fetched me a drink, I went over to an untidy desk near the window. It had all the trademarks of my father's presence. Books lying open, loose papers weighted down by random objects. I recognised my father's scrawl in a journal and his briefcase propped up against the chair.

The pair of us had endured an excruciating half an hour of small talk before Father arrived. This was followed by an even more excruciating half an hour of questions from me and recriminations from him before I left.

Mrs Keats rose from the armchair. I could tell by her wary expression that she was recalling our last encounter. 'Iris. How lovely to see you again. Please call me Katherine.' To my alarm, she reached out to embrace me.

I pulled away quickly. 'Would you excuse me? I should go and see Lizzy.' I bolted from the room and headed for the kitchen.

5

'I could box your ears,' Lizzy muttered. She enveloped me in a hug instead. This time, I returned the embrace with pleasure.

'I'm sorry.' I breathed in her familiar scent of lavender water mingled with the Hudson's soap powder she used liberally to wash all the clothes and linen in the house. It felt good to be back in her well-ordered kitchen.

Lizzy had looked after me since I was a baby, and she was the one I'd felt truly guilty about leaving. She was the only person I'd written to regularly during my travels.

'Are you coming home?' She held me tightly. 'Your room's just as you left it.'

Unconsciously, I pulled away and glanced towards the drawing room. So, Mrs Keats hadn't gone so far as to rearrange the bedrooms.

'Mrs Keats doesn't stay here overnight,' she said, as if reading my thoughts. 'She has a flat in London.'

My father living in sin would be a step too far for Walden. And Lizzy.

'She seems nice,' I said, for the sake of something to say.

'She is. It will be good for you to get to know her.' She seemed to force herself to push me away. 'Why don't you go and speak to her, and I'll bring in some tea.'

I returned to the drawing room, but Katherine stood to leave.

'I'm sure you and your father have a lot to talk about. I must get back to London. I can see myself out, Thomas.' She kissed him lightly on the cheek, wisely making no move towards me.

Father insisted on following her to the front door, and I could hear the murmur of low conversation. I stood awkwardly by the mantelpiece, not wanting to sit in the armchair Mrs Keats had just vacated. I felt like I'd pushed her out of the house. But I couldn't suddenly sit in my father's usual spot. The two chairs against the wall were only pulled out when visitors came, and if I took one of those it would seem as if I was casting myself in the role of a guest. Very rarely, someone would perch on the cushioned seat in the bay window, but that was practically the Outer Hebrides.

I'd never realised the dilemma familiar chairs could present. I squirmed uncomfortably as I sat in the still warm armchair Mrs Keats had occupied, her musky perfume lingering in the air.

My father returned and sat in his usual chair opposite me. 'I'm sorry for what I said when you came to Paris. I know how difficult things were for you last year.'

'I'm sorry for...' I trailed off. What was I sorry for? I'd needed to get away, and I had, though I felt I should acknowledge the hurt I'd caused. 'I'm sorry if you were worried about me.'

'You're back now. And George?' He tried to move his lips into a smile and didn't quite succeed.

'He's still travelling. We...we parted company.' It was an odd way to phrase it, as if we'd dissolved a business partnership or something. But George and I had never had a conventional relationship and we'd never made promises to each other. Our adventure had run its course and there was no more to be said.

My father was silent, looking as if he was running through things he'd like to say, dismissing each one until he found the right sentiment.

I didn't try to fill the silence. I was interested in this new approach he was taking. Usually, he'd issue a command, I'd become annoyed, and then we'd argue. This time, he seemed to be considering his next move. Was this Mrs Keats' influence?

'The thing is…' He hesitated. 'The thing is, I'd like you to come back here to live. If you think you could.'

Lizzy came in at that moment, saving me from having to answer. My father got up and pulled over a chair for her to join us.

'Have a think about it anyway,' he murmured. To my surprise, he wasn't even demanding an answer immediately.

'Let's catch up with all the news.' Father sounded jovial, although the rigid set of his jaw gave him away. The atmosphere was far from relaxed, and following these words, there was an awkward pause.

The three of us were aware that if we talked about my father's recent trip, we'd run the risk of alluding to his relationship with Mrs Keats. Any mention of my travels would raise the spectre of George. We settled on the recent goings-on in Walden, the opening of a new fishmonger in town and the increase in motor cars on the roads. Half an hour passed pleasantly enough and then I took my leave.

Walking to the railway station, I remembered Mrs Keats was returning to London. Had she already caught a train? I didn't want to run into her at the station. Or worse, spend the whole journey to Waterloo Station stuck in a carriage with her.

To my relief, there was only an elderly lady in the carriage I chose. Mrs Keats probably travelled first class anyway. I could only afford third.

I settled into a seat and weighed up my options. There weren't

many. I had no money to speak of, and without a job, I was depen-
dent on my family. I had to live with either Gran and Aunt Maud
or Father and Lizzy.

If I was working with Elijah again, returning to Walden didn't
seem like such a bad prospect. But... what were Mrs Keats' plans?

* * *

I was feeling unsettled by the time I got back to Gran's.

'How did it go?' Aunt Maud asked. Ben wasn't back yet and
Gran had gone up to bed.

I slumped into a chair in the parlour and told her about my
day. I hadn't mentioned Katherine Keats to Gran and Aunt Maud
before now. I wasn't sure how serious my father was about her.
There was no point in upsetting them if the relationship proved to
be as transient as mine and George's. But I needed to confide in
someone.

Meeting Mrs Keats again had come as a shock to me. Although
I knew I should be pleased for my father, it felt like the last traces
of my mother were vanishing. It had been eight years since her
death and Father had only been forty at the time. It was wrong to
expect him to stay single. But I think I had. While women found
him attractive, he wasn't the most attentive of men. He was always
absorbed in his work and didn't go out of his way to socialise.

'How long has he known her?' My aunt's voice was light,
though her lips were drawn into a tight line. I knew what she was
asking. How soon after my mother's death had they met? I reassured her.

'Mrs Keats' husband died in the war. He was in the intelligence
corps with Father and Elijah. They both went to see Katherine to
offer their condolences. And she and my father—'

'Became friends?' Aunt Maud's expression softened.

'It turns out they already knew each other. She's from Devon. Father was at school with her brother. He hadn't known she'd married Major Laurence Keats.'

'Do they have plans?'

'They were talking about new curtains for the drawing room when I arrived.'

She looked apprehensive. 'Do you think you'll move back to Walden?'

I sighed. 'It depends on how it goes with Elijah.'

And how comfortable Mrs Keats intended to make herself at Chestnut Avenue.

* * *

Instead of following my aunt up to bed, I waited for Ben to get back from work.

'How did it go?' He sat down at the kitchen table to the supper Aunt Maud had left out.

'Not bad.'

'Elijah give you a hard time?'

'His usual sarcasm. On the whole, better than expected. He'll pay me for this article and talk to Horace.'

He grinned. 'He'd love to have you back.'

'He wants me to find out what Constance intends to do with the canal.'

'She said to tell you she's in Walden on Monday at the Tolfree & Timpson biscuit factory. She'd like to show you the set-up there.'

I nodded. In truth, I'd rather have gone back to Deptford. And maybe seen Reverend Powell again. 'Have you discovered anything more about the shooting?'

'The ballistics chap has examined the shell we found in the church tower. He thinks it's likely the shot was fired from there.'

'Has anyone else received threats? I'm thinking of Daniel Timpson or Mrs Siddons. Or any Timpson employees?'

'No... not that we know of.'

'What?' I pounced on his hesitation.

'Did you see Rosie Robson again after you left the factory?'

'The young girl hiding under the stage?'

'Yes.'

I shook my head. 'She went off with Dr Mathers to the sickroom. She wasn't feeling well. Why?'

'When the charabanc went to leave, the foreman couldn't find her.'

I smiled. 'I don't blame her. She probably couldn't face the journey back to Walden. I imagine the prospect of travelling miles in a packed charabanc made her feel ill.'

'No one knows where she went. She's only sixteen.'

'She could have taken a train home later.'

'It's been over twenty-four hours since anyone's seen her. We're keeping an eye out for her in Deptford. If you go to the biscuit factory on Monday, could you ask around? See if you can pick up any gossip from the factory floor as to where they think she might be.' Ben was clearly concerned.

'Do you think her disappearance could have something to do with the shooting?'

'At this stage, we're presuming she's gone off of her own accord. But we'd like to find her sooner rather than later to be sure.'

I thought of Rosie's round eyes and impish grin. I hoped she'd somehow managed to get home to Walden and wasn't wandering the streets of London on her own.

6

'Another of my employees is missing.' Constance Timpson buried her head in her hands.

'Another? I heard about Rosie Robson.'

My Monday morning had started tranquilly enough. I'd taken the train from Waterloo to Walden and once again sauntered around Waldenmere, enjoying the warm September sunshine.

Then, instead of heading into town, I'd gone in the opposite direction. The Tolfree & Timpson biscuit factory was situated on the outskirts of Walden on the banks of the Basingstoke Canal.

Tolfree Biscuits was famous all over the world. Established in 1850 by Isaac Tolfree, the company was one of the first to produce decorative tins that preserved the biscuits and allowed them to be sent overseas. The tins had become collectable items, and the Tolfree name was known in the farthest corners of the globe. Captain Scott famously took a tin on his expedition to the South Pole.

But the company hadn't fared so well since the war. Ingredients, particularly sugar beet, had become harder to procure and more expensive. Faced with fierce competition from other manufacturers, including Timpson Foods, the fortunes of Tolfree Biscuits had rapidly declined. Earlier in the year, Constance had stepped in, bailing out Redvers Tolfree, Isaac's grandson, in exchange for a controlling interest and the addition of the Timpson name to the famous brand.

Still operating from the premises that Isaac Tolfree had built in 1850, the factory was a far cry from the modern headquarters of Timpson Foods in Deptford. Instead of the plush furnishings of her London office, Constance sat behind a simple oak desk, surrounded by ancient wooden filing cabinets that looked as though they dated back to Isaac's day.

'Freda Bray, Redvers Tolfree's secretary, has disappeared.' Mrs Siddons, Member of Parliament for Aldershot, sat opposite Constance.

'When?'

Mrs Siddons frowned. 'Mr Tolfree is rather vague about the matter. It appears no one has seen her for nearly a week.'

'A week? And what about Rosie Robson?'

'Still no word from her. I'm very worried.' Constance looked on the verge of tears. 'I'm certain she would have contacted her family if she could.'

While Constance's distress showed, Mrs Siddons was her usual calm self. I'd rarely seen her lose her regal poise. She was dressed in her customary finery in a full-length blue silk gown with a sapphire necklace from her famous jewellery collection.

'What are the police doing?' I asked.

'Detective Inspector Yates suggested someone might have kidnapped Rosie and Freda to get to me.' Constance took a deep breath. 'He said to look out for a ransom letter.'

'A ransom letter?' I slumped into the nearest chair. 'You say this other woman has been missing for nearly a week?'

Mrs Siddons nodded. 'Superintendent Cobbe is coming over to

talk to Redvers. Hopefully, he can get more sense out of the dratted man about when he last saw Freda.'

'Rosie's only sixteen, isn't she?' I thought of how frightened the poor child would be. Is that why they'd chosen her? Because she was young and vulnerable? 'What about Freda?'

'Freda's twenty-five. She's worked for Redvers for about two years. I like her. She was one of the few members of his staff to make me feel welcome when I took over. I wouldn't have been able to unravel the mess Redvers had made of the accounts without her help.' Constance gestured to the wooden filing cabinets that surrounded her.

'Do both women live in Walden?'

Constance nodded. 'Rosie Robson lives with her mother and seven siblings in a house by the railway station. Freda lives with her father in a tied cottage on a farm that neighbours the Crookham estate.'

'When did her father last see Freda?'

'We don't know. I've been away in London for nearly a month sorting out the legal issues around closing the canal. Redvers only deigned to tell me about Freda this morning.'

It was clear Constance didn't have a high regard for her co-owner.

'This could all be a fuss about nothing, and both women are absent for reasons entirely unconnected to their work,' Mrs Siddons said.

I wasn't convinced. By her expression, neither was Constance. She pulled down the jacket of her impeccably cut navy suit and patted her elaborately rolled hair. I recognised these gestures as indications she was shielding her emotions, adopting her business armour instead.

'How did it go with Mr Whittle?' she asked.

'I can't say he welcomed me with open arms. But he's agreed to take the article I proposed.'

'Thank you. Although it won't have the circulation of the city press, it will be refreshing to have something in print that hasn't been written with the sole intention of demonising me.'

'Elijah wants to know what your plans are for the canal. He said it's causing concern locally.'

Constance sighed. 'We've offered alternative work to all the men who were on the boats. Most have accepted new jobs, though some are bitter. I understand it's hard to change when you've spent your life on the water. But it's impossible to keep the canal running when there are cheaper and faster ways to transport produce.'

'What will you do with the canal itself? Sell it?'

'No one would buy it,' Mrs Siddons interjected. 'Apart from pleasure boating, there aren't any business opportunities to be had from canals nowadays.'

'So what will you do?'

A rare smile transformed Constance's face, lighting up her dark blue eyes. I could see why Percy was smitten with her. It was a shame taking over the family business had given her so little to smile about. 'Can't you guess? It's something my brother and Percy have wanted for a long time.'

'Of course.' The canal was on the Society for the Promotion of Nature Reserves' list of desired sites. They'd had their eye on it for years, knowing it was likely to fall into disuse.

'Not the whole navigation,' Constance added. 'The section they want to turn into a nature reserve is between Walden and Odiham. The Greywell Tunnel has had another roof fall, so we can't safely get barges through there any more.'

I remembered Daniel and Percy's excitement at discovering a colony of bats had taken up residence in the old tunnel. 'When will you stop using the canal for freight?'

'The last barges went up to Deptford on Friday and won't be coming back this way. Daniel and Percy are meeting this afternoon to discuss plans. They're as excited as a couple of schoolboys. Fortunately, Millicent is on hand to keep them in order.'

'Millicent?'

'Millicent Nightingale from the Elementary School. She plans to take her pupils on field visits to the canal.'

'Oh, yes.' I remembered the teacher once allowing Percy to take a group of her young pupils paddling with nets in Waldenmere. That was a biology lesson that could have ended in disaster without the indomitable Miss Nightingale at the helm. 'They were planning to set up a Walden Natural History Group?'

'It's grown into quite a large society. They hold meetings in the town hall. They're all very...' Constance paused, trying to find the right word. 'Keen.'

I smiled, remembering how out of my depth I'd felt when I first met Percy at a talk at the Natural History Museum. The audience had been enthusiastic then too.

'They're getting together after Millicent finishes school for the day,' Constance continued. 'Why don't you join them? Daniel will be pleased to see you again. He and Percy would be thrilled if you could get something about their group into the paper.'

Elijah's intention was for me to write about the economic repercussions of the canal's closure rather than its wildlife. But I agreed to her suggestion. It might help me get back into Percy's good books.

Mrs Siddons rose to leave. 'Why don't you introduce Iris to Redvers and get him to give her a tour of the factory?'

Constance looked surprised, then smiled. 'Good idea. He does like to show off to women. His boasting will give you an insight into how this place operates.'

* * *

Redvers Tolfree was a bearded, well-built gentleman of about sixty, with grey hair and a hawkish nose. He looked a bit like King George.

Constance introduced me as the journalist from *The Walden Herald*, which was overstating my role, but I let it pass. She made a few flattering remarks to Redvers about how eager I was to see his famous company, then swept from his office, giving me a wink as she went.

'My family has made the best biscuits in the world for over seventy years.' Redvers pointed to a portrait of Isaac Tolfree, a portly gentleman who looked as though he'd enjoyed a biscuit or two.

'My aunt always buys your Garibaldis.' This wasn't true. Aunt Maud and I were loyal to Chiltonian Biscuits, whose factory was in Hither Green.

'These are some of our most famous decorative tins.' He gestured to a glass display cabinet. In pride of place, next to the tin celebrating Queen Victoria's Golden Jubilee in 1887, was Redvers Tolfree's OBE.

I knew my cue. 'The king awarded you the OBE for your war efforts, I believe?'

'He did indeed. It was an honour I never sought. I was proud to do my duty.' He puffed out his chest.

During the war, the company's tin-making factories had switched to manufacturing cases for artillery shells. At the same time, the production of luxury biscuits was discontinued in favour of army biscuits to send to soldiers fighting overseas.

'Come and see the factory.' He ushered me out of the door and past the vacant desk in the outer office.

'If you're sure it's not too much trouble. Miss Timpson

mentioned that your secretary has gone missing.' I motioned to the empty chair.

His lips curled into something between a smirk and a grimace. 'Fuss about nothing. Miss Bray always had too high an opinion of herself. I'm glad to see the back of her.'

'You're not worried?'

'No. I think she decided Tolfree Biscuits wasn't good enough for her and found a new position.'

'She resigned?' I noticed he'd omitted the word 'Timpson' from the company name. 'Did she leave a letter?'

'Probably. My secretary usually takes care of that sort of paper-work for me. So I wouldn't know.' He gave a bark of laughter at this bizarre joke.

I followed him out of the door, wondering at his strange response.

7

'Come and meet my foreman, Jack Osmond. He's been with me for fifteen years.' Redvers Tolfree led the way down a curved metal staircase.

Once on the factory floor, the sweet smell that had been pleasant in the offices became overwhelming. I wondered if working there put you off eating biscuits. The sugary scent was making me feel nauseous. As we walked through the rows of conveyor belts, I noticed there appeared to be an even mix of male and female employees, old and young.

'Did you take on more female employees during the war?' I asked.

'We did. Good workers they were too.'

'Did you let many of them go after?'

'Had no choice. I took back all the men that had been with me before the war. They fought for their country, and they deserved to have a job to come back to.'

I nodded. It would have been a dilemma many factory owners faced.

'Some of your staff must have worked for you for a long time,' I said.

'There's still a fair few from the old days. A lot of the women went to the tin factories when I switched production there to munitions works, then came back here when it was over. Ask Nora about making shell casings. She'll tell you tales about nearly getting blown up and turning yellow and all that.' Redvers nodded to a woman with chestnut hair whose skin still had a slight yellow tinge.

Workers in the munitions factories had been exposed to TNT, a chemical used to fill shells that turned the skin yellow. Some women had even given birth to yellow babies. After they'd left the munitions factories, their skin returned to its normal colour, but at the time, the women had been nicknamed the Canary Girls.

'You carried on making biscuits here?' I prompted. Redvers was clearly enjoying his trip down memory lane.

'Not fancy biscuits. We supplied the army with the basics, thanks to young Jack here. He's been with me since he was eighteen and worked his way up from errand boy to become foreman.'

'Mr Tolfree even got stuck in with the baking himself,' Jack Osmond remarked, somewhat sycophantically. He was a stocky man of about thirty with a florid complexion. He wore a waistcoat that was a little too tight for his bulging waistline.

I tried unsuccessfully to imagine Redvers Tolfree in an apron with his sleeves rolled up, covered in flour. But we'd all done strange jobs during the war. I'd been a volunteer in a military hospital by day and helped clear up bomb-damaged streets at night. It was during this time I'd taken to wearing trousers. Unlike other women, I hadn't stopped wearing them after the war, much to the disapproval of the staider residents of Walden.

Redvers laughed and slapped his foreman on the back. 'We made a formidable team.'

'You were here during the war?' I wondered why Jack hadn't been away fighting.

'Problem with my eyesight.' Jack pushed his glasses further up his nose.

'Nothing wrong with his eyesight,' I heard Nora mutter under her breath.

'I was glad of it. I needed him here with all my other men away fighting,' Redvers said. 'Those were the good old days. We did valuable war work.'

It may have been valuable work, but I couldn't help thinking they'd both stayed in the safety of the biscuit factory rather than handling explosives as poor yellow Nora had done. As well as turning skin yellow, TNT was responsible for a large number of deaths in munitions factories. Fifty tonnes of TNT had exploded in Silvertown, Essex in January 1917, killing seventy-three people and injuring around four hundred more.

I guessed the good old days for Redvers Tolfree was the time when business was booming, and there'd been no need for Constance Timpson's money. I was getting tired of their reminisces. 'Were you at the factory in Deptford on Friday when Miss Timpson was shot at?'

I saw their expressions falter at this abrupt change of subject.

'I organised the trip at Miss Timpson's request. Not quite the day out we were expecting.' Jack laughed, then stopped when he saw his boss's warning glance.

'It was terrible what happened. Shocking.' Redvers adopted a lofty tone. 'I've told Miss Timpson she might want to rethink some of her plans. For her own safety.'

Despite his concerned expression, I detected a hint of hostility in his words. Jack was quick to follow his boss's lead and nodded gravely. I got the impression Jack would always regard Redvers as the owner of this company, even though Constance Timpson held the purse strings. Did he resent the changes she'd made and the female staff she'd employed?

'I met one of your workers that afternoon. Rosie Robson. Has she turned up yet?' I turned to look around the factory floor.

Jack's face clouded. 'No one's seen Rosie for a few days now.'

'I heard she didn't return on the charabanc with you. I thought she must have got the train instead.' I noticed the workers nearby had gone quiet, evidently listening to our conversation.

'That's what we thought. Typical of Rosie not to tell anyone what she was doing.' Jack rubbed his stubbly chin. 'We still haven't heard from her. Some of the girls are getting worried.'

'She was feeling unwell when I saw her. Dr Mathers took her to the sickroom,' I said.

'Sickrooms,' Redvers scoffed. 'She's installed one here too.'

So Redvers wasn't enamoured with Constance's changes.

Jack placed a hand on his boss's arm. 'Would you excuse us for a few moments, Miss Woodmore? I need Mr Tolfree to sign some dockets.'

We were standing outside a corner office with windows that looked out onto the factory floor.

'Of course.' I drifted back towards the conveyor belts, keeping an eye on Jack as he closed the office door. He didn't produce any papers for Redvers to sign. Instead, they appeared to be having an intense exchange of words.

'Excuse me, Miss.'

I turned to face Nora. She was about thirty with shrewd blue eyes that stood out against her pale, tinged skin.

'I'm Nora Fox. I work with Rosie Robson. I heard you asking about her. Do you know her?' She lifted her apron to wipe away the shimmer of sweat on her brow.

I explained how I'd met Rosie on Friday and that she'd been taken to the sickroom by a doctor.

She gave a vague nod, and I guessed she already knew this. 'Dr Mathers. He's a good man. He holds surgeries in the sickroom here and treats anyone who's ill or gets injured.'

'Would there be any reason why Rosie would want to stay in London and not come back with the rest of you? I'm in contact with one of the policemen in Deptford who's investigating her disappearance. He'd like to know anything that might help to find her.'

'She was sweet on a young man who worked on the barges. Luke Denton. He won't be coming here any more now the canal's closed. Friday was the last day. We think she might have gone looking for him.'

I remembered Dr Mathers' comment about Rosie wearing her pretty dress and suggesting she was going to meet a young man. 'I'll get the police in Deptford to look into it.'

'Will you let me know if you find out anything?'

'Of course.' I glanced towards the office to check Redvers was still occupied. 'Do you know anything about Freda Bray? Were she and Rosie Robson friends?'

She shook her head. 'Miss Bray didn't mix with us. I don't know much about her, but I reckon she's gone to get away from those two. She and Jack hated one another.' She jerked her head towards the office, then scurried away as Jack Osmond and Redvers Tolfree emerged.

I wondered what they'd been talking about. Two women had gone missing, a shot had been fired, and Redvers was suggesting Constance might want to rethink some of her plans for her own safety. Was there a threat behind those words? Were all these events connected with the sole intention of getting Constance to stop her radical new working practices?

8

I spotted Percy leaning against Blacksmith's Bridge, smoking a cigarette.

The first time I'd seen this particular stretch of water was in April 1920 when Constance's mother, Lady Timpson, had announced she'd purchased the Basingstoke Canal from the army.

At the time, Lady Timpson was standing as the Conservative candidate against Mrs Siddons in the local by-election. Lady Timpson had paid the army over the odds for a stretch of canal that was of no use to them.

Hoping to gain the support of both military and farmers, which was a large proportion of the constituency of Aldershot at that time, Lady Timpson had intended to use the abandoned navigation for its original purpose of allowing local farmers to transport flour and other produce to London on barges that returned with coal and fertiliser. Constance had made valiant attempts to make the canal work, but with a surplus of lorries left over from the war, it was much cheaper and faster to transport goods by road.

'What are you doing here?' Percy stubbed out his cigarette.

It wasn't the warmest welcome I'd received. 'Elijah asked me to find out about Constance's plans for the canal. She told me you were meeting here. She said Daniel would be pleased to see me again.' I emphasised the last sentence in a futile attempt to show I wasn't as unpopular with the rest of the world as I was with him.

He perked up a bit. 'You saw Elijah? How is the old boy?'

'Same as ever.' I wasn't sure Elijah would be too thrilled at being called an old boy. 'Do you remember the day Lady Timpson announced she'd bought the canal?'

'Oh yes. She'd erected a marquee over there.' He pointed. 'And all the local bigwigs were getting stuck into the free booze. The champagne was rather good, as I recall.'

I smiled. Percy had been fun, carefree, even silly then. I wished we could go back to those days.

'And Daniel was upset because of the otters.' I wanted to remind Percy of the time we'd been friends. More than friends if he'd had his way.

'He knew they'd disappear once the canal was used commercially again. We've got plans to get them back.'

I saw the sparkle in his eyes. This was more like it. 'Where is Daniel?'

'At the hall with the magnificent Millicent. I thought I'd give them some time alone together.' He tapped the side of his nose. 'If you know what I mean.'

'Oh.' Daniel Timpson was heir to Crookham Hall, and Millicent Nightingale was a schoolteacher at Walden Elementary School. It was a nice idea but would raise eyebrows. And with Percy acting as matchmaker, things could go badly wrong.

When Daniel and Millicent arrived, I had to admit they made an interesting couple. Both had a studious air about them. Daniel Timpson was a handsome young man, though he'd lost some of his boyishness and looked older than when I'd last seen him. He nodded a formal greeting, seeming embarrassed by my presence.

'Iris. How lovely to see you again.' Millicent's welcome was warm enough. She was the same as I remembered. Long dark unruly curls, intelligent blue eyes, and a mischievous smile.

Interesting that Millicent, respectable schoolteacher and daughter of a vicar, appeared unconcerned by my dubious reputation, whereas the two supposed men of the world seemed uncomfortable.

I liked Millicent, not least because she'd once read one of my articles to her class. When Waldenmere had been under threat of development by London and South Western Railway, I'd written a series of features on the natural history of Waldenmere and what would be lost if the railway company's plans went ahead. Millicent had been one of the few people in Walden to grasp the long-term impact of building on the lake, and it had led her to form the Walden Natural History Group.

'I expect you'll be pleased to get rid of the warehouses,' I said to Daniel.

While Constance had inherited a canal transportation business that was doomed to failure, her brother had been lumbered with a series of ugly warehouses spoiling a once beautiful part of his family's estate.

'I can't wait to tear them down,' he replied with relish.

'Has there been much hostility from the canal workers?' It occurred to me that someone bitter at losing their livelihood might have taken a shot at Constance. But would they have gone so far as to abduct her female employees? That was a cruel and extreme act of retaliation.

'Most accept the situation and have taken jobs at the factory or on the estate. It's happening to canals across the country, and they know we kept it going for as long as we could.'

'What about Luke Denton?'

'Luke?' Daniel seemed surprised. 'He's taken a job at the

factory in Deptford. His mother already works there. I know he'd prefer to stay on the boats, but he realises those days are over. Others have been less understanding.'

'Have you had any threats?'

He shook his head. 'They seem to target Constance.' Creases appeared on his forehead. 'I can't understand it.'

I could. Constance was an intelligent, strong-willed young woman daring to publicly challenge the male establishment. By contrast, Daniel was a gentle soul who, like many young men, was still suffering from his time in the trenches. He preferred a quiet life in the country and didn't venture into the city much.

'I'll be writing a series of articles on why Constance has introduced new working practices. I hope to gain some support for her and Mrs Siddons. Maybe even sympathy after what's happened.' I'm not sure my voice held much conviction. I believed in what I was doing, though I was realistic about my chances of success. At present, no one was sure exactly what was going on, or even if events were connected to the changes Constance had made.

Daniel seemed grateful. 'Anything you can do to make them less hostile towards her would help. It's unfair the way she's been treated.'

'I'll certainly try,' I promised. 'I'd also like to write about what you plan to do here.'

Daniel was more relaxed with me after that, and to my satisfaction, so was Percy. We spent a pleasant hour discussing their plans for a nature reserve, and I could see what Constance meant about Millicent. She was the practical one who had to temper some of Percy and Daniel's more outlandish ideas.

When we'd finished, Millicent and I headed back to Walden along the towpath while Daniel and Percy sauntered towards Crookham Hall. I guessed Percy had probably invited himself to dinner in the hope of spending time with Constance.

'Did you enjoy your travels?' Millicent asked. 'I do envy you.'

This was something new, someone envying me. I described the route George and I had taken and the places we'd stayed.

She sighed with what seemed like genuine longing. 'Walden must seem dull after that. What are you going to do now you're back?'

'I've spoken to Mr Whittle about returning to my old job at *The Walden Herald*.' I hesitated. 'It's not settled. Mr Laffaye will need to agree.'

She smiled. 'I'm sure Mr Whittle would love to have you back. Miss Vale keeps a tight rein on him.'

'Does she?' I was intrigued by this.

'She tells me she's trying to get him to smoke less. And take exercise.'

I gave a bark of laughter. 'I wish her every success with that.'

We stopped to look across the water to where a new housing estate had been built.

'Mrs Siddons kept her word,' I said.

Millicent nodded.

A collection of neat brick houses had replaced the caravans and poorly constructed shacks that had once graced the site. I'd visited the squalid makeshift homes two years earlier with Mrs Siddons during her election campaign. She'd made good her pledge to the families living there to build them decent affordable housing.

'So much has changed,' Millicent said. 'No more barges and soon no more warehouses.'

We carried on walking along the canal towpath until we reached Crookham Wharf. There were no longer any barges moored there and the despised warehouses that had been built alongside it were deserted. A single boat was tethered at nearby

Carnival Bridge. It bore the name *Sugar Mary* and the logo of Timpson Foods.

'Constance told me all the boats would remain in Deptford,' I said.

We walked over to it, and Millicent peered through the porthole into the cabin. 'Oh.' She stumbled backwards.

'What is it?'

'I'm not sure. Is that...?'

I took her place at the porthole and on the floor of the cabin saw a foot emerging from beneath a long pink skirt. It seemed to be twisted at an odd angle.

I jumped onto the deck, scaring a crow, who was perched like a figurehead on the bow. I tried to open the door to the cabin, but it was locked and there was no sign of a key. When I pulled at the wooden door again, it rattled, seeming to give a little.

'We need to lever this open,' I called.

Millicent searched along the canal bank and joined me on the deck, brandishing a branch with leaves still attached. I wedged it into the gap between the door and frame and levered it while she pulled at the door handle. It moved slightly. She rested her boot on the side of the boat and gave a stupendous tug. I rammed the stick in harder, and this time, the wood splintered. Another tug, and the lock broke.

I bent low and entered the cabin. A body was lying twisted on the floor. The face was blue but still recognisable, as was the pink dress. A strange sour smell emanated from her.

'It's Rosie Robson.'

'Rosie.' Millicent pushed me out of the way and crouched over her. 'I used to teach her.'

'There's nothing we can do. We need to fetch the police.' I took Millicent's arm and dragged her back out onto the deck.

Rosie Robson was beyond saving.

9

'It's Rosie Robson. From the Tolfree & Timpson biscuit factory,' I said.

While I'd stayed at Carnival Bridge, Millicent had fetched PC Sid King. He'd called Superintendent Cobbe, and police officers were now examining the *Sugar Mary*.

Millicent and I were driven to the station house in Walden to be interviewed by the superintendent who'd come over from Aldershot police station. It had been a year since I'd last seen Superintendent Cobbe. And I didn't like to dwell on the circumstances of our last encounter.

'You're very well informed, as usual.' He looked grave but raised a quizzical eyebrow. 'Are you back working with Mr Whittle?'

'I'm writing some articles for him. I may return to *The Walden Herald*.'

'No doubt I'll be seeing more of you.'

I couldn't tell from his expression if he thought this was a good or bad thing. Possibly the latter.

'I've been staying in Hither Green with my grandmother and

aunt. I was at the Timpson Foods factory in Deptford when someone fired a gun at Constance Timpson.'

'Detective Inspector Yates told me what happened when I spoke to him about Miss Robson's disappearance.' He tapped his pen on his notebook.

'That's when I met Rosie. At the factory in Deptford. Later, Ben – PC Gilbert – told me she'd gone missing.'

He nodded. 'I've no doubt PC Gilbert will have done a thorough search for her on his patch. I'll be speaking to him and Detective Inspector Yates to tell them her body's been found. May I ask what you and Miss Nightingale were doing at Carnival Bridge?'

Millicent explained about the meeting with Percy and Daniel.

The superintendent turned to me. 'Percy Baverstock?'

I nodded.

'I remember Mr Baverstock well,' he said dryly.

Most people did. Again, I couldn't tell if this was a good or bad thing.

'We left Daniel and Percy at Blacksmith's Bridge,' I continued. 'We were walking back to Walden along the canal towpath and saw the boat moored by Carnival Bridge. I thought this was odd because Constance had said all the Timpson Foods boats would be staying in Deptford and not returning to Walden. We were curious to see what was on it and took a quick look.'

'That doesn't surprise me.' This was directed at me rather than Millicent. 'But you didn't just take a quick look, did you? You smashed open the door of the cabin.'

'We saw that someone, a woman, was lying on the floor,' Millicent said reprovingly. 'We may have been able to offer her some assistance.'

Despite her hair being a tangled mess of curls after her frantic dash back to town, Millicent still had the demeanour of a respectable member of the community.

'Of course, Miss Nightingale.' He inclined his head towards her. 'I'm sorry.'

I had to suppress a smile at the superintendent being spoken to like a schoolboy and offering an apology. I wished I could be more like Millicent.

'Miss Robson used to be in my class. I still teach her younger siblings.'

'Have you seen Miss Robson recently?' Superintendent Cobbe asked.

Millicent frowned. 'It's strange. The last time I saw her was in the carnival procession in June. She was this year's carnival queen.'

'Does this have some association with the bridge?'

'The canal carnival is a local tradition. Every year, decorated boats sail from King John's Castle in Odiham along the canal to Carnival Bridge. Everyone disembarks at the bridge and follows a procession led by the carnival queen,' Millicent explained. 'I believe in the last century the procession would finish at Crookham Hall. In recent years, it's carried on into Walden and ends at the Drunken Duck.'

I imagined local tradespeople had seen the commercial potential of a boisterous carnival procession and changed the route.

'Do you know if Miss Robson had a boyfriend?' The superintendent asked.

Millicent shook her head.

'When I was at the Tolfree & Timpson factory this morning, I spoke to a woman called Nora Fox who worked with Rosie. She told me Rosie was keen on one of the young men that came down from Deptford on the barges. Luke Denton is his name. When she didn't get on the charabanc to go home, Nora thought Rosie might have gone looking for him.'

'Interesting.' He made a few notes.

'You know that another woman is missing from the Tolfree &
Timpson factory?' I added. 'Miss Freda Bray.'

'I do indeed. However, the circumstances around the disappearance of the two women are very different, and I wouldn't like
to assume a connection at this stage.' Before I could question this
statement, he stood, making it clear the interview was over. 'Thank
you for your time, ladies, you've been most helpful. Miss Woodmore, will you be seeing Mr Whittle before you return to London?'

I nodded. I was tired, but I'd be heading straight over to the
office to share this with Elijah before I went back to Gran's.

Superintendent Cobbe smiled. 'Perhaps you could pass on a
message from me?'

* * *

'What were you doing up at Crookham?' Elijah picked up his pen
and turned to a fresh page in his notebook.

I'd marched into his office and closed the door on Miss Vale so
we could talk privately.

'I met Percy, Daniel Timpson and Millicent Nightingale there.
You asked me to find out what Constance's intentions are for the
canal. She plans to give the section of navigation that runs from
Odiham to Walden to the Society for the Promotion of Nature
Reserves.'

Elijah leant back, smiling. 'That must have made young Mr
Baverstock happy. And I'm sure he's delighted that you've deigned
to return to our shores.'

I didn't dissuade him of this view. 'Millicent and I were walking
back along the towpath when we saw a boat moored at Carnival
Bridge. We looked inside and Rosie Robson was lying on the floor
of the cabin.'

He put down his pen and lit a cigarette. 'Poor child. I remember her from the photos we published of the carnival. Could you tell how she'd been killed?'

I shook my head. 'There were no obvious marks. Her body's been taken to the cottage hospital mortuary to be examined by a pathologist. It could be natural causes.'

He exhaled smoke toward me. 'Healthy girls don't just keel over.'

'Constance was shot at, two women in her employ go missing and one turns up dead. It can't be a coincidence, can it?'

'You say Detective Inspector Yates suggested both these women could have been kidnapped. Yet no one's made any demands.'

'If they can't get to Constance, they get at her through her workers?' I'd been mulling this over while waiting at the bridge for Millicent to return with the police. It seemed a strange place to leave a body.

'You think they killed this poor girl to get at Constance Timpson?' He rubbed his chin. 'It's possible, though extreme.'

'Shooting at someone is extreme. Why else would they leave the body on the boat? It must have been done to direct the threat toward the Timpsons. The bridge isn't far from Constance's home and it's on the canal she's closing.' I shrugged. 'Or someone became obsessed with Rosie when she was carnival queen and took her to the bridge to re-enact some weird pageant?'

'But Rosie went missing in Deptford. You said she had a boyfriend who worked on the barges. Isn't he a more likely suspect?'

'I'm not sure if he was a boyfriend. She was sweet on him, and her friends at the factory thought she might have gone looking for him. If she found him, perhaps he wasn't too pleased to see her,' I conceded. 'Although I'm not sure why he'd leave her body on the barge. Unless he's particularly stupid, he must realise that would incriminate him.'

'True. But he's more likely to have a motive for murdering her. I find it hard to believe someone would go to the lengths of killing a young girl to undermine Constance Timpson.' Elijah stubbed out his cigarette and picked up his pen. 'What does Cobbe want me to print?'

He and Superintendent Cobbe had an understanding. Or, to be more accurate, Horace Laffaye, *The Walden Herald*'s owner, used his considerable influence to ensure the paper enjoyed a mutually beneficial relationship with the local police. If the superintendent wanted Elijah to publish certain facts, it would be in exchange for exclusive information later on.

'He asked if you could hold off from saying too much at this stage. Report that a young woman was found dead at Carnival Bridge. He particularly wants you to include the location but don't speculate on how she died. He'll send Sid over once he gets information from the pathologist on the cause of death. He doesn't want us to mention the other missing woman, Freda Bray. He said the circumstances are very different.'

'How?'

I shrugged. 'He wouldn't tell me.'

We sat in companionable silence for a few minutes. I drained the last of the coffee while Elijah scribbled notes.

'I met Redvers Tolfree this morning, and his foreman, Jack Osmond. I'm not sure they like being told what to do by a woman.'

Elijah laughed. 'Tolfree hated going cap in hand to the Timpsons. But he had no choice. He'd borrowed too much, and the banks were about to close on him. One more week, and he'd have gone under.'

'He was going on about the Tolfree glory days, the Royal Appointment, and his OBE. Seeking financial help would have been bad enough, then to be forced to change his company's name...' I paused. 'If something were to happen to Constance, what would that mean for Tolfree & Timpson?'

'He wouldn't get his shares back if that's what you're thinking. Timpson Foods would still have the controlling interest.' Elijah tapped his pen against an ashtray, causing black ink to splash over his desk. I imagined Miss Vale mopping up ash, ink and coffee stains at the end of each day. A task I used to attempt.

'He was rather disparaging about the sickrooms that Constance has set up in her factories.'

Elijah stretched back in his chair and yawned. 'Staff welfare wasn't one of the Tolfree family traditions. Like his predecessors, Redvers thinks his employees should be grateful for the privilege of working for such a famous company.'

This gave me the opening I needed to broach the subject of my next article.

'Constance and Mrs Siddons want me to write about the working practices introduced in Timpson Foods' factories and why other business owners should follow suit. It's not just about equal pay for women, it's about staff welfare. A doctor comes and holds surgeries at the factories. Paid for by the Timpsons. I'd like to mention that and a home in Deptford they fund for ex-servicemen who've fallen on hard times and need to find work. I could talk to the vicar who runs it.'

'This wouldn't happen to be the vicar of the church where the sniper is supposed to have hidden?'

I tried to look innocent. 'Yes. He's the vicar at St Mary's.'

'Hmm. Be careful. Concentrate on writing about the factory here in Walden first and the canal's closure. You can go snooping around in Deptford if—'

'If?'

'*If* Mr Laffaye decides to employ you. He wants to see you.'

10

I could sense the atmosphere as soon as I walked onto the Tolfree
& Timpson factory floor. It was uncomfortably warm and airless,
and there was none of the usual larking about or chatter. The staff
had their heads down, getting on with their work. The sweet smell
seemed even more cloying than before.

Nora Fox spotted me and came scurrying over. 'You and Miss
Nightingale found Rosie, didn't you?'

I nodded.

She wiped her hands on her apron. 'How did she seem?'

'Peaceful.' I didn't know what else to say.

'Was she clothed?' Wisps of damp hair stuck out from under
her white cap and beads of sweat glistened on her forehead.

'Yes. She looked just like she had when I last saw her.' This
sounded foolish given the circumstances. Poor little Rosie had
looked nothing like the impish young girl I'd seen hiding under
the stage. She'd been cold, blue and lifeless. 'I'm sorry.'

Nora nodded and went back to the conveyor belt.

Jack Osmond offered me a subdued greeting. His eyes were

bloodshot and his chin was red and sore as though he'd shaved roughly. 'Miss Timpson is in her office with Mrs Siddons.'

I hadn't been surprised to receive the message from Mrs Siddons to meet her and Constance at the factory. Rosie Robson's death cast a grim shadow over what they were trying to achieve.

'I can't believe it.' Constance ran a hand through her hair. 'Have you heard anything? About what happened to Rosie?'

'The police aren't saying,' I replied. 'Not until the pathologist has examined her.'

'It's my fault,' she sobbed. 'That's what it said in the letter. Something about young girls suffering. I thought they meant me.'

'The letter you received on the day of the shooting? Do you still have it? What did it say?' I desperately wanted to see this.

'Ben took it. I can't remember the exact words.' Constance closed her eyes and inhaled deeply.

I didn't push her. I could see she was struggling to contain her emotions.

Mrs Siddons turned to me. 'Do you think Rosie was murdered?'

'I don't know. Detective Inspector Yates is investigating where she went after she was last seen in Deptford on Friday afternoon. When we found her, she was wearing the same pink dress.'

'Healthy girls don't just turn up dead on boats.' Mrs Siddons echoed Elijah's words.

'Then it's my fault,' Constance said. 'Whoever did this was trying to punish me. Or scare me. Why did she end up on the *Sugar Mary*? It can't be a coincidence. Not straight after my announcement that I was closing the canal.'

'Why was the boat there?' I pulled over a chair and sat opposite her. 'I thought all the working barges were going up to London and wouldn't be returning.'

'We're going to refurbish the *Sugar Mary* to use as a pleasure boat. The Timpsons have always provided the carnival queen's boat and the old one is falling apart.'

'When was it moored at Carnival Bridge?'

'Luke Denton sailed her down from Deptford on Friday.'

Luke Denton, the boy Rosie liked.

'He left Deptford Creek at six o'clock on Friday evening and would have arrived at Crookham sometime on Saturday night,' Constance said. 'He'd been given money to catch a train home. If it were too late, he would have stayed at the old Lockkeeper's Cottage on the estate and got a train in the morning. I've told the police this. They're going to question him, though I can't believe he'd hurt anyone.'

'Whoever did this is dangerous.' Mrs Siddons glanced at me. 'The article in *The Walden Herald* gave nothing away. You found the body. Mr Whittle could have got some mileage out of that. I presume he's acting on Superintendent Cobbe's orders?'

'He asked us to keep it vague for the moment.'

'In exchange for more details later?'

I nodded. 'We're hoping he'll share the results of the autopsy with us. The superintendent also asked us not to mention Freda Bray yet. He said the circumstances of the two women are very different?' I posed this as a question to Constance.

She looked perplexed. 'It turns out Freda's father died recently, which meant the tenancy on his tied cottage came to an end. Freda cleared the place out and gave the keys back to the landowner, so it appears she'd made plans to leave.'

I was astounded. 'Did Redvers Tolfree know this?'

Constance shook her head. 'Superintendent Cobbe told us. I've asked him to keep trying to find her. Although it seems she's gone of her own accord, I find it hard to believe she would leave her position here without informing me. She wasn't that type of woman.'

This was getting more curious by the minute. 'With Superintendent Cobbe's permission, perhaps we could publish something in the paper asking anyone with knowledge of Freda's whereabouts to contact the police?'

Constance nodded. 'Please do. I can't bear the thought that something might have happened to her too. I need to know she's safe.'

'Are you back at *The Walden Herald*?' Mrs Siddons asked.

I hesitated. 'I have a meeting with Mr Laffaye this afternoon.'

She smiled. 'Perhaps you could mention to Mr Laffaye that I'd be most grateful for any support he can offer my election campaign.'

Constance gave a bitter laugh. 'Have you thought about distancing yourself from me? You could end up losing your seat if you're associated with all this.'

'No.' Mrs Siddons reached out and took Constance's hand. 'What you're doing is right and long overdue and I'll continue to encourage other industries to follow your lead. But we have a fight on our hands.'

* * *

Heron Bay Lodge was tucked away in a copse of trees on the southern shores of Waldenmere. It was a modern wooden-clad house, painted a soft shade of grey with a high veranda that offered a spectacular view of the lake.

'Welcome home, my dear.' Horace gestured for me to take a seat on the veranda where Elijah was waiting.

'Thank you, Mr Laffaye.' I tried to appear calm despite the knot that had formed in my stomach. I wondered if he was going to chastise me for leaving *The Walden Herald* without notice.

Horace Laffaye chose to give the appearance of being a mild-mannered, retired bank manager who'd led a quiet, uneventful life. In reality, he was a financial wizard who'd travelled the world and traded on Wall Street. He'd settled in Walden nearly ten years ago and decided that the peaceful town should stay just the way he liked it. And he used his considerable influence to ensure that it did.

As usual, he was impeccably dressed in a beige linen suit with a Panama hat on his closely cropped grey hair. Elijah sat next to him in a rumpled brown suit, cigarette in hand. They may have looked a mismatched pair, but something drew them together.

A thought suddenly occurred to me that more might have changed in my absence than I realised. Elijah and Horace may no longer be a couple. It was difficult to tell. They generally spoke to each other in a formal manner, giving the impression they were nothing more than business colleagues. I'd have to wait and see.

'Did you enjoy your travels?' Horace asked.

'I did, thank you.' I took the glass of lemonade he handed me. He and Elijah were drinking whisky.

'I'm glad. Travel is so good for the mind. It's not only educational; it makes you appreciate what you have at home.'

I wasn't sure what aspect of my home life I should appreciate, though I didn't say this.

'You're currently staying in Hither Green, I believe?'

'That's right.' I pulled my cardigan closer around me and gazed out at the lake. There was a melancholy stillness about it on this September afternoon. Despite, or perhaps because of all the memories it held for me, I was drawn back to it.

'Do you intend to return to Walden?'

The prospect of Mrs Keats becoming a permanent fixture weighed heavily on my mind. I wanted to be near Waldenmere. But did I want to go back to Chestnut Avenue? 'My father would like me to.'

'And I would too. I understand why you left the way you did. What happened to your friend was a dreadful tragedy. Now you're back, I'd be pleased if you'd consider returning to work full-time for Mr Whittle. He may not say it, but he missed you while you were away.'

'I enjoyed the peace and quiet,' Elijah retorted. He and Horace exchanged an affectionate glance, which told me they were still together.

'I missed... Waldenmere.' Like Elijah, I wasn't given to sentiment. But I was grateful to them for letting me back into their lives. 'I'm sorry for leaving the way I did. I'd love to come back to *The Walden Herald*.'

'That's settled then. Now let's talk about this unfortunate case. You met the poor girl, I believe?'

I nodded. 'At the factory in Deptford. She was sweet. Constance Timpson blames herself. She's terribly upset.' The knot in my stomach melted away as I spoke. This was like the old days, and I realised it was Elijah and Horace and *The Walden Herald* I'd been homesick for, not 9 Chestnut Avenue.

'I'm sure she is. It's somewhat of a coincidence. She gives a speech to announce she's closing the canal, then on top of an assassination attempt, the body of one of her employees is found on the last barge that travelled along that navigation.' Horace tutted. 'It seems symbolic to me.'

'A cruel thing to do.' Elijah lit a cigarette. Despite the grim subject matter, his expression showed that he too was pleased we were back together again.

'Indeed,' Horace agreed.

'Rosie was last seen at the Timpson Foods factory on Friday afternoon. Luke Denton left Deptford on the *Sugar Mary* on Friday evening at around six o'clock and moored it at Carnival Bridge sometime on Saturday evening. We found Rosie's body in its cabin on Monday afternoon,' I recounted. 'It could very well have nothing to do with the Timpsons.'

Elijah nodded. 'Luke Denton must be the main suspect.'

'Will this cause Miss Timpson to tone down some of her plans?' Horace asked.

I shook my head. 'She intends to continue implementing changes in all her factories: no child labour, equal pay and no dismissing women from her employ when they marry. Mrs Siddons is calling on other business owners to follow suit, and Constance is supporting Mrs Siddons in her election campaign.'

'And how is the campaign going?'

I shrugged. 'Recent articles have implied Mrs Siddons is turning her back on her election promise to help ex-servicemen find work. She asked me to say that she'd be most grateful for your support.'

'Did she.' Horace smiled, seeming to weigh up the matter.

The Walden Herald had championed Mrs Siddons as the Liberal candidate in the 1920 by-election. With a General Election coming up would Horace and Elijah get behind her again? Horace might find some of Mrs Siddons' reforms too radical. However, the Labour Party had gained considerable support, and I couldn't see him welcoming a Labour government.

'I'll call on Mrs Siddons to discuss the matter. In the meantime, I'm agreeable to you continuing to report on Miss Timpson's work. I'd also like *The Walden Herald* to be the first to publish any news on the sniper attack or this poor girl's unfortunate death. And, of course, we'd like to help in the search for Miss Bray.'

I nodded, understanding his message. If he were to extend his support to Constance and Mrs Siddons, he'd expect it to be mutually beneficial. He was happy for me to stay close and publish stories on their good works in exchange for first-hand information on any developments.

11

'Are they for me? How kind.' I smirked at Percy's discomfort.

He clearly hadn't expected an audience when he'd bounded into Constance's Deptford office clutching a highly fragrant bouquet of lilies. I was seated by her desk, drinking coffee, while Ben stood by the window looking over at St Mary's Church.

'They're to thank Constance for gifting the canal to the society.' Percy seemed highly pleased with himself. No doubt the society had given him full credit for acquiring part of the canal as a nature reserve.

Constance smiled and thanked him. But I noticed her eyes kept drifting towards Ben. That was an interesting development.

'Ben's worried someone's going to shoot me through the window.' Constance gave a silvery laugh.

'No. The angle's all wrong.' Ben swung around, seemingly satisfied that there was no chance of a sniper being able to target the office.

'Thank you for looking after me.' Constance reached out to touch his arm and I felt a pang of sympathy for her. Ben was unlikely to reciprocate her feelings. His heart had been broken by the loss of his first love, and I suspected he'd closed his mind to any romantic notions. Percy was watching them with a crestfallen expression.

'Only following orders,' Ben said.

Constance's smile faltered. She got up and went over to the rosewood cabinet. Filling a crystal vase from the water jug, she began to arrange the flowers.

'Have you received any more threatening letters?' I asked.

'No. Only that one.' She returned to her desk, opened the top drawer, and took out a sheet of paper. She slid it across to me. 'Detective Inspector Yates has the original. This is what it said. The words were typed.'

I read the message.

Men work in factories and run them. Not young girls. Restore things to how they should be, or there'll be more suffering.

'Has Detective Inspector Yates found out who sent it?'

Ben shook his head. 'The paper is cheap. From the Lion Brand range that can be purchased from anywhere, and it could have been typed on any typewriter. It was left on Constance's desk, and there was no envelope.'

It didn't need saying that whoever put it there must be familiar with the layout of the factory to be able to access the office without being noticed.

'I've got my old job back at *The Walden Herald*.' I changed the subject, hoping to lift Constance's mood, which had dropped as fast as Percy's high spirits.

Ben smiled. 'I thought you would. Will you be moving back to Walden?'

'Once I can arrange for a car to take my cases.'

'Percy can do that, can't you?' Constance seemed to take it for granted that he would jump at her every command.

'There's no need,' I said hastily.

'He loves driving people in his car. Will it be big enough?'

'I just have some clothes and books.' I'd travelled light. Most of my belongings were still in my old bedroom in Walden.

'I'd be delighted to help.' Percy mustered a faint smile. I gratefully accepted the offer.

'Mr Laffaye plans to call on Mrs Siddons. I get the impression he'll agree to *The Walden Herald* supporting her.'

'Good.' Constance suddenly looked tired. 'We need all the help we can get. You also mentioned you wanted to talk to Reverend Powell and Dr Mathers about Creek House?'

I nodded. 'I think we can counter some of the criticism directed at you and Mrs Siddons by highlighting the work you do for ex-servicemen.' I stood up, glad of an excuse to escape the office. 'I'll see if anyone's over at the church.'

* * *

As I was walking through the gates of Timpson Foods, I stopped to look at the tower of St Mary's Church. Was the person who fired that shot responsible for Rosie Robson's death?

'Has Superintendent Cobbe been in touch?' I asked Ben, who'd followed me out.

He brightened at this. 'Yes. Detective Inspector Yates has said to give him every assistance. Yates seems to think the shooting and the disappearance of Rosie Robson and Freda Bray are linked. His theory is that a kidnapper murdered Rosie to show what he's capable of. He's told Constance to look out for a ransom demand for Freda.'

I frowned. This theory didn't feel quite right.

Ben continued, 'The superintendent disagrees with Yates. He doesn't think Freda's been kidnapped. It's possible the shooting was some sort of diversion connected to Rosie. Either way, we need to know where she went that afternoon. How did she get to Walden, and was she killed before or after she got there? WPC Jones saw Rosie leaving the factory shortly before five on Friday. After that, we have no idea where she went.'

'There was a PC stationed at the gate at the time of the shooting, wasn't there? No one could have come in or gone out without being seen?'

'Yes.'

I looked up and down the road. 'A rifle would be hard to conceal, wouldn't it?'

'The ballistics expert says the bullet and shell came from a Lee Enfield SMLE Mark III. That type of rifle is nearly forty-five inches long. You'd be noticed carrying it down the street.' Ben followed my gaze to the few houses dotted along the road. 'The small cottage to the left of St Mary's is where Reverend Powell lives. It's owned by the church and comes with the job. Creek House is to the right of St Mary's. It's the home I told you about for unemployed ex-servicemen. Timpson Foods owns it along with the row of terraced houses next door.'

'Who lives in the terrace?' I nodded towards the row of five houses.

'The tenants are mostly employees who need financial help and pay a low rent for living there. Mrs Blanche Denton lives in the end one nearest the church and Dr Mathers in the last one at the far end of the road. The three in the middle are occupied by the families of barge workers who have moved from the boats to work in the factory.'

'Mrs Blanche Denton? Any relation to Luke Denton?'

'His mother. He lives there too. Blanche works in the factory.'

He jerked his head back to Timpson Foods. 'They say they were in the crowd when the shot was fired. We have witnesses who saw Blanche but not Luke. He told me he was keeping out of the way of Rosie. He admitted she was keen on him, and he didn't want to encourage her. He says he saw Rosie getting off the charabanc but didn't see her again after that. He was at the factory for the rest of the afternoon and then left on the *Sugar Mary* at about six o'clock.'

'What about the men living in Creek House?' I looked over at the imposing grey-stone building.

'There are currently six occupants. Some of them are disabled. The Timpsons pay the bills and Dr Mathers' medical fees. With the help of Reverend Powell, they try to get the men back into work, sometimes giving them jobs in their factories or on the farm at Crookham Hall.'

'Have you questioned them? They live next to the church; didn't they see anything?'

He shook his head. 'They say not. Whoever was hiding in the tower could have been there for some time before the actual shooting. Reverend Powell was with a parishioner. He'd intended to be at the factory for Constance's speech but got held up. It was all over by the time he got back.'

'Whoever it was must have left the church straight afterwards,' I commented. 'They would have known the police would search the tower.'

'In the chaos, the person could have left without anyone noticing. All attention was on the factory. We've searched the church and surrounding area but haven't found the rifle.'

'You're worried they might try again?' We walked over to St Mary's.

He nodded. 'WPC Jones and I are still keeping an eye on Constance. And, of course, she has Percy to protect her.'

I smiled. 'Between WPC Jones and Percy, I think my money is on WPC Jones. Are they recruiting more female police officers?'

Ben laughed. 'Please don't tell me it's a career you're planning to take up.'

'Why is that funny?'

'Because you have to abide by the rules, take orders. I'm not sure you'd be a suitable candidate.'

'A rebel, eh?' A low voice came from behind one of the columns at the entrance to the church. 'You question those in command?'

Reverend Powell was watching us with a smile. I felt myself blush.

His clerical garb still took me by surprise. I wasn't a church-goer, and my view of religious men had been formed by Reverend Childs, the vicar of Walden, a fussy but kind man who delivered sermons with gentle persuasion. Reverend Powell looked like he'd bark orders from the pulpit like a sergeant major. I could imagine him leading soldiers into battle, not tending to his flock.

'Isn't that a good thing?' I took in his intense green eyes and dark blond hair. It was his masculinity that was unnerving. I couldn't help wondering how old he was. He had the physique of a young man but mature features. I guessed he must be over thirty, how near to forty, I wasn't sure.

He held up a hand to concede the point. 'It is in peacetime. It's not such a good trait in wartime. Men had to obey commands without question, which is why some of them find it difficult to manage their lives now they're back home with their families. The expectation is on them to make the decisions. Be the head of the household.'

'Could I talk to you about Creek House? I'd like to know about the ex-servicemen you take in and what you do for them.'

'Miss Timpson said you want to write about our work. I'll show you the church first, then take you over there.'

'Thank you, Reverend Powell.'

'Call me Archie. It's Iris, isn't it?'

I nodded, faintly pleased he'd remembered my name.

'Coming in for a cup of coffee, Ben?'

He raised a hand in response. 'Thanks, but I've got to get back to the station.'

I followed Archie into St. Mary's. It was built of grey Portland stone with columns on either side of the aisle. The church was cold and had that musty smell often found in ancient places of worship. The altar was simply decorated with a cross and an urn full of fresh flowers.

'He's a good lad, that one. Is he your beau?'

I smiled at the old-fashioned term and shook my head. 'Ben's like a brother to me.' I felt an unexpected swell of emotion as I said those words. I'd never described him that way before, but I suddenly realised it was how I felt.

'You've known him a long time?' Archie looked at me curiously.

'Since we were children.'

'In Walden?'

I nodded.

'It's a lovely place. Daniel lets me stay in a cottage on the Crookham estate at the weekends when his workers aren't using it. I go there to paint.'

'I believe Luke Denton stayed at a cottage on the estate after he left the *Sugar Mary* at Carnival Bridge?'

'Yes, it's the same one, Lockkeeper's Cottage. The bargemen sometimes used it. Let's go through to the vestry, and I'll make us some coffee.'

I followed, noticing the narrow, winding stone staircase between the main body of the church and the vestry to the side.

'Does that lead up to the steeple?' I asked.

'It does.' He grinned. 'Go on. I guess you're dying to take a look.

Be careful. The staircase is steep. It's a bit tight for two people, so come and find me in the vestry when you're done.'

I climbed the winding staircase. The stone steps were uneven and there was no handrail to hold onto. At the top of the stairs was a low wooden door that led outside. You could walk in a circle around the base of the steeple, which sat on top of the cylindrical tower. It was a narrow space. There wasn't even enough room for two people to pass each other. I examined the dull stone floor and low wall, but there was nothing of interest. The shell casing had been removed.

From this vantage point, you could see down to the river, the surrounding streets and into the forecourt of the factory. A lone sniper could easily have hidden behind the low wall and focused on their target without being seen. I shivered at the thought of a shot ringing out as Constance walked through those factory gates.

12

I made my way down the steep steps and into the vestry. It was a simple room with a worktop and wall cupboards along one side and a solid oak table at its centre. A wardrobe in one corner presumably contained ecclesiastical robes.

There was a back door and, peering out of the vestry window, I saw that it led to an enclosed courtyard with a high wooden gate that must open onto the road. The sniper could have accessed the tower from either the vestry or the church's main entrance. I suspected they used the vestry. That way, they could check all was clear from behind the cover of the gate before making their escape. It would have been safer than coming out of the front of the church and down the steps onto the street armed with a rifle. I wondered if they'd had a car parked nearby.

'You're a reporter?' Archie was watching me with an amused expression as he boiled water on a small gas ring. 'Do you like investigating crimes?'

'It's not something I do very much. Walden's usually a quiet place.'

'That's why I like it. Particularly the meadows and woodland at

Crookham. It's the perfect place to paint.' He placed a coffeepot on the table and gestured for me to sit down. I watched his long, slender fingers as he poured two mugs of coffee. 'It's where you found Rosie Robson, I believe? At Carnival Bridge?'

'On the *Sugar Mary*.'

'Poor girl.' His voice held anger as well as sorrow. 'I don't know how she got there, but I can tell you it wasn't Luke Denton's doing.'

'How do you know?'

'Because I do,' he said simply. 'He's not capable of harming someone, least of all a young girl. His mother, Blanche, keeps this place clean for me and does the flowers for the church. She's taken care of me since I was posted here a couple of years ago. I've grown close to her and Luke. They're good people.'

'What about the sniper? Do you have any idea who that could be?'

To my surprise, he laughed. 'I'm afraid that could be anyone. The idea of taking a pot-shot at Constance Timpson would appeal to quite a few men I know.'

My nostrils flared. 'Why? What makes them hate her?'

'I don't think they hate her. They're angry at what she represents. I'm not convinced anyone intended to kill her.' He sighed. 'It's a complicated situation.'

'Why is it?' I couldn't believe how dismissive he sounded. A woman's life had been threatened. On the day of the shooting, I'd been willing to believe it was done to scare Constance. But now Rosie Robson was dead, and I'd seen the anonymous letter, I was persuaded the danger was real.

'There are two main issues. The first is that factory owners don't want to dig into their pockets and pay women the same as men. Less profit for them.'

'If they don't, they might end up with a strike on their hands.'

'Unlikely. Most women don't belong to a trade union because

most male union leaders try to stop women from getting any training. They only want men in skilled positions.'

I nodded. It was true and it appalled me. 'What's the second issue?'

'There aren't enough jobs to go around. In some factories, young women make up three-quarters of the workforce.'

'Because they're cheaper to employ?'

'Precisely. Many are the same age as Rosie Robson. During the war, women did a good job for a low wage. Factory owners didn't want to get rid of them. But there are men who fought for their country who want their jobs back.'

'Surely paying women the same as men makes it fairer for men, too? They're not being undercut by a cheaper female workforce?'

He leant forward. 'I don't know what the answer is. I believe in trade board rates, which means there's a minimum wage. Some employers think they can get away with murder and pay a pittance.'

'What about equal pay for women?' I was curious to see how he'd answer this.

He gave a sheepish grin. 'I support that. But...'

'But what?''

'You probably won't like this, but maybe a woman should give up her job when she marries. After all, she'll be looked after by her husband.'

'Many families need both wages. And why should it be women that have to leave their jobs?'

'Because, as I said, there aren't enough jobs to go around. George Cadbury has it right. A married woman's duty is to her husband and children, and she can't be in two places at the same time. He looks after his workers, and the female staff at his Bournville factories have to resign when they wed.'

'His factories are filled with women in the most menial, lowest-paid jobs, and the poorest of them can't afford to leave and get married. How can that be right? I can see it's a problem. But why is there such hostility toward Constance and Mrs Siddons for trying to tackle the issue?'

'People fear change. And equal pay and conditions is a radical change. It's part of a new way of life that men and women have to adjust to.' He spread out his hands. 'My role is to help them adjust and show greater tolerance for each other.'

We finished our coffee and he stood up. 'I'll take you next door to Creek House to meet some of the men.'

We went back through the church, and I noticed a woman was sitting in the front pew, staring dreamily at the altar. Despite our footsteps clicking on the stone floor, she seemed unaware of our presence.

'Blanche,' Archie said softly.

'Oh, Reverend, I was just...' She raised a thin hand to touch her wispy grey-blonde hair. I caught a waft of gardenia scent, similar to the one my grandmother wore.

'It's alright, stay here as long as you want. We're going next door, so you'll be alone. This is Iris Woodmore. She's a reporter. She's writing about Miss Timpson and the work we do at Creek House.' He turned to me. 'Iris, this is Mrs Blanche Denton. She does a marvellous job with the flowers. When we can get them.'

'They're lovely.' I nodded towards the display at the altar.

'Woodmore.' Blanche Denton stared at me with sorrowful pale blue eyes. 'I shared a prison cell with a woman named Woodmore.'

I stiffened.

'Mrs Denton was a suffragette,' Archie explained.

I smiled at Blanche and nodded my understanding. But I stayed silent. I told myself it was because I didn't want to discuss my past with strangers.

As I followed Archie out of the church and down the stone steps, old feelings of grief and resentment floated to the surface. I knew I should be proud of Mother. Not angry. So why hadn't I acknowledged it was her in that prison cell?

I shut out those feelings and turned my attention to a Ford sedan motorcar I'd noticed parked outside the factory before. 'Whose car is that?'

'Constance Timpson bought it to help us with our work. Dr Mathers uses it the most. He has patients to see here and in Walden. I drive it occasionally, although I try to make sure it's on hand for the doctor in case of an emergency.'

'Was it here on the day Constance was shot at?'

His eyes narrowed. 'I expect so, though I couldn't swear to it. What are you suggesting?'

'Just that it would be handy for anyone leaving the church to drive away in it.' I assumed Dr Mathers had been in the factory grounds at the time of the shooting. He would have been caught up in the commotion and perhaps wouldn't have noticed if someone had taken the car and put it back later.

'One of the men living at Creek House, you mean?' His voice was low, and there was a hint of displeasure.

I didn't answer, saying instead, 'Was anyone in the church when you left that afternoon?'

Archie frowned. 'No, it was empty. Micky Swann, one of the current occupants of Creek House, asked me to call on his wife. When I got back, no one was around, and a police constable told me what had happened.' His eyes were hard, and I could tell he didn't like my questioning. 'I can't remember if the car was there or not.'

Archie opened the front door of Creek House and led me into a hallway which reeked of cheap cigarettes.

'It's not much. The men's bedrooms are upstairs. There's a

kitchen and dining room at the back of the house.' He gestured to
the doors at the end of the hall. 'This is the office that Mathers and
I share, and in there is a communal lounge.'

The office door was open, and I glanced inside to see if I could
spot a typewriter. There was no sign of one. 'What's in there?' I
pointed to a closed door next to the office.

'It's a junk room. It was supposed to be a second office for the
men to use, but they tend to do everything in the lounge.' With
this, he opened the door opposite the office and ushered me into a
smoke-filled room. I peered through the smog to see about half a
dozen men sitting around engaged in various occupations. Some
were reading, and to my alarm, one man seemed to be recon-
structing a pistol.

'What's that you've got there, Micky?' Archie strolled over
to him.

'Jerry gun. Souvenir,' he grunted back.

'Don't fire it at anyone. We've had enough near misses around
here.' Archie didn't appear to be troubled by the weapon. 'This is
Miss Woodmore. She's going to be writing an article about what
we do here. You can tell her how grateful you are to your bene-
factress.'

To my alarm, Archie then swept from the room, leaving me
with five sets of hostile eyes staring at me. A sixth man sat in the
corner. He wore dark glasses and held a white stick.

Micky Swann got up and came towards me, pistol in hand.
'Why are you wearing trousers?' he asked.

13

Micky Swann examined me as though I was a specimen in a laboratory. He was a stocky man with sandy brown hair, who looked to be in his thirties. His most arresting feature was his strange amber eyes, which were currently trained on me.

'Told ya. Women wear the trousers nowadays.' This came from a young redheaded man seated in an armchair, a book resting on his lap. He was missing his right hand.

I ignored the sniggers and held Micky's gaze. 'I wear them because they're comfortable.'

'Women take our jobs; now they're wearing our clothes,' said a grey-haired man reading a newspaper. A crutch was propped up against the wall next to his chair. I could see that each man apart from Micky had a disability.

'It's not practical to wear a skirt when you're clearing up debris after a zeppelin raid. Or driving an ambulance or working in a munitions factory. That's why women started wearing trousers.'

'You're right. But the war's over. It's time women went back into the home and started dressing properly again,' Micky said.

'I think you'll find there's no going back. Women have proved they can do most jobs just as well as men.' I realised this wasn't the most diplomatic thing to say in the circumstances.

He scowled. 'You didn't fight for your country.' He ran the muzzle of the gun along his left arm. 'You didn't get shot at.'

'No, I didn't. I appreciate the sacrifices that have been made. I hope we never have to endure anything like that again. Perhaps with women entering politics, we can avoid more wars.' I couldn't resist saying it, even though I wasn't speaking to the most receptive audience.

Micky laughed. 'Women haven't got a clue about politics. They should stay out of Parliament and business.'

'You benefit from Miss Timpson's generosity, yet you believe she shouldn't be running her family's company. Do you feel threatened by her?' I stared at the gun in his hand, my implication clear.

He moved closer. 'Are you trying to suggest I had something to do with that shooting?'

I stood my ground. He held the gun in a threatening way, though I didn't think he'd risk firing it in a room full of people. At least, I hoped he wouldn't.

Archie appeared at the door. 'Dr Mathers has arrived. You can ask him about the car.'

Relieved, I followed him into the hallway. I had a sneaking suspicion he'd been listening at the door.

'Did you find that intimidating?' His green eyes appraised me.

'No,' I replied untruthfully. Dr Mathers was in the office, and I was aware he could hear our conversation. 'Why would I?'

'I thought you might have found them a little rough. These men spent years living in appalling conditions and endured hardship and injuries you couldn't imagine.'

I noted the edge to his voice.

'I spent over two years in a Voluntary Aid Detachment, the majority of it in Lewisham Military Hospital taking care of men shipped back from France. I've a good idea of what they went through,' I replied. 'You didn't need to leave me in a room with an armed man to prove your point.'

He waved a hand dismissively. 'Micky Swann wouldn't hurt a fly.'

'What does he plan to do with that gun?'

'It's a souvenir. Micky loves guns, even though one nearly killed him.'

'What's he doing here at Creek House?' I asked. 'You said he was married?'

'His wife, Polly, kicked him out. His own fault. Micky used to drink. He's packed up since he's been here. All he wants is to get a job to provide for his two children and show Polly he can still take care of them all. He's desperate to go back home. We just need to get him stronger and find him suitable work.'

'What did he do before?'

'He was a labourer. He took a bullet to his left arm, and his chest's not good, so he can't go back to that, though Mathers has worked miracles.'

Dr Mathers, who'd been rummaging in a large black medical bag, looked up at the mention of his name. 'I just gave Micky exercises to improve his breathing and strengthen his arm. He's the one that's done all the hard work. His rehabilitation has been a joy to watch.'

'He has significantly more movement than before,' Archie said. 'He'll never be able to go back to heavy manual labour, but he could do a factory job as long as there's not too much lifting involved. We start them off doing odd jobs across the road to see how they get on.'

I thought of the way Micky had placed the muzzle of the gun to his arm. He'd been on the receiving end of a bullet that had ruined his life. Perhaps he thought it was someone else's turn. I wondered whether his arm was strong enough to handle a rifle. And if the men did odd jobs at the factory, it wouldn't have been difficult for one of them to have sneaked the letter onto Constance's desk.

'Mathers does sterling work,' Archie said. 'You wouldn't get many doctors running surgeries in between shifts at the hospital.'

Dr Mathers smiled. 'It's only thanks to the generosity of the Timpsons that I can afford to give my time here and at the factories. They fund the work and pay for the medicines needed.'

Archie glanced at his watch. 'I have to be at a meeting of the diocese. I really do need to leave you this time.'

I raised my eyebrows at this admission. So he had left me in the lounge on purpose. I nodded in response and didn't bother thanking him for his time. By the curl of his lips, he understood the reason for my displeasure.

'Sorry,' he mouthed silently.

I watched him disappear through the front door, irritated by his behaviour.

'It's Archie that does wonders,' Dr Mathers said. 'Staying here is only a temporary arrangement for these men. A stepping-stone to a new life. Over the last couple of years, he's helped hundreds of ex-servicemen find work and places to live. But there's only so much time and money. We can't help everyone.'

'He was a chaplain in the war, I believe?' I was curious to find out more about the infuriating Reverend Archibald Powell.

Dr Mathers smiled. 'He's an intriguing chap, isn't he? And a brave one, from what I've been told. He followed soldiers into battle and tended to them in extreme conditions under heavy fire. He went wherever the men went.'

I was about to ask more about Archie, but the doctor went over to the office door and closed it. He gestured for me to sit down. His smile had faded.

'Miss Timpson tells me you were the one that found poor Rosie Robson. I'm going to call on her family this afternoon.'

'You know the Robsons?'

'I'd often see Rosie and her brother, Nicholas, on my trips to the biscuit factory. Nicholas once asked me to call on his mother when she had a nasty bout of influenza. Poor woman has to cope on her own with eight children.' He stopped, realising what he'd said. 'Seven without Rosie. Not that Nicholas is a child. He's eighteen and has been the man of the house since his father was killed in the war.'

I shook my head in sadness at what the family had endured.

'It's dreadful to contemplate, isn't it?' Dr Mathers lifted the wire-rimmed spectacles from the bridge of his nose and rubbed his eyes. 'I've no doubt Mrs Robson is going to ask me what happened to her daughter and I don't have any answers for her. Rosie was fit and healthy when I saw her, apart from her bout of sickness, which was understandable after the shocking events that afternoon. Do you know if the police have established how she died? I want to speak to them before I call on Mrs Robson.'

'I believe they're still waiting for the pathologist's report. You could ask PC King at the station house. Or Superintendent Cobbe at Aldershot police station.'

'Thank you. I'll call in at the station house while I'm in Walden.'

'Do you visit Walden much? It must be handy to have a car.'

'It's invaluable. Miss Timpson was most generous in purchasing it for us. I drive to Walden at least once a week for my surgeries and sometimes call in at Wildmay Manor. Have you heard of it?'

Wildmay Manor was an ornate country house with acres of

beautiful grounds and a farm. Once owned by a wealthy banker, it had been converted into a hospital for servicemen suffering from mental afflictions and war neurosis. It was only six miles from Walden.

I nodded. 'I went there last year. I was writing an article about the work they do.' This wasn't true. My reason for visiting Wildmay Manor had been to snoop on a patient I suspected may have committed a crime. The article had been a pretext to get me through the door. 'What takes you there?'

The doctor looked pleased I'd heard of the place. 'Some of the men that come to Creek House have more than physical ailments. In severe cases of shellshock, I try to get them a place at the Manor or at least some therapy from Dr Outen.'

When I'd met Dr Outen the previous year, he'd described treatments that included hypnosis, massage and different dietary regimes. Patients were encouraged to participate in outdoor activities in the garden and on the farm to give them a sense of purpose and to take up creative hobbies such as painting and pottery.

Initially, Dr Outen's work had been considered controversial, as during the war, many soldiers suffering from mental illnesses had been charged with desertion, cowardice and insubordination. Some were even shot. But as the term shellshock became more widely understood, Dr Outen's therapies gained credibility.

'Are any of the men at Creek House ever aggressive?' I hoped the question wouldn't antagonise Dr Mathers in the way that it had Archie.

He hesitated. 'They're all former soldiers. They've been trained to fight. Most are harmless, but... well, let's just say there are some you'd be wise not to provoke.'

'Trained to fight and to shoot?'

'I know what you're thinking.' Dr Mathers didn't seem as appalled by this suggestion as Archie had.

'Was your car here on Friday? After the shooting?'

'The police asked me the same question. The truth is, I don't know. I'd driven over to the hospital that morning and got back in time for Miss Timpson's speech. I ended up staying at the factory for some time after the incident, treating people for shock.'

'Could one of the men here have taken it for a short while without you noticing?'

He shrugged. 'I suppose they could. It's a shared car, and there are a couple of keys. I'm afraid I was a little preoccupied after what happened.'

'I saw Micky Swann handling a gun earlier. Archie assured me he's harmless.'

'It's in Archie's nature to see the best in his men and try to protect them. As I said, when he was a chaplain, he tended to his flock, whatever that entailed. Even crawling across battlefields to drag wounded men back to safety. He treats all men equally, from officers like Daniel Timpson to foot soldiers like Micky Swann. The war may be over, but he still believes it's his duty to look after those who served.'

'Even if they're dangerous?'

The doctor sighed. 'Most of these men are decent souls who just need practical help to regain their self-respect and dignity. Some would benefit from the psychological treatments Dr Outen offers to enable them to adjust to life outside the army, but he can only take the most extreme cases. For the others, we try to show them how to take responsibility for themselves and their actions.'

I found it interesting that Archie seemed to think all his protégés were angels, whereas Dr Mathers took a more pragmatic view. Was one of those decent souls so intolerant of women that they decided to aim their gun at Constance Timpson? I remembered Archie saying he hadn't been in the church at the time of the shooting because Micky Swann had asked him to call on his wife. Had that been a ploy to get him out of the way?

And what about Rosie Robson? Could she have witnessed something that put her life in danger? Or stumbled into the wrong person when she left the factory that evening?

'Delighted to meet you, Mrs...' Percy looked at me for guidance.

'Armitage,' I supplied.

'Delighted to meet you, Mrs Armitage and Miss Armitage.'

Aunt Maud welcomed Percy into the parlour. Gran sat in her upright chair and glared at him. 'Are you another boyfriend?'

'I'm the only true love.' Percy put his arm around my shoulder and squeezed me.

Introducing him to Gran was never going to go well. I wanted to get it over with as quickly as possible.

'I've told you about Percy, Gran. He works at the Natural History Museum.' I thought this would make him sound respectable.

'Are you a professor?'

'Good lord, no. Too dim for that.' He pushed his hair back over his brow. 'I catalogue records in the herbarium and go on field trips, that sort of thing.'

'That sounds very interesting,' Aunt Maud enthused.

'The records can be dull, but the trips out are fun.'

'You have a motor car?' Gran peered at him over her spectacles.

'I don't like motor cars. Dangerous things. I was almost run over by one.'

'Do you think they did it on purpose?' Percy asked with interest.

I elbowed him in the ribs.

'I haven't killed anyone yet,' he assured her.

'Yet?' Gran's voice rose. 'That sounds like you intend to run someone down?'

'I'll try not to,' Percy replied gravely. 'You'd best stay in the house just in case.'

I stifled a laugh.

'Would you like a cup of tea?' Aunt Maud hovered in the doorway to the kitchen.

'No,' Percy and I said in unison.

'We'd better get going. We might get held up if we...' I floundered.

'If we hit any pedestrians on the way,' Percy finished cheerily. 'But thank you for the offer.'

My cases and a few boxes were lined up in the hallway. Percy and I hurried to load them into the car.

I waved to Aunt Maud as Percy drove off at a sedate speed. He was a careful driver who kept his eyes on the road. Unlike Mrs Siddons, who liked to tear along country lanes, regardless of what she might encounter around the next bend.

'This is kind of you,' I said to him.

'I was going to Walden anyway.'

I got the message. He didn't want me to think he was doing me a favour. I tried again. 'I'm sorry about my gran. Thanks for helping me escape.'

At this, he seemed to thaw a little. 'A charming lady. Though I can understand why you want to move back to Walden.'

I laughed. 'I'll miss Aunt Maud.'

'She seems a decent sort. I pity Ben, though. Poor chap probably doesn't get a moment's peace.'

'They do fuss over him. I think he'd like more time to himself, even if he does appreciate being well-fed.'

'I could find him new digs. I did consider introducing him to a few friends of mine. Female ones, if you see what I mean. Try to get him back...' He faltered. '...back into the swing of things.'

'I'm not sure he's ready.' I wondered whether Percy's concern was because he'd noticed Constance's fondness for Ben.

When we pulled up outside 9 Chestnut Avenue, I was embarrassed by the welcoming committee that emerged from the house. I could see the neighbours' curtains twitching. As if Gran wasn't bad enough, there was the rest of the family to face. On first meeting Percy, my father had viewed him with suspicion. Since then, I'd absconded with a man Father considered far worse – so there was the possibility Percy would now be looked upon more favourably.

Elijah was in attendance, and he and Percy greeted each other like long lost friends. Lizzy hugged me while Father took my cases from the car. Fortunately, there was no sign of Mrs Keats. I hurried everyone inside and closed the front door on the prying eyes.

Everything seemed to be going smoothly. That is until Percy grabbed a case. 'Shall I take this up to your bedroom?' He gave a sudden, panicked laugh. 'Not that I know where that is.'

'That won't be necessary.' My father took the case from him. 'I can manage.'

'I expect you'd like a cup of tea after your drive.' Lizzy disappeared into the kitchen.

'Bet you'd like something stronger.' Elijah ushered Percy into the drawing room and helped himself to the contents of the drinks cabinet while Father and I ferried my belongings upstairs.

Lizzy insisted on Percy staying to lunch and, to my surprise, he accepted with enthusiasm. 'Terribly kind of you. I'm meeting Miss Nightingale later, and I'll be famished by then.' He turned to me. 'She asked if you'd like to come along. There's something she wants to talk to you about.'

Elijah stayed too, and contrary to my expectations, it was an enjoyable lunch. My father was interested in the society's plans for the canal, which gave Percy the chance to shine.

Ever since I'd known Percy, he'd had a mercurial temperament, switching in an instant from silly to serious and daft to knowledge-able. He was well versed in this subject, and my father nodded in agreement at much of what he said. I watched them with some pride and affection until I felt Elijah's eyes on me. I knew he secretly hoped that Percy and I would become an item. That wasn't on the cards. All I wanted was our friendship back.

After lunch, Percy drove us into town to call at the red-brick end-of-terrace house where Millicent Nightingale lived with her Great Aunt Ursula.

I hadn't known Millicent well before I'd embarked on my trav-els, but I'd felt we were on the brink of forming a friendship. Now I was back, I was keen to get to know her better, especially after our shared experience of finding Rosie Robson.

Millicent showed us into a room that smelt of old books and sweet sherry. It was part library, part curiosity shop. Floor to ceiling shelves were crammed with journals and strange ornaments.

'You're admiring my table, and I'm admiring your hair.' Great Aunt Ursula scrutinised me. 'My father brought it back from India around a hundred years ago.'

Ursula was a diminutive woman with a heavily lined, weather-worn face and wild grey hair. The table in question, made of teak, was embedded with jewels and decorated with carvings of tigers and elephants. Though scuffed and marked, it was still an extraordinary piece of furniture.

'I've never seen anything like it.'

'It's a beauty, isn't it? Where do you get a haircut like that? Not in Walden, I'm sure.'

I touched the ends of my sharply bobbed hair and told her about Dolly Dawes' salon in Lewisham.

'Shame Millicent's got such a wild curly mop. It would never suit her. I reckon I could carry it off.'

I didn't know whether she was joking or not.

Percy kissed Ursula's hand. 'You'd look ravishing. I'll take you to the Foxtrot Club after you've had it done to show you off. We'll make a handsome pair.'

I was glad he hadn't attempted that kind of flirtation with Gran. The repercussions might have been fatal.

Great Aunt Ursula hooted with laughter. 'Don't tempt me, young man. Stop flirting and let me show you what I've found.' On the table was a pile of books, and Percy pounced on one entitled *Waterways of India*.

'There's a country I'd love to go to.' He sank into an engraved teak chair and stretched out his long legs.

'You could learn a lot from some of the practices they employ. I've marked the relevant chapters.'

'Ursula is advising us on the canal,' Millicent explained. I noticed she used her great aunt's first name. 'She's seen first-hand how similar projects have worked in other countries.'

'Ursula should be put in a museum and preserved forever.' Percy rested his feet on a battered leather footstool.

'I'm not a dinosaur.' Ursula pushed another book towards him. 'Though perhaps I am.'

'You're a goddess,' Percy decided.

'That's better.'

'I'll make tea.' Millicent beckoned me to follow her to the kitchen, where it was evident she and her great aunt took most of their meals. Lizzy and I always ate at the kitchen table rather than in the dining room when my father was away.

'I'm going to visit Mrs Robson and wondered if you'd come with me? Rosie's brother, Nicholas, has been to see me. He wants us to tell his mother that Rosie looked like she was asleep and having a lovely dream when we found her. He thinks it would bring her some comfort.' She paused. 'I know it's not true...'

'Of course.' I wished it had been true. I'd willingly lie if it would offer a crumb of consolation to Rosie's mother.

15

'I know you enjoy it, but don't keep shutting the door on Miss Vale.'

It was true. I took great pleasure in swinging the door closed behind me, even though it did make Elijah's den even more suffocating. I strode over and opened the window.

'I'll catch my death of cold.' Elijah tugged at his jacket.

'Shall I get Miss Vale to put a blanket over your knees?'

'She thinks I should get more fresh air.'

'Then we have something in common.'

'God help me,' he grunted.

I wondered whether Horace ever nagged him about his health. I suspected he did, though I knew I'd be overstepping the mark to ask. It crossed my mind that Miss Vale could have been installed to keep an eye on Elijah.

'What's going on with you and young Baverstock?' He obviously didn't feel any qualms about commenting on my relationships.

'Nothing's going on. We're friends, just about. Didn't you catch the whiff of disapproval?' I pulled my cardigan around me and sat closer to the open window.

'His nose has been put out of joint, has it? He'll come round.' He stubbed out his cigarette and immediately lit another one, probably to annoy me.

'I don't care if he doesn't.' This wasn't true. I was relieved Percy's initial frostiness was beginning to thaw. Before Elijah could reply, there was a tap on the door.

Miss Vale poked her head in. 'PC King is here to see you.'

'Send him in.' Elijah waved his cigarette at her.

It used to be PC Ben Gilbert who brought us messages from Superintendent Cobbe. I remembered the days when he would slump into the nearest chair while I reheated coffee for him.

Sid King sat down as if he was preparing for an interview. He had a boyish face that made him look considerably younger than his twenty-five years. From what Ben had told me, Sid was a competent policeman. But while Ben had a natural gravity that instilled trust, Sid had a cheeky grin that made him look like a naughty scamp from a comic. He coughed and flicked through the pages of his pocket book.

'Come on, lad, spit it out. Has Superintendent Cobbe had the pathologist's report?' Elijah asked.

'The thing is.' Sid eyed me uncertainly. 'The thing is, Rosie Robson was pregnant. She'd undergone an abortion. Not a safe one.'

'She was only sixteen,' I exclaimed.

'Poor child,' Elijah muttered.

'The pathologist thinks she would have been in a great deal of pain. She'd been bleeding heavily.'

'I didn't notice any blood.' I pictured the scene inside the cabin of the barge.

'Er, under her skirts,' he mumbled.

I remembered the strange odour coming from her body.

'She died from internal injuries?' Elijah asked.

Sid shook his head. 'She'd been asphyxiated.'

'She'd undergone a backstreet abortion, then someone strangled her?' Elijah was incredulous.

'Not strangled. She was smothered with something. The pathologist thinks it was probably a pillow or cushion. There were some tiny bits of blue cloth in her mouth.'

Elijah's brow creased. 'Whoever carried out the procedure may have panicked when it went wrong.'

I shuddered. How could anyone do something so brutal to that sweet young woman? I thought of Rosie's panic-stricken face after drinking the brandy Percy had given her. No wonder she'd been nauseous. It had been a traumatic afternoon for a pregnant young girl. And after she left the factory, it had got a whole lot worse. 'Do you know if she had the abortion in London or Walden?'

'Detective Inspector Yates is working on the assumption that it was in London and somehow her body was transported. Superintendent Cobbe agrees this is the most likely scenario.'

'Luke Denton could have been the baby's father,' I suggested. 'Maybe she'd got on the barge with him, and when she told him she'd had an abortion, they argued?'

Sid nodded. 'That's what Yates thinks. The only problem is, there are witnesses at Deptford Creek who swear Luke Denton was the only person on the *Sugar Mary* when it set sail. He's been questioned and says he saw Rosie get off the charabanc earlier that afternoon but didn't see her again after that.'

'Why would he leave her body on the boat and incriminate himself?' Elijah shook his head. 'There's a lot of water between London and here. He could easily have thrown her in.'

'Did Luke know she was pregnant?' I asked.

'He says not. He denies being the father.'

'He's hardly going to admit to being involved,' I commented. 'What time did he get to Carnival Bridge?'

Sid checked his notebook. 'He says it was around ten o'clock on Saturday night. He moored at the bridge and went to a cottage on the Crookham estate. The cottage is owned by the Timpsons and is occasionally used by their workers, mostly bargemen on weekdays. At weekends, a friend of Daniel Timpson, a vicar, sometimes goes there to paint, but he wasn't there that weekend.'

'Reverend Powell mentioned Lockkeeper's Cottage to me. I'm not sure where on the estate it is,' I said. 'Carnival Bridge is a quiet spot, especially now the warehouses are closed. It was deserted when Millicent and I found the body. I don't imagine many people would be up that way on a Saturday night.'

Sid nodded. 'No one saw Luke Denton while he was in Walden, apart from the ticket master at the railway station who confirms he caught the nine-thirty train to Waterloo on Sunday morning.'

Elijah posed another theory. 'If Rosie Robson knew that Luke Denton was taking the *Sugar Mary* to Crookham, perhaps she caught a train home after having the abortion and went to the bridge to meet him?'

'Rosie was known to go walking along the canal from the biscuit factory to Crookham Wharf after work,' Sid said. 'But it's unlikely she could have walked all the way from Walden railway station to Carnival Bridge in the state she was in. I've checked, and no one reports picking her up in their car or carriage. Her family are certain she would have gone home if she'd returned to Walden. She'd know her mother would be worried about her.'

'So where did she go after she left the Timpson Foods factory?' I sighed. 'Did she stay in Deptford or travel somewhere else?'

'Detective Inspector Yates' officers are talking to people in the vicinity to see if anyone saw Rosie on Friday or Saturday. And Superintendent Cobbe has got us searching Crookham Wharf and the area by Carnival Bridge. We're asking around to see if anyone saw her or Luke Denton that weekend.'

Elijah picked up his pen. 'What does the superintendent want me to put in the paper?'

'He wants you to confirm that Rosie Robson was murdered, but not to specify how. Ask anyone with information to contact the station house. He's also agreed to your request to put in an appeal for information about the whereabouts of Miss Freda Bray. Under the circumstances, he'd like to know where she is.'

'Has Rosie Robson's family been told?' I asked.

'Superintendent Cobbe and I went to see them.' Sid's voice quivered.

'Not an easy task.' Elijah stubbed out his cigarette.

'Mrs Robson was very distressed. We need to ask her some questions.' Sid chewed his thumbnail. 'They're a bit delicate. And she was too upset. I'll have to go back and see her again.'

'Nicholas Robson asked if Millicent Nightingale and I would visit his mother. Millicent taught Rosie, and some of the other Robson children are still in her class. She might be able to help.'

Sid's eyes widened with relief. 'Miss Nightingale would be the best person under the circumstances. We need to know about boyfriends. Was Rosie seeing anyone, or had anyone shown an interest in her? Had she been anywhere recently that was out of the ordinary? The pathologist thinks she must have got pregnant sometime in June.'

I noted down his questions. 'June? That's when the carnival was.'

Sid nodded.

'What does Superintendent Cobbe make of this?' Elijah asked.

'In view of the pregnancy and subsequent abortion, he thinks it has the appearance of an argument with a lover. It's the placement of the body that bothers him. Why the boat?'

'There's something almost symbolic about it,' Elijah agreed. 'The carnival queen found at Carnival Bridge on the *Sugar Mary*, the only boat the Timpsons kept after closing the canal. It's possible Rosie encountered someone with a vendetta against Constance, though it seems unlikely.'

I couldn't believe someone would do something so hideous to Rosie to get at Constance. But my thoughts drifted back to that obscure anonymous letter.

Men work in factories and run them. Not young girls. Restore things to how they should be, or there'll be more suffering.

16

'Hello, Miss Nightingale.' A solemn-faced girl of about eight opened the door.

The Robsons lived in a picturesque but neglected house near Walden railway station. It had a gabled roof and ivy growing up the walls.

'Hello, Sally. Is your mother home?' Millicent lightly touched the little girl's blonde head.

'She says to come in.'

Sally took Millicent's hand and led her along the hallway to a parlour at the back of the house. At her heels was a small boy of about five, who looked curiously up at me as I followed.

Mrs Robson was seated in an armchair next to the fireplace while a tall, slim young man placed teacups on a round occasional table in front of her. The shape of his mouth and the colour of his eyes reminded me of Rosie.

Millicent greeted them and introduced me.

Nicholas Robson smiled shyly. 'Thank you for coming. Please, sit down.' He gestured to the faded sofa next to his mother's armchair.

'How are you, Mrs Robson?' Millicent asked.

'I can't stop thinking about her. My beautiful young girl.'

The words 'young girl' instinctively made me think of the threatening anonymous letter.

Mrs Robson took a handkerchief from the pocket of her pinafore and blew her nose. 'When you found her, did she... Was she—'

'She looked like she was asleep,' Millicent replied. 'And having a lovely dream.'

I nodded in agreement.

'She wasn't messed up or anything?' Her grey eyes pleaded with us.

'No, not at all.' Millicent took the teacup Nicholas handed her and gave him a reassuring smile.

'She was just the same as when I'd last seen her at the factory in Deptford. In her pretty pink dress,' I added.

'That was her favourite dress.' Mrs Robson smiled at me. 'She did look lovely in it.'

'Yes, she did.'

Her smile faded, and she pulled at the strings of her pinafore. 'She was too pretty and too innocent. Some man took advantage of her.'

A brief silence followed. We sipped our tea.

Millicent placed her cup on the table. 'Did Rosie mention anyone to you? Someone who may have paid her particular attention. Perhaps when she was carnival queen?'

Mrs Robson shook her head, her eyes filling with tears. 'I wished she'd told me. I should have noticed, but the children take up so much of my time. It's my fault.'

Nicholas perched on the arm of her chair and put his hand on his mother's shoulder. 'It's not your fault. It's mine. I should have gone with her to Deptford.' He looked at me and Millicent with a sad, apologetic expression. 'They wanted some of us to stay at the factory. I needed the overtime.'

'You must stop blaming yourselves,' Millicent said firmly. 'I know it's difficult, not knowing what happened.'

'She was a good girl.' Mrs Robson's tears flowed. 'I don't know how we're going to manage without her. She looked after the children when I was working. And gave me money each week.'

'I can go to work, Mummy,' Sally piped up. 'Don't cry. I can help.'

Her little brother clambered onto his mother's lap and dabbed his hand on her cheeks to wipe away her tears. This gesture only made Mrs Robson sob even more.

'Not just yet, you can't.' Nicholas picked up Sally and sat her on his lap. He turned to his mother. 'I'll look after us. There's nothing for you to worry about.'

Millicent glanced at me and then at the children. 'PC King wanted me to ask you a few questions. About Rosie's condition.'

'I could take Sally outside to play,' I suggested, knowing the little boy would likely follow.

'I'll show you my room.' Sally jumped off her brother's lap and took my hand. 'Come on, Peter.'

I looked at Mrs Robson. She raised a handkerchief to her face and nodded.

As Sally pulled me into the hallway, Peter slid off his mother's lap and trotted after us up the stairs. I passed furniture that was a bit battered, which was hardly surprising with eight children in the house, but the place was clean and smelt of fresh laundry. I followed Sally into a small bedroom that contained a wardrobe, a chest of drawers with a washbasin on top, and three single beds.

'Is this where you sleep?' I asked.

Sally nodded and pointed to the beds. 'I sleep there. Jane sleeps there. And Rosie sleeps there.' Her face screwed up in confusion. She clearly didn't understand that her older sister would never be coming home.

She sat on Rosie's bed, frowning. I sat next to her.

'Rosie brushes my hair for me.' Her lower lip started to tremble. 'With her special brush.'

'You have pretty hair.' I smiled at her.

'Rosie has pretty hair.' She jumped off the bed and reached under it, pulling out a wooden box. She took out a silver hairbrush to show me.

'That's lovely. Is it Rosie's?'

She nodded.

I crouched down next to her on the floor and glanced at the contents of the box. It contained face cream, a pot of rouge, hairpins, ribbons, and a few copies of *Picturegoer* magazine. I noticed that tucked away behind the box was a pile of newspapers.

'Does Rosie like to read the newspapers?'

The little girl wrinkled her nose. 'She doesn't really read them. She looks at the funny adverts and the pictures.'

I pulled out the bundle of newspapers and flicked through the pages. Rosie had circled a few advertisements. She appeared to have been interested in tablets made from the herb pennyroyal. From the wording, it wasn't clear what these pills were for.

Hearing Millicent calling me, I put the newspapers back under the bed along with Rosie's wooden box. I glanced over at Peter, who was happily curled up on Sally's bed, reading a comic.

'Thank you for showing me your room, Sally.' I smiled at her, and she grinned with pleasure. She took my hand and led me downstairs to where Millicent was waiting.

'What did they tell you?' I asked as we strolled along Walden High Street.

'Not much,' Millicent replied. 'Mrs Robson assumed Rosie was a virgin. She's adamant that some man must have forced himself on her. Nicholas didn't seem too sure. I don't think he wanted to say anything that would upset his mother.'

'Did they give you the names of any possible boyfriends?'

'Nicholas said Rosie's friendship with Luke Denton hadn't amounted to much. It sounds like Luke wasn't as keen on Rosie as she was on him.' Millicent sighed. 'Mrs Robson is upset that Rosie didn't confide in her. She feels she let her down.'

'It can't be easy with all those children to provide for.'

'She's a good mother. Better than some of the parents I encounter. But she's struggled without her husband. He was killed in the war before little Peter was born.'

'What could she have done, even if she'd known about Rosie's condition? It was a hopeless situation. I'm not surprised Rosie sought a way to end her pregnancy. With the family struggling already, she must have dreaded the thought of her mother finding out.' I told Millicent about the newspapers under the bed. 'She'd been looking at some advertisements for a herb.'

'A herb?'

'Pennyroyal and steel pills. The wording was cryptic, and I'm not certain what they're supposed to be for. Under the circumstances, I can hazard a guess.'

'Ursula knows all the old herbal remedies. We can pop in and ask her if you have time.'

I was happy to keep Elijah waiting as I was eager to meet the fascinating Ursula again.

'How would you go about getting an abortion?' I pondered.

'You're probably more worldly about these matters than I am.'

I looked at her oddly, and Millicent went bright red, realising what she'd said.

'That wasn't what I meant. I meant... I thought you might hear stories through your work.'

I smiled, pretending to brush off her comment, but I could feel myself blushing too. I was ashamed to admit that George and I had sometimes taken risks in the heat of the moment. What would I have done if I'd found myself in Rosie's situation?

'If you're rich enough, your parents pack you off for a continental education,' Millicent said jovially. I knew she was diverting the conversation to cover her embarrassment.

I was happy to go along with it. 'A continental education? What does that mean?'

'Well-off families often send unmarried daughters abroad if they become pregnant. They tell everyone their daughter's studying art or learning a language. The girl comes back with no baby – and no knowledge of the subject she's supposed to have been studying.'

'What happens to the child?'

'It's taken away as soon as it's born and found a place in a suitable family. The girl returns home, and no one is the wiser.'

'For someone like Rosie Robson, a backstreet abortion was probably the only option.'

'I'm not surprised she took it. When she was at school, she was adamant she didn't want to end up the same way as her mother. She yearned for a more glamourous life. Working at Tolfree & Timpson biscuit factory wasn't what she'd hoped for.'

Millicent unlocked the front door and called out to Ursula. We found her seated at the jewelled table, book in hand, snoring softly.

Millicent woke her and explained about the newspaper adverts. The next moment, Ursula was out of her chair, pulling books off the shelves. For an old lady, she was surprisingly sprightly.

'Nostrums,' she declared. She pounced on a small blue volume and handed it to me. It was a report published by the British Medical Association in 1912 entitled *More Secret Remedies*.

'Nostrums?' I asked.

'Medicines prepared by an unqualified person and generally considered not to be effective,' Ursula explained.

I flicked through the pages until I came to a report on pennyroyal. It was what I'd suspected. 'According to this, the herb pennyroyal is thought to induce miscarriage. "Pennyroyal and steel pills are often sold illicitly through newspaper advertisements aimed at women wishing to end a pregnancy",' I read. 'That's what Rosie had circled. Adverts for pennyroyal and steel pills.'

'What newspapers were they?' Millicent asked.

'One was the *Hampshire Chronicle*.'

Millicent rummaged in a wicker basket and produced a sheaf of newspapers. She laid them on the table and we began to trawl through the classified pages.

We quickly found what we were looking for. I was astonished at how many of these adverts there were.

'A Women's Unfailing Friend' was the headline of one, followed by the crude promises to 'correct all irregularities', 'remove all obstructions' and 'relieve the distressing symptoms so prevalent with the sex'.

'Good grief. I'd have assumed this was a cure for constipation.' I shook my head in disbelief.

Ursula chuckled. 'Constipation is all that it would induce.'

Millicent smiled. 'I think that would have been my assumption. I suspect Rosie's friends in the factory told her what to look for.'

'A women's unfailing friend.' I stared at the words in disgust. 'These pills certainly failed Rosie.'

Ursula slapped the pile of newspapers. 'Fraudsters. Making money from the gullible and the vulnerable.'

'I'm going to tell PC King about this,' I seethed. 'These people should be prosecuted.'

Ursula waved a dismissive hand. 'That's why the wording is so cryptic: to avoid breaking the law. The police can't prosecute someone for offering to "remove all obstructions".'

'Could it be a ploy?' I mused.

'What do you mean?' Millicent asked.

'When the pills inevitably fail, the woman becomes desperate,' I explained. 'She panics and resorts to more desperate measures.'

Ursula nodded slowly. 'You could be on to something. These fraudsters have no morals. Money is all they care about. If Rosie contacted them to say the pills hadn't worked, they could have tricked her out of even more money and arranged for a surgical procedure. She was probably frightened enough to go along with whatever they suggested.'

'It's disgusting.' Millicent's lips were tight with fury. 'They take this poor child's money and then butcher her.'

I shared her anger. But this still didn't explain why Rosie had ended up dead on the *Sugar Mary*.

17

'What is this?' Elijah ran a nicotine-stained finger over the classified section of the *Hampshire Chronicle* I'd placed in front of him.

'No, not that one. That's a cure for impotence. This one here.'

Since I'd discovered the world of small ads, I couldn't stop searching for ones that promised miraculous medical cures. My father and Lizzy were not amused when I read them aloud at the breakfast table.

Miss Vale came in with a cup of coffee for Elijah. She hadn't poured one for me. I noticed her peer at the advert, which declared;

New life and vigour. Stimulates the functions of various organs, increases their secretions!

Her eyebrows shot up.

Elijah covered the newspaper with his hand. 'Perhaps you'd better close the door after you, Miss Vale.'

'Of course.' Her face was rigid.

I smirked.

Elijah uncovered the newspaper, lit a cigarette, and scrutinised the page. I directed him to an advert claiming to be from a Mrs Yearsby.

'Sid's been through all the newspapers that were under Rosie's bed. He thinks she sent off for these pills.'

'If she did, they probably wouldn't have done her much harm. They're usually chalk.'

'But what would she do when they didn't work?'

'Which they undoubtedly wouldn't.'

'She might have written again to this address, and they could have responded and offered her a more drastic alternative?'

He shrugged. 'It's possible.'

I breathed in the tobacco fumes and coughed. 'We need to contact this Mrs Yearsby.'

'I doubt there is a Mrs Yearsby.'

I nodded. 'The address is a boarding house in Aldershot. Sid checked, and there isn't a Mrs Yearsby living there. But he doesn't know which of the occupants is posing as her. He wants you to help him find out who it is.'

'I'm not sending off for any pills or potions,' Elijah spluttered.

'You don't have to. He wants you to write to this Mrs Yearsby and ask if she'd be interested in advertising in *The Walden Herald* at a low rate.'

'Horace will not permit this type of advertisement to appear in his newspaper. And neither will I.'

'It won't get that far. You just need to set up a meeting. Sid will go with you as your assistant.'

'God help me,' Elijah groaned. 'I'm a newspaper editor, not a detective. You read too many crime novels.'

'It was Sid's idea. Sort of. Once he knows who Mrs Yearsby is, he can take them to Aldershot police station for questioning and find out if they communicated with Rosie Robson.'

To my delight, Sid shared my fascination with the classified section. We'd cried with laughter at the adverts for 'magnificent male stamina' as we trawled through the newspapers. I'd wanted to go to the boarding house with him, but he said Superintendent Cobbe was only likely to give permission if Elijah was the one who made contact.

Elijah grunted. 'I'll talk to Sid. In the meantime, do you think you could do what we pay you for? I want a heartrending piece on how Rosie's death has affected the town. Go to the biscuit factory and talk to her friends. I want quotes from anyone she was close to, saying how distraught they are. The more affecting, the better. We want people to feel upset enough to come forward with information. And if you want to gain sympathy for Constance, say something about how she's helping her staff come to terms with this tragedy. I need the piece by tomorrow.'

I didn't argue. I'd already planned to visit the factory that afternoon. Rosie must have confided in someone about her pregnancy, and her fellow workers were the best bet.

* * *

'You can't get enough of this place, can you?' Jack Osmond's greeting was far from welcoming. I noted his bloodshot eyes and how the buttons of his creased shirt strained against his protruding stomach. He had the appearance of a man who liked his ale.

'Miss Timpson has given me permission to talk to the staff about Rosie Robson's death.'

'Can't say no then, can I?'

'No, not really.' I marched past him along the rows of conveyor belts until I found Nora Fox.

'Could I talk to you for a few minutes?' I asked her.

She looked towards Jack Osmond, who nodded. Her colleagues watched us in silence.

'Let's go to the sickroom,' she suggested.

I followed her off the factory floor and along a corridor into a pleasant room furnished with a couple of sofas and numerous chairs.

'Is this where Dr Mathers holds his surgeries?' I asked.

She nodded. 'He puts a sign on the door and holds private consultations with anyone who wants to see him. We use it as a messroom when he's not here.'

I sat down on one of the sofas. 'Did Rosie ever go to see him?'

Nora shook her head. 'Some of the staff think that if they tell him something, it will get back to Miss Timpson. I don't believe that's true. Doctors take oaths, don't they? I think he's a kind man. He explained why the chemicals in the munitions factory had turned my skin yellow. He told me not to keep scrubbing at it and promised it would fade with time. And it has. Rosie avoided him because she thought he'd be able to tell she was pregnant just by looking at her.'

'You knew she was pregnant?'

Nora hesitated. 'She made me promise not to tell anyone. I caught her looking at one of those adverts you see in the paper. It didn't take much working out.'

'Did she send off for pills to make her lose the baby?'

'I don't know. I told her not to waste her money. I can't deny, I hoped she'd lose it. It sounds terrible, but I could picture her mother's reaction when she found out. There's no room in that house for any more children.' She sighed. 'Poor kid. Is it true she'd had an abortion?'

I nodded. 'Do you know where she might have gone to have it?'

'Not a clue. She may have had a few shillings to pay for some pills, but I didn't think she'd have enough to do much else. I told her to try to persuade the father to do the decent thing. She said she was too scared to tell him.'

'Did she mention a name? It might have been someone she got together with at the carnival. The pathologist thinks she became pregnant around that time.'

She shook her head. 'She was thrilled when Reverend Childs chose her to be the carnival queen. She loved dressing up and showing off. Poor kid just wanted some attention. It went to her head and she became a bit flirty. At the time, I didn't think there was any harm in it, but...' She gave a sad smile. 'Some bloke must have paid her too much attention.'

'Is there anyone else Rosie might have confided in? Someone in the factory I could talk to?'

'They won't speak to you. They know you're a reporter.'

'I don't want to get anyone into trouble. I just want to find out what happened to Rosie. And stop whoever did this to her from doing it to anyone else.'

Nora scrutinised me for a moment. 'I'll see if I can find out anything. They're more likely to tell me.'

'Is there any news on Freda Bray?'

'No. But one of the girls said she saw Miss Bray going into Miss Timpson's office and leaving a letter on her desk.'

'A letter? When was this?'

'A few days before we went up to Deptford for the speech. Miss Bray didn't come in the next day, and no one's seen her since.'

I wondered why Constance hadn't mentioned a letter to me.

'There's one other thing.'

'What?'

'Jack Osmond didn't come back on the charabanc with the rest of us either.'

I leant forward. 'He told me he got everyone back on board.'

'He rounded up all the stragglers and saw us on our way. But he didn't get on himself.'

'Where do you think he went? Do you think he was with Rosie?'

'At the time, he seemed genuinely annoyed that he couldn't find her. Now...' Her mouth was pinched. 'Now, I'm not sure what to think.'

'How did they get on?'

'He fancied her. But she turned him down. Said he was far too old.'

'I bet he didn't like that.'

She gave a bitter laugh, and I wondered whether she too had been on the receiving end of Jack's advances. 'You know what men are like. Think every woman should fall at their feet. Rosie kept out of his way. That's why I didn't think she was with him when she didn't come home. I thought she'd gone to find that boy, Luke. Now I wonder.'

'You think it's possible Jack was the baby's father?'

'Maybe he tried his luck with her again. And this time, she didn't turn him down. Or he didn't take no for an answer.'

I stared at her. If Rosie had plucked up the courage to tell Jack she was pregnant with his baby, what would his reaction have been? He probably didn't want to marry her any more than she wanted to marry him. It wouldn't have been difficult for him to have found the money to pay for an abortion. He was on good terms with Redvers Tolfree and could easily have asked his boss for a loan.

Had Jack Osmond found a backstreet abortionist and persuaded Rosie to undergo an illegal operation?

18

They were an interesting foursome: Miss Constance Timpson, Mrs Sybil Siddons, Reverend Archibald Powell and Dr Granville Mathers. The factory owner, the politician, the clergyman and the doctor made an unusual but formidable team. I watched as they listened to Ben.

We'd gathered in Constance's office in Deptford at her request. Ben had been asked by Detective Inspector Yates to explain the circumstances of Rosie's death.

'I wished she'd come to me.' Dr Mathers stroked his beard. 'It's believed that taking pennyroyal will induce miscarriage. Nonsense, of course.'

'That's not what killed her, though, is it?' Archie said dryly. He stood at the window, contemplating the church. 'What could you have done if she had come to you?'

'I couldn't have done much about the pregnancy,' Dr Mathers admitted. 'And once she'd started bleeding after the procedure, she would have needed to see a surgeon at the hospital.'

'These practices should be stamped out,' Archie growled. 'It's against God's will.'

'You say she was asphyxiated?' Dr Mathers took off his glasses and cleaned them with a handkerchief. 'Why? Why would someone do that?'

'Perhaps the father of the baby found out what she'd done and was angry,' Mrs Siddons suggested.

'Do we know who the father is, or was, I should say?' Constance's manner was brusque. She might be trying to appear in control, but her drooping eyelids and sallow skin told of sleepless nights.

Ben shrugged. 'The only name we've been given is Luke Denton. Rosie went out of her way to be friendly with him whenever he delivered a shipment to the biscuit factory. When she didn't return on the charabanc, a few of her friends thought she might have gone looking for him, knowing that his trips to Walden would be coming to an end.'

'Luke's a good lad. I can't believe he had anything to do with this,' Archie said tersely.

Dr Mathers seemed perplexed. 'She was found on his boat?'

Archie turned on him. 'It's not his boat. It's Miss Timpson's. You know Luke as well as I do. He wouldn't hurt a fly.'

He'd used those exact words about Micky Swann, and I hadn't been convinced then.

Ben interrupted to quell the dispute. 'With Miss Timpson's permission, WPC Jones and I would like to continue talking to the staff here. We need to establish where Rosie went. Did she confide in anyone about her plans? Superintendent Cobbe needs the same access to the employees at Tolfree & Timpson in Walden.'

Constance nodded wearily. 'Of course.'

'Has anyone come forward with any information about Freda Bray?' Mrs Siddons asked.

I told her what Nora Fox had said about Freda leaving a letter on Constance's desk.

Constance's brow creased. 'I didn't receive a letter. I was away when Freda went missing, but there was nothing in my office when I returned.'

'Could your secretary have moved it?' Mrs Siddons asked.

'She would have given it to me.'

'Unless...' Mrs Siddons paused. I noticed her exchange a glance with Ben. 'If it was a threatening letter, she may have decided to remove it before you could read it. She is protective of you.'

Constance's groan reflected her frustration and despair.

'Could you check?' Ben asked her gently.

Constance nodded, then rested her forehead on her hand, covering her eyes.

* * *

I walked through the factory gates with Dr Mathers and Archie, sensing the underlying tension between the two men.

'You're wrong about Luke, you know,' Archie said to the doctor.

'You may be right. It's the shock. I don't know what to think.'

Dr Mathers nodded goodbye and walked slowly towards his house. Lacking his usual ebullience, he had the appearance of a much older man.

'I'm being hard on him,' Archie admitted. 'I know he feels responsible for the girl. But it's not right to blame Luke.'

I didn't reply.

I turned to go and spotted Blanche Denton enter St Mary's. 'Could I come into the church for a moment?' I asked.

'Of course. My door is always open to you.' To my surprise, he reached out and tucked a stray lock of hair behind my ear.

'I'd like to have a word with Mrs Denton,' I said hurriedly.

A scowl replaced his smile. 'Why don't you leave the investigations to the police? I'm sure Luke and his mother have enough to deal with.'

'It's not that. I want to talk to her about something else.'

He strode towards the church without replying. As he'd just said that his door was always open to me, I followed, deciding to take him at his word.

Inside, I found Blanche seated in the front pew, gazing at the altar with the same dreamy expression as before.

'Blanche.' Archie touched her arm. 'Why don't you come through to the vestry and we'll have some tea?'

Blanche peered at him with watery eyes and nodded.

In the vestry, I sat at the wooden table opposite her. She stared at me without recognition.

'I'm Iris Woodmore. We met the other day.' I paused. 'You said you'd once shared a cell in Holloway Prison with a woman called Woodmore. That would have been my mother, Violet.'

Something in Blanche's eyes flickered to life. 'I thought so.'

Archie, who'd been putting the water on to boil, turned to look at me in surprise. He hovered for a moment and then said in a low voice, 'Would you like me to leave you to talk privately?'

'Oh no, Archie,' Blanche exclaimed. 'Let's all have tea.'

I nodded at him to stay. Blanche clearly felt reassured by his presence.

'You look like Violet,' she said. 'You have her eyes.'

'I am proud of her. What she did.' Since my first meeting with Blanche, I'd questioned why I hadn't admitted to her that my mother had been a suffragette too. It had seemed like a betrayal, and I felt like I had to tell Blanche the truth to make amends.

'Of course, you are. She was a brave woman. It was terrible what happened to her.'

I nodded but couldn't find any words to respond. Archie came over and placed his hand on my shoulder, then went back to making the tea. This gesture left me even more tongue-tied.

'I remember the day it happened. Such a tragedy,' Blanche continued. 'I still don't know what went wrong. I was on the march to Buckingham Palace.'

'Were you arrested?' I tried to steer the conversation away from the events that had led to my mother's death. I knew the truth, and I wasn't about to explain it.

Blanche nodded. 'I was taken to Bow Street, but they let me go. I don't know what I'd have done if I'd ended up back in Holloway. My sister had to look after Luke when I went inside.' She sighed. 'Sometimes I wonder what it was all for.'

I could understand Blanche's doubts. It had taken me years to come to terms with my mother's commitment to the Women's Social and Political Union. I still felt a low burning anger at losing her to the cause. But when Mrs Siddons had been elected to Parliament, it had helped me to realise that my mother's death hadn't been in vain.

'Your mother used to talk about you.' Blanche smiled at Archie as he placed a mug of tea in front of her. 'She worried for your future. She wanted you to have more opportunities than she'd had in her life.'

'I do. The suffragettes made that possible.'

'Did it? I look at the young girls in the factory and think: what have they got? Did we make it better for them?'

It was a difficult question to answer. A lot more needed to be done before there would be any equality for the Rosie Robsons of this world.

'And look at me.' Blanche touched her lined face. 'I'm forty-seven, and what have I got to show for it?'

Before I could reply, the back door of the vestry crashed open, and a young man stumbled in.

Archie put out a hand to steady him. 'What is it, Luke?'

So this was Luke Denton. Long lashes framed intense brown eyes and thick dark hair fell over a wide brow. It was easy to see why he'd captured Rosie's attention.

'They want to question me at the police station.' He reached out to grip Archie's shoulder. 'I never touched her, I swear.'

'Never touched who?' Blanche was on her feet, wrapping her arms around her son.

'Rosie Robson was pregnant. They think the baby was mine.'

'You didn't even know the girl.' Blanche held him tightly. 'Did you?'

'We kissed once. It was just a kiss.'

'Oh, Luke.' Blanche's eyes filled with tears.

19

Sid dragged me off the street and into the station house before I had a chance to speak. For a brief moment, I thought he was arresting me.

'This Mrs Yearsby turns out to be a six-foot former sergeant major who got kicked out of the army. He tried to run for it as soon as he cottoned on to what we were up to. I blocked his way and was trying to get my handcuffs out when cool as anything, Elijah comes up behind him, gets him in an arm lock and holds him till I can cuff him.' Sid's eyes were even rounder than usual. 'I never knew he had it in him.'

I sat open-mouthed in the interview chair, listening to the words tumble out. Sid's astonishment was as funny as the tale of Elijah's sudden transformation into the hero of the hour.

'I was so shocked I nearly dropped the bloody cuffs. Where did he learn how to do that?'

I cursed I hadn't been there to see it for myself. 'He was in the intelligence corps during the war with my father. But they've never told me what they got up to.'

'I tell you what, I'll never look at him in the same way again.'

'What happened to this sergeant major?'

'His name is Alan Pickles. We took him to the station, and he confessed to peddling remedies for unwanted pregnancies and, er, male physical problems.' He gestured to the bundle of newspapers on his desk. 'He claims the pills he prescribes are harmless. I'm not sure the magistrate will see it that way.'

My laughter dried up. 'They weren't harmless to Rosie Robson. They made her even more desperate. Are you sure he's not somehow involved in her death?'

He shook his head. 'She was one of hundreds taken in by the rubbish he peddled. We've been through all his correspondence. She posted the money, and he sent her the pills. But he never heard from her again.'

'Where would Rosie turn next?'

'I got the feeling her brother, Nicholas, knew more than he was letting on. He doesn't want to say anything for fear of upsetting his mother.'

'What about Jack Osmond?' I asked.

Sid rifled through a sheaf of badly typed notes strewn across his desk. Apart from the messy paperwork, it was surprisingly clean in the station office, although there was a faint whiff of unwashed socks.

'He's a dodgy character. He was happy to let us believe he'd taken the charabanc home with the others. When he realised we knew he hadn't, he changed his story. He claims to have been to a few pubs. Said he'd needed a drink after what had happened.'

'Did he meet with anyone?'

'He said he got drinking with some blokes he'd never met before, got drunk and slept on the floor of one of their houses. He caught the train back to Walden the next day.'

'Not the best alibi I've ever heard.'

'He was up to something. Probably something illegal. But I'm not sure it has anything to do with Rosie Robson. Ben's going to speak to his boss. Detective Inspector Yates knows which villains to tap for information.' Sid's voice held a note of admiration.

The villains of Walden only consisted of poachers and the occasional rowdy drunk. With its busy docks, Deptford would have a different class of criminal underworld.

'What's it like being here on your own without Ben?' I glanced around the office. I realised Sid was more capable than his appearance suggested. It was just unfortunate that as a police officer, he had the look of a boy who needed his mother to tell him to wash behind his ears.

He grinned. 'Mrs Gilbert still comes in to clean the place. Sometimes she brings me hot meals. I think she misses cooking for Ben. I don't mind standing in for him, especially when she's cooking suet pudding.'

'After Rosie's murder, Superintendent Cobbe might decide Walden needs a second policeman again,' I mused.

'How about Constable Whittle?' he suggested.

I snorted. 'I'd love to see Elijah on a bicycle.'

* * *

That afternoon, I went back to the Tolfree & Timpson biscuit factory to see if Nora Fox had managed to find out anything.

Rather than seek Jack Osmond's permission to speak to Nora, I approached a young woman standing by the door to the factory. She'd just stamped out a cigarette and was about to head back inside and I asked her to pass on a message.

I walked around to the yard at the rear of the building and was relieved to find it deserted. Cigarette butts dotted the ground and upturned wooden pallets leant against a wall. I waited behind a stack of old oil tins.

I remembered Millicent saying Rosie had yearned for a more exciting life. This factory wouldn't have provided it. But nearby was the wharf, where barges from London came to load and unload their cargoes. It was a picturesque stretch of the canal with banks of pine trees on either side and swans gliding through the water. I could imagine Rosie leaving the sickly-sweet stench of the factory behind and strolling along the towpath, watching the men steer their boats down the navigation. When she'd spotted Luke, with his handsome features, had she dreamt of a great romance?

A few minutes later, Nora appeared accompanied by a large woman with curly blonde hair and a red face.

'This is Gwen.' She glanced back at the factory to make sure no one was watching.

'I wish I'd never said anything about it now.' Gwen's pout indicated she had no desire to talk to me.

'Go on, tell her.' Nora prodded her. 'And be quick.'

Gwen twisted her apron in her hands. 'Rosie was in a state. The pills she'd sent off for hadn't worked. I said there were other ways. I wasn't to know what she'd do...'

'What did you tell her?'

'There's a shop in Deptford. Hopkins Tobacconist. It's around the corner from the Timpson Foods factory. I heard about it from one of the girls up there. You go in and ask if Mrs Quentin is available. The man behind the counter says he often sees Mrs Quentin and that if you come back on a certain day, he'll tell you where you'll be able to find her.'

'Does this man ask for money?'

'No. You just have to buy some baccy or sweets or something to make it look like you're a normal customer. You go back on the day he tells you, and then he gives you an address of where to find Mrs

Quentin. When you go there, you pay her the money, and she does the deed.'

'You think that's what Rosie did?'

'Go on. Tell her.' Nora prodded her again.

'I wouldn't have done it if I'd known. It wasn't my fault.' Gwen stuck out her lower lip.

'Done what?' I was growing impatient.

'Rosie knew I had to go up to Deptford on the Monday before Miss Timpson's speech. She wanted me to go into this tobacconist for her. Make the arrangements. I went in, and this creepy man appeared. I told him my friend was coming up on Friday, and he had to arrange for her to see Mrs Quentin that day. He said he couldn't guarantee she'd be available, and I said she's bloody desperate, so you better bloody guarantee it. He went all quiet, then he nods and says to tell her to come at five o'clock on Friday.' She shrugged. 'I didn't think she'd go through with it. Didn't think she could afford it for one thing. It's not cheap.'

'Do you know where she might have found enough money?'

'No idea. They ain't got two ha'pennies to rub together in that house.'

'Did she say anything to you on that Friday when you went up to Deptford on the charabanc?'

'I didn't go. I had to stay here.' Gwen sniffed. 'I feel dreadful about it. I'd never have done it if I'd known what was going to happen. I won't get in trouble, will I?'

I shook my head. Nora gave a quick nod of approval. We both knew Gwen should have gone to the police. But the reality was that many working-class families had a deep-seated mistrust of anyone in authority.

'We've got to get back.' Nora pulled on Gwen's arm.

'Thank you,' I called after them.

Had Rosie got the money from Jack Osmond? He might have

thought she'd been trying to trick him and decided to go with her to make sure she went through with it. What would he have done afterwards when Rosie was in pain and bleeding? It must have been obvious she needed to go to a hospital. But what she'd done was illegal. Could he have killed her to make the problem go away once and for all?

20

Once Elijah had approved my articles for the latest edition, I'd persuaded him to let me write some pieces about the ex-servicemen who passed through the doors of Creek House. And the factory owner, politician, vicar and doctor who helped them rebuild their lives.

'You want to go up to Deptford to talk to Ben and snoop around this tobacconist,' he'd grunted. 'You have told Ben, I take it?'

I nodded. 'Detective Inspector Yates is investigating what Gwen told me.'

'Good. Alright, I'm going to agree because I like the sound of these articles.' He waved a finger at me. 'Make sure you don't forget what you're supposed to be researching. Vicars may seem boring in comparison to murderers or assassins, but they're generally safer.'

This particular vicar was far from boring, and I wasn't entirely sure how safe he was.

I'd intended to go straight to St Mary's Church, but when I turned onto Creek Road, I saw the Ford sedan parked outside Dr Mather's house. I knocked on the door and the doctor answered.

'Hello, my dear. Did you want to talk to me? I'm afraid there's not much I can tell you about my work. Patient confidentiality and all that.'

I followed him into a consulting room that smelt strongly of mothballs. It was a small room, crammed with a large desk, an examination couch, a couple of wooden chairs and a medicine cabinet. Bookshelves lined one wall while medical charts covered another.

'One of the women at the biscuit factory told me that some staff don't come to your surgeries because they're afraid it will get back to Miss Timpson.'

'It doesn't matter how many times I reassure them and explain the Hippocratic Oath.' He sat down slowly, rubbing his back. 'Most of the staff are happy to be treated by me. But you can't change the minds of those who've been brought up to distrust authority figures.'

'How did you come to know the Timpsons?'

'Miss Timpson's mother, Lady Timpson, visited the South Eastern Fever Hospital where I work. She was a member of a health board that was looking into isolation practices. This was during the war, and at the time, I needed somewhere to live that was near the hospital. She offered me this place.' He waved his hand. 'It's small, but it's a roof over my head and a place to treat patients. When Miss Timpson took over the business, she wanted a doctor to tend to her factory workers, so we came to an agreement.'

'When did you become involved at Creek House?'

'Towards the end of 1919. Archie had just taken on St Mary's. After the war, he and Daniel Timpson had discussed doing something to support ex-servicemen. At that time, Lady Timpson was running the show, and Daniel had told Archie he could persuade his mother to let them use the houses and factory here to help unemployed soldiers. I think that's why Archie took the post in Deptford. Most army chaplains opt for a quiet countryside parish to recover. Not Archie. He went where he was needed most. It wasn't long before I got involved.' He smiled, though his usual enthusiasm was lacking.

'Your work must give you a great deal of satisfaction.'

He nodded slowly. 'It does. But these last few weeks have left me feeling rather despondent. I wonder if it's time for me to retire. I'm beginning to feel my age. My back aches and my feet are sore. The lament of many an old doctor.' He gave another weak smile.

'What would you do with yourself if you retired?'

'Settle somewhere in South Devon and pootle up and down the coast in a small boat. The scenery is stunning. I've had enough of city life. When my wife was alive, we used to go to the theatre and restaurants. Since being a widower, I've felt I'd rather be somewhere quieter.'

'My grandparents live in Exeter. My father was born there. We always used to go on holidays to Dawlish.'

That had been when my mother was alive. The holidays stopped after she died and I suppose other things had too. The war had brought so much disruption I'd never noticed. With Katherine in his life, my father could enjoy going to restaurants and the theatre again. I resolved to make more of an effort to get to know her for his sake.

'Ah, Dawlish. A charming little place. Perfect for a tired old man like me.' He lifted his wire-rimmed glasses and rubbed his eyes. It was a gesture I was becoming familiar with. 'I still have much to sort out here, but one of these days...'

'What about Creek House?'

'That's best left to younger men like Archie. He has an energy and passion that I'm starting to lack. I've been talking to a young doctor at the hospital who's interested in what we do there. Once he's finished his training, I plan to introduce him to Archie and see how they get along.'

I was touched by Dr Mathers' commitment to the continuation of Creek House. I left his consulting room hoping he would one day enjoy the quieter life he dreamt of.

* * *

'You back again?'

I found Archie in the office at Creek House. The front door was unlocked and I'd walked in without knocking. I was still curious to know if the men there had access to a typewriter. The threatening letter to Constance bothered me, and I'd hoped to take a peek in the mysterious second office. But its door was closed, and I didn't want to incur the wrath of Archie by brazenly opening it and having a nose around.

'I came to see if any of the men here would talk to me about their personal circumstances and what led them to Creek House.' Judging by the smell of cheap cigarettes drifting from the lounge, some of them were home. 'And I wondered how Mrs Denton is?'

'She's worried about Luke. The police questioned him, but there's no evidence against him.' He paused. 'Thank you for talking to her about your mother. It must have been painful for you. Blanche told me what happened to her. How old were you when she died?'

'Fourteen.'

I'd wondered whether she would tell him. It wasn't something I wanted to discuss.

'I'm sorry.'

I didn't respond. I never knew what to say when people sympathised about Mother.

Archie seemed to sense this. 'Ben tells me you've gone back to live in Walden with your father. How's that going?'

'He has a girlfriend.' I blurted it out before I could stop myself.

'Ah. How do you feel about that?'

'I don't mind. It's just...' I floundered, trying to find the right words.

'You're used to having him to yourself?'

'I suppose so.' I hated to admit it. 'That makes me sound like a spoiled child, doesn't it?'

'It's natural. When I go home, my mother and sisters still fuss over me. I've always been the man of the house. I don't know how I'd react if I wasn't the centre of attention. I'd probably sulk.' He grinned.

I laughed, but I could imagine Archie sulking. Or at least scowling a lot. 'What happened to your father?'

'I'm not sure.' He shrugged. 'He was an alcoholic. He went out one day when I was a kid and never came back. We weren't sorry he'd gone. When I met Blanche and Luke, they reminded me of home. Blanche left her alcoholic husband and brought up Luke on her own.'

'Blanche likes to look after you,' I noted.

He smiled. 'She's become like a second mother to me. Don't tell her I said that. There are only nine years between us.'

I got the impression Blanche wouldn't mind Archie describing her this way. It was how she seemed to view herself. There was something worn and defeated about her while he had the energy of a younger man. I couldn't help calculating his age. Blanche had told me she was forty-seven, which made him thirty-eight.

Rather than dwelling on the fifteen-year age gap between Archie and me, I tried to focus on other matters. 'Luke stayed in Lockkeeper's Cottage after he left the *Sugar Mary*. Is it far from Carnival Bridge?'

'You think Luke did it?' His eyes narrowed.

'If someone saw him walking to the cottage, they may have passed the *Sugar Mary* and peered in, like Miss Nightingale and I did. If Rosie wasn't there, it might help him.'

He seemed to thaw a little. 'Unlikely, I'm afraid. The cottage isn't far from the bridge but it's secluded. Few people go that way. I should've been there myself that night. I'd planned to drive down on Saturday and return with Luke on Sunday. But after the shooting, the police needed me at the church.' He stood up and I rose to follow him. When I reached the door, he stopped me. 'Why don't you come and see the cottage for yourself? I'm planning to spend the day there on Sunday. I can show you my paintings if you'd like to see them.' His green eyes held mine. The challenge in his voice made it clear he was testing me.

Did I want to be alone with this man – in what he'd just told me was a secluded cottage?

'I'd love to.'

21

After leaving Archie, I went in search of Ben. I'd achieved what I came to Deptford for. I had background information on Dr Granville Mathers and Reverend Archibald Powell and had heard how Creek House was established.

Archie had come with me into the lounge this time, to see if any of the men would be willing to talk to me. In the presence of Archie and the absence of Micky Swann, they'd been more welcoming. I'd spoken to Frank, the grey-haired man with the crutch who'd made the comment about 'women taking men's jobs'. I had to work hard to overcome his initial distrust, but when I explained the purpose of my articles, he became more receptive to my questions. His right leg was amputated below the knee, and after five years of setbacks, he was about to resume his career as a draftsman in an architect's office. Kevin was the redheaded young man who'd lost his right hand. I'd swallowed hard as I listened to the story of how his fiancée had broken off their engagement and he'd tried to take his own life. Despite having excellent references, he'd so far been unable to find work in his former profession as a bookkeeper.

I came away feeling I'd been too suspicious of the occupants of Creek House. Neither Frank nor Kevin could have been involved in the shooting due to their physical limitations. But I wasn't yet convinced of Micky Swann's innocence.

I found Ben on the factory floor at Timpson Foods and asked him if he'd visited Hopkins Tobacconist.

'We're keeping an eye on the place,' he replied. 'I've asked Mr Hopkins if he saw Rosie Robson on Friday the fifteenth or Saturday the sixteenth. I said we were asking everyone in the area, which is true. He denied seeing her.'

'Can't you take him in for questioning? Frighten him a bit?'

Ben shook his head. 'That wouldn't get us anywhere. There's nothing we can charge him with, and Hopkins knows it. All he's doing is passing on an address. Nothing illegal in that. I'm sure he's paid for this service, but we have no way of proving that. Hopkins would incriminate himself if he gave us any information, and he's not about to do that.'

'He must know what happened to Rosie,' I remonstrated.

'Not necessarily. He may not even know who carries out the procedures. We have to find that person. For the moment, Detective Inspector Yates doesn't want Hopkins to know we're on to him. Yates wants to stop the whole operation, not just the messenger. He's been in touch with some of his contacts, trying to find out who's involved and if it's local or if it covers a wider area.'

I looked around the factory floor. 'Did anyone here know Rosie? Is there someone she might have confided in?'

'She rarely came to Deptford. A few remember seeing her on Friday afternoon with the others from Tolfree & Timpson, but no one saw her outside the factory grounds.'

'Did you get anything from Luke Denton?' I spotted the young man at the far side of the factory, loading boxes onto a pallet.

'He didn't tell us much. He was seen leaving Deptford Creek on the *Sugar Mary* at about six o'clock on Friday evening. No sign of Rosie and witnesses swear they would have noticed if she'd been on board. He moored up near the River Wey junction for a while to get some sleep. A few people saw him and said he appeared to be alone.'

'She could have been hiding in the cabin.'

'Someone had cleaned the boat before Luke got on board. She wasn't there.'

'He could have picked her up en route?'

'It's possible, I suppose.' He shrugged, seeming doubtful.

'Say she started bleeding on the journey, and he didn't know what to do?' I suggested.

'He could have stopped if there was an emergency.'

'She'd had an illegal operation. He might have panicked and smothered her when she screamed in pain.' I was warming to my idea.

'Why leave her body on the barge to be found when there would have been opportunities to dispose of it on the way?'

'Because he felt guilty and wanted to return her to her home-town and her family.'

'If he had a guilty conscience, he would have confessed. He said he moored the *Sugar Mary* at Carnival Bridge at about ten o'clock on Saturday night and went straight to Lockkeeper's Cottage to get some sleep. He was seen catching the nine-thirty train from Walden to Waterloo on Sunday morning. That gave him plenty of time to get rid of her body. Yet he just left her there to be found?'

I had to admit he had a point. 'Do you think he was the father of the baby?'

'He said he liked her, and they'd kissed on one occasion. When he found out she was only sixteen, he ended it. He said she was too young, and he knew his time on the boats was coming to an end and he wouldn't see her any more.'

'Maybe he's not as innocent as he pretends to be. Perhaps he did take it further with Rosie precisely because he knew he wasn't likely to see her again once his trips to Walden stopped.'

'Too many "what ifs". There's no real evidence to say Luke Denton was involved.'

I sighed. Ben was right, there were too many holes in my theory. 'Sid told me that Jack Osmond doesn't have much of an alibi for Friday evening?'

'That's a strange one.' He dropped his voice. 'Osmond said he went to a pub and got talking to some blokes he didn't know. But he was seen out with someone he did know. Someone who could have provided him with a credible alibi. If their activities were innocent.'

'Who?'

'Redvers Tolfree.'

I thought of the intense conversation in Jack's corner office. Something odd was going on between Redvers and his foreman. Before I could ask any more questions, we were interrupted by Constance's secretary, asking if we'd go to Miss Timpson's office.

We made our way up the stairs and along the green-tiled corridor to the mezzanine that overlooked the factory floor.

In Constance's office, we found her seated behind her rosewood desk. She wasn't alone. Opposite her sat a tall, angular woman with high cheekbones and a strong jawline.

Constance raised a slender white hand and gestured to the woman. 'This is Miss Freda Bray.'

22

'I'm sorry. I should have told you in person rather than in a letter. But I couldn't wait any longer. I had to get away.'

Freda Bray's dark hair was cut into a bob that was shorter and more precise than mine. I wanted to know where she had her hair done, but I was aware there were more important questions to ask.

'Told me what?' Although Constance seemed relieved by Freda's reappearance, she was clearly apprehensive over what she was going to reveal.

'Redvers Tolfree and Jack Osmond have been stealing from you.'

'How?' Ben asked before Constance could say anything.

'They set up a fake company that's supposed to supply oil. Osmond creates an invoice and gives it to Mr Tolfree to sign off. The accounts department then pays this company.' Freda Bray had a self-assured manner that left you in no doubt as to the accuracy of what she was saying.

Constance stared at her. 'Doesn't that leave us short of oil?'

'When Osmond records the amount of each ingredient used, he overestimates the quantity of oil, so it's not noticeable.' Freda took a sheet of paper from the large bag she held on her lap. 'Here are all the details. The name of the company and the dates and amounts of each invoice. This is what I put in the envelope along with my letter of resignation.'

Constance breathed heavily as she read the document. 'You've been working on this for some time. Why didn't you tell me?'

'I suspected something was going on, but it took me a while to figure out what. When I finally had the proof, you weren't around, and I had to get away.'

'Why did you have to get away?' I recalled Redvers Tolfree's strange comments about Freda's disappearance. No wonder he was vague about whether she'd resigned from her post.

'My father died and I lost the house I'd lived in all my life. I decided to move to London to be with my sister and she found new lodgings so I could move in with her. Jack Osmond was being vile to me – I think he suspected I was on to them – so I left as soon as I could.' She looked at Constance. 'I gave you my address, hoping you'd contact me. Then, with the shooting and everything, I assumed you were too busy with other matters. I didn't know you hadn't received my letter.'

'Why didn't you come forward sooner?' Ben asked.

Freda gazed at him apologetically. 'I had no idea anyone was looking for me until I managed to get hold of all the recent editions of *The Walden Herald*.'

'Why did you want copies of the paper?' I asked in surprise.

She smiled. 'Because I'd heard you were back.'

'Me?' I spluttered.

'Yes. I used to read all your articles. I want to be a writer. I am a writer,' she corrected herself. 'Have you heard of *Time and Tide*?'

Constance and I nodded. Ben looked mystified.

'It's a weekly journal run by women. Lady Rhondda is one of our founders,' Freda explained. 'I manage the office and write the occasional article. My sister got me the job. She already worked for Lady Rhondda.'

Margaret Haig Thomas, now Viscountess Rhondda, had been an active member of the Women's Social and Political Union. She'd once famously set fire to a post box. Like my mother and Blanche, she'd spent time in prison, where she went on hunger strike in protest at being held as a common criminal rather than a political prisoner.

'Is the journal looking for new writers?' I was intrigued. *Time and Tide* was a feminist magazine launched two years previously. It was political and literary but maintained it was independent of political parties.

'Absolutely,' Freda exclaimed. 'We'd love to reprint some of the articles you've published on Miss Timpson and Mrs Siddons.'

Ben held up his hand. 'Could you discuss this later? I need to report Miss Bray's reappearance to Detective Inspector Yates and Superintendent Cobbe.' He turned to Freda. 'I'm guessing Tolfree and Osmond snoop around when everyone's gone home. They must have spotted your letter on Miss Timpson's desk and removed it. That's something we'll have difficulty proving. I'm more concerned about Rosie Robson. Did you know her?'

Freda shook her head. 'I'd seen her at the factory but didn't know her personally. I read what happened to the poor girl. I'd no idea you thought me leaving had anything to do with her.'

'Do you think Tolfree or Osmond could have been involved with Rosie?'

She considered this. 'It's possible, I suppose. They think all women are whores put there for their pleasure.'

Constance gasped at this.

Freda shrugged. 'It's true. Mr Tolfree seemed to think he could touch me whenever he felt like it. He'd place his hand on my back, then it would find its way down to my buttocks.'

Constance steepled her hands under her chin. 'You should have told me.'

'What could you have done? He owns half the company.'

'He won't for much longer.'

I noticed the glint of steel in Constance's eye. After weeks of looking tired and defeated, the set of her jaw indicated she was about to do battle once more.

'If we could concentrate on the criminal investigation first,' Ben interrupted. 'What about the sniper attack on Miss Timpson? Do you think they could have had anything to do with that?'

'I overhead one of the women on the factory floor say there was nothing wrong with Jack Osmond's eyesight,' I said.

Freda laughed. 'Apparently his glasses are just that. Plain glass. His eyesight deteriorated when conscription came in. He's a coward. I'm not sure he's got the nerve to try something like that. It's money he and Redvers are after and I don't think they'd do anything that might jeopardise their scam.'

'On the evening of the shooting, Jack Osmond didn't return with the others from the Tolfree & Timpson factory,' Ben said. 'He was seen out with Redvers Tolfree. Have you any idea what they were doing?'

Freda grimaced. 'Probably visiting brothels. It's a regular pastime. I have evidence of that too.'

'Good grief.' Constance leant back, a look of disgust on her face. 'I've never liked Redvers, but I never suspected he could be quite so odious.'

Ben took out his pocket book. 'I have to get back to the station and report this. Could I have your address, Miss Bray? I'll need to talk to you again.'

Constance rose from her desk. 'I'd like to come with you to the police station. I need to speak to Detective Inspector Yates. Then I'll arrange a meeting in Walden with Superintendent Cobbe.'

Ben seemed uncertain. 'I can pass on any messages you have.' He glanced at Constance's expensive attire: a mauve silk dress and patent shoes. 'Deptford police station isn't a suitable place for a—'

'I'll survive,' Constance interrupted. 'I have a few suggestions on the best way to handle Tolfree and Osmond. I need to control the timing. I'm planning to hold a party at Crookham Hall for Mrs Siddons. All the factory workers are invited and I'd rather delay any unpleasantness until after the event. Perhaps even until after the election.'

With that, Constance strode from the room. Ben finished noting down Freda's address and shot me an apprehensive glance as he hurried after her.

'I'd like to see Tolfree and Osmond publicly humiliated,' Freda said bitterly.

'I think we'll have to wait until after the election. Once that's over, I'm sure that between us we'll be able to come up with something.'

She grinned. 'I'm sure we will.'

23

After I left Timpson Foods, I couldn't resist going to see Hopkins Tobacconist for myself.

With more than enough research completed for my articles, I felt I could indulge in a little snooping. Inspired by Freda's work in uncovering Tolfree and Osmond's scam, I wanted to play detective.

To Elijah's amusement, I was a fan of Maud West. Maud claimed to be Britain's only female detective. Newspaper stories exaggerated her exploits, and although not all of her tales were true, she'd undoubtedly solved some famous cases. In one article, she described how she shadowed people, explaining it was imperative to keep your distance yet never lose sight of the person you were following.

I waited across the road from Hopkins Tobacconist for some time, but nothing out of the ordinary happened. No likely suspects appeared for me to shadow.

Maud was also famous for using disguises to pass unnoticed in different venues. It occurred to me that, in this case, a disguise wouldn't be necessary. Hopkins expected young females to make enquiries. I just needed to appear nervous.

I crossed the road and pushed open the door. A bell tinkled above my head, and a middle-aged man in a brown apron emerged from the back of the shop.

'Can I help you?' With his polite deference, stooped shoulders and thinning hair, he wasn't the cartoon villain I'd pictured. But Gwen was right. There was something a little creepy about him.

'I'm enquiring about a Mrs Quentin. A friend of mine told me she may be able to...' I let my voice falter, then become a whisper, 'help me.'

'Indeed?' Mr Hopkins maintained the same polite expression. 'Mrs Quentin helps a great many ladies. May I enquire how you heard about her?'

'A friend of mine works at the Timpson Foods factory. She told me you might be able to arrange for me to see Mrs Quentin.' I dabbed my dry eyes with the corner of my handkerchief.

'I often run into Mrs Quentin. Perhaps if you come back on Friday afternoon at about four o'clock? I might have had the chance to speak to her by then. If she's accepting visitors, I can let you know where to find her.'

'That would be most kind.' I attempted a sigh of relief, but it sounded more like a dog panting.

'What sweets would you like?' He indicated the rows of jars on the shelf behind him.

'Oh, yes, of course. A quarter of barley sugars, please.'

He took a glass jar from the shelf and carefully poured the sweets onto the brass weighing scales. Then he tipped them into a paper bag.

'Thank you.' I tried for breathy gratitude. This time, I sounded like Elijah after he'd walked up the stairs to the office. I decided not to attempt any acting if I returned on Friday. I paid him and left the shop.

I hovered outside, considering his proposal. He'd agreed to

Gwen's ultimatum of five o'clock on Friday without consulting the mysterious Mrs Quentin. Had he known she'd be available at that time? Or had he just wanted to get loud-mouthed Gwen out of his shop as quickly as possible? Factories generally closed early on a Friday. That would make it a convenient time. I wondered if Mrs Quentin was a factory worker.

* * *

'You're planning to stay at Gran's again?' My father put down his knife and fork. 'You've only just left.'

I knew it was foolish to go back to Hopkins Tobacconist. What would I say if I confronted Mrs Quentin? But I'd decided to chance it and see how far I could take my charade.

'Only on Friday night.' I'd noticed how anxious he became when I mentioned staying away. I suspected he was afraid of me leaving again. Since I'd moved back, he'd been more considerate than before. I wasn't sure if this was Katherine's influence or because my flight abroad had scared him.

'Why?' His tone was light, but he'd stopped eating.

'To see Constance Timpson.' I knew this hardly required an overnight stay.

'Why can't you see her when she's in the Walden factory or at Crookham Hall?' He took a sip of water.

'Not just to see Constance. I'm writing about Creek House and the work Reverend Powell and Dr Mathers do.'

He nodded. 'Interesting set-up they've got there. I'd like to see it for myself.'

The thought of my father accompanying me to Deptford on Friday made me choke on the lamb chop I was eating.

I changed direction. 'Dr Mathers holds surgeries at the factories. Mrs Siddons has been trying to persuade other business owners to follow Constance's lead.'

He nodded in approval.

'Constance is holding a party for Mrs Siddons at Crookham Hall. The Tolfree & Timpson factory workers are invited. I'm sure Constance would be happy for you to come along.'

'I'd like that. Katherine would be interested too.'

'I'll ask her to invite you both,' I said hesitantly. How did my father plan to introduce Katherine on these occasions? Girlfriend and boyfriend seemed idiotic terms for a couple of their age.

'Katherine's coming to dinner on Saturday evening. You'll be home by then, won't you?' His anxious look had returned.

My heart sank. I'd enjoyed having Father to myself at breakfast and dinner, but I remembered my resolve to be more accommodating of Katherine. 'I'll make sure I'm back in time.'

* * *

At a minute to four on Friday, I took a deep breath and pushed open the door to Hopkins Tobacconist. The bell sounded and Mr Hopkins appeared from the back of the shop.

He smiled pleasantly. 'How nice to see you again.'

'I wondered if you happened to run into Mrs Quentin?' My voice sounded nervous and high pitched. This time I wasn't acting; I was genuinely petrified.

'I did indeed. And you're in luck. She's accepting visitors, but you'll have to be quick. She's expecting you. Twenty-six Dolphin Street. Do you know where that is?'

I nodded. It was only a few streets away.

'Some barley sugars?' he asked.

'Oh, yes. A quarter, please.'

'Warm for the time of year, isn't it?' He shook the contents of a glass jar onto the brass weighing scales.

'Yes, very.'

My hands were clammy as he handed me the paper bag of sweets.

Outside, I tried to steady my breathing. Twenty-six Dolphin Street. I kept repeating the address to myself. I started to walk and felt the tremor in my legs. What would I do when I got there? It would be sensible to let someone know where I was going in case I was murdered. I couldn't tell Ben. I knew what his reaction would be. Then I spotted Percy sauntering out of the factory gates. I dashed over to him.

He looked at me in surprise. 'Hello. What are you doing here?'

'Would you like a barley sugar?'

'Alright.' He took one and popped it in his mouth.

'Would you do me a favour?'

'It depends.' He eyed me warily.

'Walk with me to Dolphin Street? It's not far from here. Then stand outside a house. If I don't come out within half an hour, knock on the door.'

'Iris, what are you up to?' He sighed, pushing his floppy hair back over his forehead.

This familiar gesture made me smile and I suddenly felt more confident. 'I'm trying to find out something.'

'Is it safe? I know what you're like.' He sucked loudly on the barley sugar.

'It is if you're there.'

'And if I say no?' He made another sucking noise.

'It's alright. I shouldn't have asked.' I walked away but at a leisurely pace. I hoped he'd rush after me. He didn't. By the time I reached Dolphin Street, I'd slowed to a dawdle.

Then I felt a hand on my arm. 'I don't have much choice, do I?

This is typical of you,' he said. 'You're going to do whatever it is anyway, and I have to stand outside like an idiot while someone murders you.'

'Thank you.' I stood on tiptoe and kissed his cheek.

'If anything happens to you...' He floundered for the right words. 'If you get hurt or end up dead, I'll be very angry with you, and I won't speak to you again.'

'If I'm dead...'

He cupped his hand over the back of my head and pulled me towards him. 'You know very well what I mean,' he said roughly into my hair, then let me go.

This made my knees tremble. I stumbled across the road and rapped on the door before I could change my mind. An elderly woman opened it.

'I'm here to see Mrs Quentin.' My voice shook despite my best efforts. But that would be expected in the circumstances.

'Down there.' She pointed a bony finger to a door at the end of a dark hallway.

I went down the corridor and hesitated outside. The floor smelt strongly of damp, and wallpaper was peeling from the walls. All was quiet. It was impossible to tell how many people were in the house. Or who was behind the door. Mrs Quentin may not be a woman – Mrs Yearsby had turned out to be a six-foot sergeant major. I'd anticipated walking out after confronting the person. However, recent events proved it might not be that easy.

'In there.' I jumped at the old lady's voice. She was standing right behind me.

With a shaking hand, I tapped on the door and opened it. To my relief, the figure standing beside the examination couch at the far end of the room was a woman and not a particularly large one.

My relief turned to shock when I recognised her. It was Blanche Denton.

24

'Iris.' The colour drained from Blanche Denton's face. Her body drooped, and she rested her hand on the grimy brown couch to steady herself.

I stayed by the door, taking in the sparsely furnished room. Apart from the examination couch, there was an old pine table and a pair of mismatched chairs. On the table was a black medical bag.

The bare wooden floorboards creaked as I walked across the room. I pulled open the bag and grimaced. Inside was a collection of medieval-looking metal instruments. Alongside the bag was a pile of greying towels and some swabs.

'Why?' I didn't attempt to hide the revulsion I felt.

'I help women who are in trouble,' she whispered. 'Are you in trouble?'

'No, of course not,' I snarled. 'I'm trying to find out who murdered Rosie Robson.'

Blanche gripped the side of the couch. 'I didn't mean it to happen.'

'You butchered her.' I pictured Rosie in this drab room, lying on the disgusting brown couch, and felt sick. How much pain and fear would she have experienced when those gruesome instruments invaded her body?

'I don't know what went wrong. It's never happened before.' Her voice was a whimper. She raised a hand to her wispy blonde-grey hair, and I caught a whiff of her gardenia scent.

'Are you sure it's never happened before? Perhaps some of your other victims hid their injuries?'

She shook her head. 'I know what I'm doing.'

'I don't think you do.' The windowless room was dimly lit. I couldn't imagine Blanche would have been able to see well enough to know what she was doing.

She stared at me in silence.

'I thought you were a suffragist. How can you abuse these women? Young girls like Rosie? Take their money?'

'I don't do it for the money. The money enables me to rent this room.' Her eyes pleaded with mine. 'I do it to help them.'

'What you do helps no one.' I was biting back my fury.

This seemed to spark something in her. 'What do you know?' She waved a trembling finger at me. 'You may not be rich, but you're not poor. Not truly poor. Have you ever had nothing to eat and no roof over your head?'

It was my turn to be silent.

'Because that's what having another baby does to some families. Young girls with no future ahead of them except to go on the streets. Older women barely surviving with the ten children they've already got. Another one would kill them.' Spittle flew from her mouth.

'What you're doing is a crime.' But I'd lost my conviction. I knew what she'd said was true. It wasn't about birth control; it was about life and death. Poor nutrition, working long hours in physically demanding jobs, and multiple pregnancies. One more baby did mean death for some women.

'When I became pregnant again, after Luke, I had a daughter, Ivy. She was a sickly child. I couldn't afford to give her the food and medicines she needed to get better and she died. When my husband made me pregnant again, I couldn't go through with it. I didn't want to bring another child into this world. I had an abortion without him knowing. Then I left him and took Luke with me. I'd be dead if I hadn't. I do this to make life better for other women.' She held my gaze, though her fight had gone. She collapsed into one of the rickety chairs.

'It's wrong.' The words sounded futile even to my ears.

'Your mother would have understood. She was kind. She didn't look down on people. She wanted to help them.'

'My mother would—' I stopped, my cheeks flushing. I didn't know what my mother's views had been on this subject. She'd supported wider education on birth control. But this? All I knew was she would have hated what took place in this squalid room.

'What did you do to Rosie?' That was all there was left to ask. I'd heard enough and wanted to escape from this miserable musty-smelling house.

'She was fine when she left here. I would never have let her go if I thought she was hurt.' She stared into the distance.

'She wasn't fine,' I said in a low voice. 'She was bleeding internally.'

Blanche closed her eyes. 'I'm sorry,' she whispered.

'Do you know what happened to Rosie?'

Blanche opened her eyes and looked up at me. 'No. Please believe me. I would never have harmed her. Nor would my son.'

I made a choking sound, realising the horror of the situation. If Luke Denton was the father of Rosie's unborn baby, then Blanche had aborted her own grandchild.

'Will you go to the police?' she whispered.

My anger had evaporated. But I couldn't risk her performing another operation. 'Yes.'

Blanche's body sagged so far forward I thought she would topple from the chair. She didn't cry. She just sat motionless, staring at the floor. All I could feel was pity for a woman so beaten down by life that she had no tears remaining.

I left her like that. I didn't think she'd attempt to run away.

25

'You did this on purpose, didn't you?' Percy rushed over to me, his face pinched and tense. 'Left me standing here like a plum, hanging on. I didn't know what I was supposed to do.'

'I'm sorry. I didn't mean to.' I felt a wave of nausea wash over me. I gripped his arm. It was a relief to escape from that dark, claustrophobic room.

He put his arms around me and pulled me into a hug. 'What happened? Are you hurt?'

I shook my head. 'I need to find Ben.'

'He's at the factory. With Constance,' he said, a note of despondency in his voice.

He took my hand and we walked along Dolphin Street. I looked back at the door of number twenty-six. I'd slammed it closed and no one had come out after me. I guessed Blanche was still sitting where I'd left her.

Percy followed my gaze back to the house. 'Who was in there?'

'I'll tell you when we find Ben.' I didn't want to have to repeat this tale more than once.

Ben was with Constance in her office, discussing plans for the party at Crookham Hall. He was concerned she was putting herself in danger, and I sensed she was enjoying his attention. I glimpsed the flash of annoyance in her eyes when Percy and I interrupted them.

'What is it?' she asked with a hint of impatience. Since Freda Bray's revelations, Constance seemed to have rediscovered her sense of purpose. She planned to gain full control of Tolfree & Timpson. And she was determined to ensure Mrs Siddons retained her seat in the general election.

With trepidation, I told them what I'd done. I'd expected Ben to be first to explode, but Percy beat him to it.

'For goodness sake, Iris. You went into that house, pretending to be...' He flapped his arms, unable to finish the sentence.

'Blanche Denton.' Constance closed her eyes. 'I can't believe it.'

Ben picked up the telephone and asked to be put through to Deptford police station. He didn't look at me.

Percy scowled and paced the room while Constance sat still at her desk. I was hoping someone would offer me a stiff drink. No one did.

Ben spoke for some minutes with Detective Inspector Yates before replacing the earpiece on the cradle. Constance and Percy looked at him expectantly, but he ignored them.

'Iris.' Ben's voice was hard with anger. 'Don't ever do anything like that again.'

He strode out of the room before I could reply.

* * *

I walked out of the factory gates feeling sorry for myself. I'd soon tired of Percy's ranting. All I wanted to do was get out of Deptford and catch the tram back to Gran's. But before I did, there was one other person I needed to see.

The church was empty, so I made my way to the bottom of the tower steps and called out. I didn't relish telling Archie. He'd probably be furious with me too.

'In here.' The voice came from the vestry. I found Archie standing by the table, rolling up a large length of canvas.

'I'm taking this down to the cottage for—' He stopped when he saw my face. 'What is it?'

'Sit down.' I dropped into one of the wooden chairs. 'I need to tell you something. About Blanche.'

'Is she ill? She didn't look well this morning.' He sat down and leant toward me.

Trying to sound as calm as possible, I told him what I'd witnessed at Dolphin Street.

'I can't believe it.' He stretched out his hands. Once again, I was transfixed by his long, slender fingers. I wanted to reach out and touch them. 'Blanche?'

I nodded.

'She did that to Rosie Robson?'

'She performed a procedure on her, but swears Rosie was fine when she left.'

I watched his disbelief turn to rage and felt a shiver of fear pass through me. His nostrils flared, and I jumped in fright as he slammed his fists on the table. Archie may be a man of God, but he was still a man. And a strong one.

I stood up. I'd had enough for one day. I didn't want to be on the receiving end of his temper.

He reached out and gripped my wrist. 'Where's Blanche now?'

'Probably where I left her. I got the impression she didn't plan to run away. I don't think she'll leave Luke.' I tried to pull free of his grasp. 'Let go of me. I want to go home.'

He came to his senses and released his hold, appearing surprised that his hand was on my wrist. 'I'm sorry. I didn't mean to frighten you. Sit down. I'll get you a drink.'

He pushed his chair back and went over to a cupboard by the sink. I was tempted to walk out, but when he fished out a bottle of brandy, I changed my mind. He rinsed out two teacups, poured a measure in each and placed one in front of me. I took a large gulp.

'Steady on. Take it slowly.' His voice was calmer. 'It must have been an ordeal for you.'

'It was horrible. And now everyone's cross with me.' I realised this sounded petulant. After all, I'd brought it on myself.

'I'm not cross with you.' His voice was low and soft. 'I'm angry with Blanche. Angry that she felt she had the right to do such a thing.'

I nodded. I felt the same. We sat in an eerie silence, sipping from our teacups. It felt odd to be in the vestry of a church drinking brandy with a priest. Then again, it hadn't been a normal day.

'Who is it that's cross with you?' he asked after a few minutes. His fury had subsided, and he looked drained and sad.

'Ben. And Percy.'

'Percy?' He smiled. 'Is he capable of being cross? I think he's the most easy-going chap I've ever met.'

'He seems to manage it when it comes to me.' I rubbed my eyes, tiredness settling on me.

'He cares about you. He's upset with you for putting yourself in danger. So is Ben.'

'It's not just today. Percy's been annoyed with me for some time. For going away.' I didn't stop him when he topped up my glass.

'Oh yes, that. Running away with a man, I believe?'

I saw the tiny flicker of amusement in his eyes and flushed. So even Archie knew. 'He seems to have a hard time forgiving me.'

'Do you need forgiveness? Perhaps I can help?' He pointed to his white collar.

'I'm not repentant.' I was sick of being judged.

He gave a bark of laughter. 'That's good to hear. I find people often repent or regret things instead of learning from the experience. Perhaps even coming to relish it.'

'Isn't that contrary to most religious teachings?'

He leant forward, his lips close to my ear. I could smell the brandy on his breath. 'I'm of the view that God isn't as judgemental as people think. Especially when it comes to relationships. We were put on this earth to love one another in whatever form that takes.'

I was enjoying his closeness too much and knew it was time to leave. I took a last gulp of brandy and got to my feet unsteadily. 'I'm tired.'

He stood up and rested his hands on my shoulders. For a moment, I thought he would pull me into an embrace. But he just said, 'Do you want me to drive you home?'

I shook my head. I wanted to be alone.

Outside, it was darker than I'd expected. It wasn't yet eight o'clock, but the October nights were drawing in. I squinted up at the tower of St Mary's. The dull illumination of the streetlamps made it look like the turret of some gothic castle.

When Rosie disappeared in September, it must still have been light when she left the house on Dolphin Street. Where had she gone? She'd been at her most vulnerable, far from home, bleeding and in pain. Why had no one seen her?

I started to walk briskly. I too was far from home, and I didn't want to be wandering about these dark streets on my own. The factory was closed, and there was no sign of Ben or WPC Jones. I passed Creek House and could see the outline of figures behind the curtains of the lounge.

The sudden yelp of a dog somewhere in the distance made me jump. Then I heard another noise. It sounded like footsteps close by. I quickened my pace, wishing I hadn't refused Archie's offer to take me home. I could have asked him to drive me to Gran's.

I heard more footsteps and knew someone was following me. They could be heading to the same tram stop. Or they could be about to attack from behind. I had to know which it was.

I swung around and found myself staring into the strange amber eyes of Micky Swann.

'Are you following me?' I demanded.

He didn't seem bothered by my reaction. 'You shouldn't be wandering about on your own at night. But I suppose you think you can do whatever you like.' He sunk his hands in his pockets and rocked back on his heels.

'All I'm doing is going home.' It came out more tremulously than I'd have liked. I was too exhausted to summon up any more authority.

'You've been to see the vicar? Asking more questions?' His eyes gleamed under the light of the streetlamp. 'Didn't you get all you needed the other day?'

'It was a social call.' I wasn't in the mood to be threatened by Micky Swann. And I wasn't going to tell him about Blanche Denton. No doubt he'd find out soon enough.

'The vicar is good to us men. That's all you need to know. Come on, or you'll miss your tram.' To my surprise, he fell in step alongside me.

'There's no need for you to walk with me.'

'I want to make sure you go.'

I decided there was no point in standing around arguing. We walked in silence. When we reached the tram stop, Micky shuffled around next to me. I tried to ignore him.

He said nothing until the tram arrived.

Before I could board, he put out his arm to stop me. 'I think you've been spending too much time around here. If I were you, I'd stay away,' he whispered. Then he removed his arm and strolled back in the direction of Creek Road.

26

I was glad to return to Walden on Saturday morning.

Ben had yet to forgive me. The night before, I'd sat in the kitchen waiting for him to come home. With a stony expression, he told me that Blanche Denton had been arrested. She was later charged with intent to procure a miscarriage and was being held pending further investigations into the case of Rosie Robson. Ben believed that Detective Inspector Yates intended to charge Blanche with Rosie's murder.

Mr Hopkins had been let off with a warning. He claimed he had no idea Mrs Quentin wasn't who she said she was and he hadn't been aware of the type of service she offered.

At home, Lizzy was busy with preparations for dinner.

'Where are you going now?' she demanded as I dumped my bag in the hallway and headed for the door.

'To see Elijah.'

'Make sure you're back in time to get washed and dressed for dinner.'

Washed and dressed for dinner? I caught the scent of roses and saw a vase of fresh flowers on the table. What was so special about Katherine coming to dinner?

Realisation dawned. 'Oh. Is he—'

'Iris.' Father stood at the door of his study. Lizzy disappeared into the kitchen, shutting the door behind her. 'I was worried you wouldn't get back in time.'

'Back in time for what? Dinner?' I swallowed, my mouth dry. 'Or is something else going on?'

'I wanted to talk to you about it, but you're never here. I've asked Katherine to marry me.'

I was silent.

'I want you to get to know her,' he continued. 'That hasn't been possible. Now we're engaged, I see no reason why Katherine shouldn't spend more time here.'

I took a deep breath. 'I'd like that,' I lied. I guessed this meant she would be staying overnight. That would give the gossips of Walden something to get flustered about. After all, being engaged wasn't the same as being Mr and Mrs Woodmore. But then, I was hardly in a position to criticise.

He relaxed and gave me a brief hug. 'We'll celebrate tonight at dinner. I've asked Lizzy and Elijah to join us.'

I mumbled something into his chest about being happy for them. As soon as he released me, I darted out of the front door.

* * *

Elijah was dozing in his chair, and there was no sign of Miss Vale. I brewed some coffee, which roused him.

'What have you been up to?' He yawned, reaching for his cigarettes.

'Why should I have been up to anything?' I put a mug in front of him.

'Because you didn't come here on a Saturday morning to make me a cup of coffee.'

I recounted the events of the previous day, knowing what was coming.

He groaned. 'What were you thinking? Rosie Robson wound up dead. You could have ended up the same way.'

'That's what everyone keeps telling me. But Blanche doesn't have the strength. I don't believe she could have suffocated a healthy young woman like Rosie.'

'You didn't know who was in that room. It could have been a stocky bloke like Alan Pickles, who you may remember pretended to be a woman.' He sighed. 'Where does that leave the case?'

'Ben thinks Detective Inspector Yates plans to charge Blanche with Rosie's murder.'

'You think she's too frail?' He frowned. 'Where did she perform this procedure on Rosie?'

'The same house I went to on Dolphin Street. Ben said they're questioning the occupants and all the residents on the road. No one's admitted to seeing Rosie arrive or leave the house.'

'How does Yates think Blanche could have got Rosie's body from Deptford to Walden?' He sipped his coffee.

'He's trying to prove that Luke helped her.'

'We're back to the question of why they'd leave the body on a boat in Walden when they could have disposed of it on the way?'

'A threat to Constance?' I still felt that the placement of Rosie's body had been symbolic.

'Why would Blanche or Luke Denton feel antagonistic towards Constance? They both work at Timpson Foods,' he said. 'Since Freda Bray turned up, I'm less inclined to think what happened to Rosie has anything to do with the Timpsons.'

'It doesn't make sense,' I admitted.

'Forget about Rosie Robson and go home. I take it you have been home since you came back from London?'

I nodded.

'You've spoken to your father?' he asked warily.

Reluctantly, I forced myself to think about the engagement. 'Do you like her?'

'Katherine? Yes, I do. I think she and your father are more suited than...' He stubbed out his cigarette, not meeting my eye and corrected himself. 'I think they're well suited.'

I knew what he'd been about to say. 'More suited than he was to my mother?'

'I didn't mean that. Thomas and Violet were young when they got married. I'm not sure they really understood one another.'

'My father didn't know how to deal with Mother when she became a suffragette.' I'd long since come to realise this. 'And now he has no idea how to cope with me.'

'You don't make it easy for him.' Although he regarded me with exasperation, I could see affection there too. 'How do you feel about him marrying Katherine?'

'I'm pleased for him. I want him to be happy.' I paused. 'But I don't need a mother.'

He sighed. 'If you say so.'

I stood up, feeling irritated. 'I'll welcome Katherine with open arms.'

He appeared to be about to say something more, then decided against it. 'I'll see you tonight. Be on your best behaviour for once.'

* * *

Dinner was relaxed until my father decided to make a toast to welcome Katherine to the family. My jaw stiffened in anticipation of the sincere smile I'd have to adopt.

He kept it brief, and Lizzy and Elijah made appropriate comments while I managed a mumbled welcome. Father seemed satisfied.

'Thank you all.' Katherine smiled at Lizzy. 'And thank you, Mrs Heathcote, for preparing such a wonderful dinner.'

Lizzy smiled back with what seemed like genuine warmth. When she got up to clear the dishes, I helped her carry them into the kitchen.

'How do you feel about Katherine being here?' This was going to affect Lizzy more than anyone. 'Do you like her?'

'Yes, I do. I'm pleased they're going to live in Walden. I'll be glad of the company. I was lonely when you and your father went off on your travels.' She stacked the dishes in the sink and began to prepare coffee. 'Although I feel she shouldn't stay here until after the wedding.'

I wrapped my arms around her. 'I'm sorry.'

She shooed me away with a tea cloth. 'Go and speak to Katherine.'

Father and Elijah were sitting opposite each other by the fire in the drawing room, deep in conversation. Katherine was by the window on the bench we never used. She patted the cushion next to her, and I dutifully went over and sat down.

'I hope our engagement hasn't come as too much of a shock to you?' She smelt of expensive perfume.

'I'm happy for you.' I realised I was repeating the same phrase I'd been using all day. Was I trying to convince myself? Sitting close to her, I appreciated the charm of her features. At a glance, she was a well-groomed woman of medium height with glossy dark hair. Close up, I noticed the character in her face. She had rich hazel eyes, a freckled nose and a smile that brought dimples to her cheeks.

'I don't want my presence to come in the way of the relationship you have with your father. I know I could never take the place of your mother. You're a grown woman, and I'm sure you don't feel the need for a stepmother.'

'I don't,' I agreed bluntly.

She smiled. 'In that case, I hope we can be friends.'

I nodded.

'Do you think we can live in harmony together?' she asked tentatively.

I sighed. 'I'm not sure.'

She looked disappointed, and I realised I wasn't making this easy for her.

'Father and I don't always...' I searched for the right words. 'Father and I don't always agree on things. I have a feeling his thoughts regarding my future probably don't tally with mine. There's likely to be conflict.'

'I see.'

'What I'm trying to say is that sometimes we argue. We probably always will, and I don't want you to think you're the cause of those rows.' I smiled. 'And I wouldn't attempt to be the peacemaker. Father and I are both too obstinate to make that a worthwhile task.'

She laughed. 'Thank you for your frankness.'

'I don't want to put you off Father. The fault is probably with me.'

'You haven't put me off him. Or you. I appreciate your honesty. You've confirmed what I already suspected.'

* * *

The next day, I left my father and Katherine at the breakfast table discussing wedding plans. I told them I was going for a walk around the lake, but I intended to go a lot further.

Out on the road, I spotted Mrs Briggs, an elderly neighbour, duck behind her curtains as I passed. It would soon be all around Walden that Katherine had spent the night.

I started at the lake and kept walking. I made my way along the canal towpath until I reached Carnival Bridge. The *Sugar Mary* was still moored there, and everything looked as it had when we found Rosie.

I followed the route that Archie had told me Luke Denton would have taken to Lockkeeper's Cottage. The path cut away from the canal through woodlands that edged the Crookham estate. It was a bright morning, not a cloud in the sky, but I passed no one else out walking. Elijah was right. Luke Denton would have had ample opportunity to have hidden Rosie's body either on his journey from London or when he got here. Late on Saturday night, he'd have had plenty of time to bury her body in the dense woodland.

I came across the cottage quite suddenly. It was a sturdy building made of dull grey stone with a tiled roof. A solitary structure with no nearby dwellings. There was nothing pretty about it, though the way it was nestled deep in the woodland made it feel like it belonged in a fairy tale.

Archie was in the garden, an easel propped up in front of him. He wore a crumpled shirt and corduroy trousers. Without the clerical garb, he had the appearance of a gardener or the lockkeeper of the cottage's name. He was absorbed in his painting, and I considered slipping back into the woods before he noticed me. Then he glanced up and gave that lazy curling smile, making something stir in my stomach.

I took a deep breath and walked toward him.

'You came.'

His painting, a wide oil landscape of the surrounding countryside, was not what I'd expected. For a start, it was very good. But what surprised me most was its serenity. I'd anticipated something darker, brasher.

I followed him into the tiny cottage. It was as plain on the inside as it was on the outside, with a basic kitchen and parlour. Despite its simplicity, there was something appealing about the place. It was cosy. A little too cosy.

Archie's tall frame seemed to fill the parlour, and I felt his closeness. Aware we were alone in this remote spot, I could feel the tension crackle to life.

Canvases were lined up against a wall. They had the same serenity as the painting Archie was currently working on. The landscapes were almost spiritual in how they depicted nature: vast open spaces with lots of natural light.

'I had a friend who painted. She would have loved these,' I murmured.

'You lost her?'

I nodded and decided to change the subject. 'Have you been to Wildmay Manor?'

He looked at me quizzically. 'Yes, frequently. Why?'

'I visited the art studio there once. Some of the paintings were quite harsh.' By harsh, I meant violent. Most of the patients at Wildmay Manor suffered from shellshock. Some had taken up painting as a way of coming to terms with the horrors they'd seen on the battlefields. This was reflected in the composition of their pictures, vivid depictions of mud, barbed wire and blood in vibrant slashes of colour.

He nodded thoughtfully. 'You expected my paintings to be more like that? I've made my peace with the battlefields. I have my faith to help me make sense of things. That's why my pictures celebrate the healing powers of nature.'

'You don't question the war?'

'I question many aspects of why we went to war. The futility of it all. That's why I want to bring some order to the chaos the war created. I'm a practical man. Giving others a sense of purpose in their lives gives me a sense of purpose in mine.'

His words resonated with me. During my travels abroad, I'd had the feeling I was floating through life. George hadn't known where he was going or what he wanted to do. By coming back to England, I'd hoped to regain my direction. But I still felt adrift.

My eyes took in the row of canvases. There was something celebratory, almost triumphant about them. 'They're beautiful.'

'Thank you. Painting is my escape from real life.'

'I could do with escaping from real life right now.' I thought of returning home to more talk of weddings.

'Are you missing your travels? Or the man you were travelling with?' He took a step closer to me.

'Neither.' My reckless instinct was doing battle with the sirens sounding in my head.

He slid his arm around my shoulder. 'Is there a vacancy to be the man in your life?'

'I suppose there is.' I tried to sound cool, but surprise must have shown on my face.

'Vicars are allowed to have girlfriends, you know. Though perhaps not too many and not too publicly.' His green eyes glinted with amusement as he pulled me towards him.

I wondered how many he'd had. I hadn't heard any rumours about him in Deptford. No one had a bad word to say about him. Perhaps he was discreet. That suited me.

'I don't believe in God, you know,' I murmured into his ear. He smelt of soap, paint and linseed oil.

'Would you like to chat about theology?' His lips grazed the top of my head.

'Not just now.' I raised my arms and wrapped them around his neck.

He lowered his mouth to mine, and his hands pushed against my back. My fingers entwined in his hair, and the heat of our bodies intensified as our kisses became longer and deeper.

I could feel his hands moving beneath my cotton blouse – my linen jacket had fallen to the floor. We stumbled against the wall, and I felt the pressure of his heavy frame as he leant into me.

Suddenly I was aware of a noise coming from outside.

'Reverend Powell,' a voice called. 'Are you there?'

27

Archie and I leapt apart.

A second later, Daniel Timpson appeared at the door of the cottage. Millicent Nightingale stood behind him.

'Daniel.' Archie was breathing heavily.

'Oh, Iris.' Daniel appeared to be taken aback at the sight of me. 'Sorry, Reverend Powell. Didn't know you had company.'

'Iris was just passing. I was showing her my paintings.' Archie slowed his breathing and managed a rigid smile. 'I've told you, call me Archie. We're not in the army now.'

Daniel gave a short laugh. 'I find it difficult to break the habit.'

'What brings you up here?' Archie's voice was a little too jovial.

Daniel turned to Millicent. 'I told Millie about your paintings. I didn't think you'd mind us taking a look. And I wanted to talk to you about a job for one of the Creek House men. It's in the factory down here.'

I stood back to let Millicent through. She was dressed in a full-length walking skirt with matching jacket, her curly locks pinned beneath a felt hat. I was conscious of my bare arms and ruffled hair.

Archie was all smiles, guiding Millicent and Daniel through the artworks stacked against the wall. I tucked myself into a corner. The parlour had been intimate with two people; four was a tight squeeze.

While Millicent and Daniel inspected an oil painting of Crookham Hall, Archie shot me a warning glance and tapped the top of his left arm. I didn't understand what he meant. Then he picked up a cloth and wiped paint from his hands. Alarmed, I looked down at my left arm. It was covered in smeared blue finger-prints. As discreetly as I could, I pulled a handkerchief from my trouser pocket, spat on it, and rubbed hard. I realised I was likely to have blue paint on my blouse as well. I edged closer to where my jacket was lying on the floor.

'Are you getting more involved with the business?' Archie asked Daniel, steering him away from where my jacket lay.

Millicent turned from the paintings to give me a curious look. I felt myself blush, conscious of my stained arms and creases in my cotton blouse. I picked up my linen jacket from the floor and slipped it on, stuffing the handkerchief into my pocket.

'I'm trying to take some of the weight off Constance's shoul-ders,' Daniel replied.

'Good. You should spend more time in Deptford,' Archie said.

'I must admit, I was hoping you'd be here this weekend so I didn't have to go up to town.' Daniel glanced in my direction. 'But I shouldn't have disturbed you. I'll come to see you at the church. The vacancy I need to discuss is sensitive.'

I grabbed this chance to escape. 'I have to be getting back. Sorry for dropping in unannounced.' I moved towards the door. 'Thank you for showing me your paintings, Reverend Powell.'

'The pleasure was all mine.' Our eyes locked, and I could feel the heat of my body rise to my face. 'We must do it again sometime.'

'I need to get back too,' Millicent announced. 'I'll come with you.'

Navigating the uneven track out of the woods made conversation difficult. Once we were walking side by side on the towpath, I knew Millicent's curiosity would get the better of her.

'Reverend Powell doesn't look much like a vicar,' she commented. 'And I should know. I come from a family of clergymen.'

'No, he doesn't,' I agreed.

There was silence. I knew she was waiting for me to say more. I could see her forming another question and squirmed in anticipation of what it would be.

'Please pass on my congratulations to your father on his engagement.'

I gave a shrill laugh that was part nervous relief, part genuine amusement at the speed of the town gossips. She stared at me in surprise.

'Sorry,' I spluttered. 'He only announced it privately yesterday. Even by Walden's standards, that was fast work.'

Millicent appeared apologetic. 'Oh, I didn't realise. I heard it when I was in the newsagents this morning. Is she nice?'

'Who? Oh, Mrs Keats. Yes, she's fine.' I didn't know Katherine well enough to describe her and felt too flustered to find any appropriate words.

'You don't sound thrilled about it. It must be difficult to adjust. My mother died when I was twenty, and I can't see my father ever remarrying. He's not handsome like your father. He's a typical vicar, if you see what I mean.' She smiled, giving me a sideways glance. 'Not remotely like Reverend Powell.'

'I'm happy for them.' My nostrils detected a faint whiff of paint, and I wondered if Millicent could smell it too.

'But?'

I was happy to stick to the subject of the engagement. 'It's the living situation that bothers me. I think I'm going to find it awkward. All of us living under one roof.'

'Have you thought about taking lodgings? Ursula and I have discussed letting a room. Only to someone we feel comfortable with, though. If you're not in any rush, I can talk to her about it.'

I pushed Archie from my mind and took a moment to let this sink in. Millicent's suggestion could be the answer. 'Would you really consider me? They're not planning to marry until next year, and I think Katherine will keep her flat in London until then.'

'When you're free, come and spend some time with Ursula. She's quite taken with you, but I think she'd like to get to know you a little better. We also need to sort out the house. The books you've seen are only the surface. There are even more upstairs.'

Sleeping in a version of Ursula's curiosity shop appealed to me. 'Thank you, I'd like that. It's very kind of you.'

At Carnival Bridge, we stopped to look at the *Sugar Mary*.

Millicent stared at the boat. 'I can still picture Rosie's body.'

'So can I.' It was a hard image to forget.

I told Millicent about Blanche Denton.

'She's the mother of the young man who brought the *Sugar Mary* back?'

'That's right. The police want to charge her with Rosie's murder, though there are some things that don't make sense.' I sighed. 'She's in prison, and Detective Inspector Yates wants to make sure she stays there.'

* * *

On Monday, I met with Constance and Mrs Siddons at the Tolfree & Timpson factory to discuss the party at Crookham Hall. Mrs Siddons was to give a speech encouraging everyone to vote in the forthcoming general election. Everyone who was eligible, that is. I wasn't.

The Representation of the People Act in 1918 had given the vote to all men over the age of twenty-one but only to women over the age of thirty who met a property qualification. In recent years, it felt like little headway had been made in the fight for equal voting rights.

'Elijah suggested I mingle with the factory workers at the party. And ask who they'll be voting for and why. He wants to know what issues they feel strongly about.' To my delight, Horace Laffaye had decided *The Walden Herald* would champion Mrs Siddons in the election.

'I've invited Mr Whittle and Mr Laffaye. I'm tempted to ask Miss Bray to come along too and write something. It would be worth it just to see the look on Redvers' face.' Constance's eyes glinted with malice. 'But I'll keep her out of sight until I've dealt with him and Osmond.'

'What are you going to do about them?' I was curious to know how she was going to play this.

'Superintendent Cobbe paid Mr Tolfree a visit.' Constance toyed with her silver fountain pen. 'He explained that Miss Bray has turned up safe and well. And that certain allegations have been made that he's looking into.'

'How did Redvers react?' I asked, intrigued.

'He's scared. So's Jack Osmond. They've been trying to get rid of evidence. But thanks to Miss Bray, I was able to secure all the documents. They're with Superintendent Cobbe,' Constance said with satisfaction.

'Is he going to arrest them?'

Mrs Siddons smiled. 'Not yet. He's agreed to take his time with the investigation. It's feasible they were behind the shooting. The superintendent will be showing up every so often to ask them more questions. They may trip themselves up.'

'Poor Redvers is getting himself into quite a state,' Constance said with mock concern. 'They're not stupid enough to try any more fraudulent invoicing, so I'll keep them here until the time's right. I don't want to be involved in yet another scandal before the election. I also need to persuade Redvers to sell me his share of the business. When he realises how expensive his legal fees are going to be, I think he'll be more amenable to selling.'

I smiled, pleased Constance was back on form. I was also worried. She didn't seem troubled about her safety, but I was. The threat hadn't gone away.

'You mentioned your father wishes to attend?' Mrs Siddons said.

I dragged my thoughts back to the party. 'He'd like to bring Mrs Keats, his fiancée.' The unfamiliar word 'fiancée' stuck in my throat.

'He's engaged?' Mrs Siddons looked astonished. She clearly hadn't been to the newsagents recently.

'Yes, they announced it at the weekend.' I wilted under her scrutiny. She'd want to know why I hadn't told her.

'Pass on my congratulations to your father and Mrs Keats.' Constance added their names to her list in perfect handwriting. 'I look forward to seeing them both.'

Mrs Siddons gave me a meaningful stare and pressed me to visit her at Grebe House soon for a 'cosy chat'. Since my return to Walden, I'd had little opportunity to speak to her privately. She'd become a close friend following my mother's death, and I guessed she was worried about how I was coping with the prospect of gaining a stepmother.

I left Constance's office, intending to go down to the factory floor to find Nora Fox. As I passed Redvers Tolfree's office, I saw him having an intense conversation with Jack Osmond. I noticed the typewriter on his secretary's desk. Freda Bray had left days before the shooting, so it wouldn't have been difficult for Redvers Tolfree or Jack Osmond to have typed the threatening letter. Could they have got someone to sneak it into the Deptford office?

Out of sight of the office window, I stopped to listen, hoping to eavesdrop on their conversation. But all I could hear were voices from the factory floor below.

'She was wearing trousers again, did you see?' I heard one woman say.

To my embarrassment, I realised they were talking about me.

'She's got balls, ain't she?' said another. This was met with raucous laughter.

I blushed.

'Too right. She caught that woman single-handed. Walked in bold as brass, pretending she was there for a you-know-what.'

I inhaled sharply. News did indeed travel fast. It must have spread from factory to factory. I already had a questionable reputation in Walden; tales like this would do nothing to improve it.

'Good for her. She's done more to find out what happened to Rosie than the police have.' I recognised this as Nora's voice. There were murmurs of agreement.

'You wouldn't catch me wearing trousers. Wouldn't feel natural.' It sounded like an older woman speaking.

'You think you've got the legs for one of those skirts Miss Timpson wears?' came the reply.

There were shrieks of laughter.

'You know the problem with them short skirts?' the older woman replied. 'Nowhere to hide anything. I once nicked a whole gammon and hooked it to my petticoat.'

I smiled at their howls of laughter. They obviously knew Jack Osmond wasn't on the factory floor. And as I couldn't hear what was going on in Redvers' office, I realised I should take advantage of his absence too.

Making more noise than was necessary, I went down the stairs. The chattering stopped and I felt dozens of pairs of eyes on me. I was relieved when Nora came over.

'I've heard all sorts of rumours about what you did,' she said. 'You've got some nerve, I'll say that.'

'I didn't expect it to turn out the way it did.'

'You think she was the one that hurt Rosie? Blanche Denton?'

'She admitted to carrying out the procedure to bring about abortion. I'm not sure she killed her.' I glanced around at the workers. 'Have you found out any more about who the father could have been?'

She shook her head. 'No one here knows.'

'What about her brother, Nicholas? Would Rosie have told him?'

'She might have, but I doubt it. Poor lad's been in a right state. He blames himself for what happened. God knows what he could've done about it. Rosie was a wilful little thing. When she set her mind to something, there was no stopping her.'

'Is he around today?'

'He's out in the yard, loading the pallets.'

I found Nicholas outside, his shirt sleeves rolled up, sweating profusely. He stopped when he saw me.

'Do you think that woman killed our Rosie?' he asked.

'I don't know. She would have needed help to move Rosie's body.'

'Luke could have helped her.'

'Do you think he was the father of Rosie's baby?'

'I don't know. She was sweet on him, though he didn't seem as keen on her. When I asked her if it was him, she said it wasn't.'

'You've no idea who else it could have been?'

'I thought it was someone local. Once she came home with a pair of pheasants and another time a brace of rabbits. Said someone had given them to her. I didn't ask too many questions. We were grateful to have them.' Nicholas suddenly dropped the box he was carrying and sat down on it. 'I should have asked more. Made her tell me who it was. It's my fault.'

I shook my head. 'It's not your fault,' I said gently.

'I gave her the money to get rid of the baby.' The words caught in his throat and he began to cry. 'We couldn't have another mouth to feed. We just couldn't. It would've sunk us.'

His words echoed those of Blanche Denton. One more child could sink a family.

'I never thought...' His body was shaking.

'You couldn't have known what would happen. It's not your fault,' I said again.

'Rosie was desperate. I was desperate. So I gave her the money I'd saved up. I just wanted her to get rid of it.'

'Did you know where she was going?'

'I assumed it was London; I didn't ask. I should've made her tell me. I should've gone with her.'

'Did anyone go with her?'

He shrugged helplessly. 'I don't think so.'

I thought of Rosie going into that dark room with the grimy brown examination couch. Had Blanche comforted her? Reassured her that everything would be alright? Perhaps Rosie had confided in her. I doubted she'd reveal the name of the baby's father, but she might have given some clue as to how the pregnancy came about.

If Blanche did know something, she'd only tell the police if it put her son in the clear. I remembered the look on her face when Luke said he and Rosie had kissed. Without knowing the truth behind the pregnancy, Blanche wouldn't risk saying anything that might incriminate her son.

It was years since I'd visited Holloway Prison, and I didn't relish going back there. But I needed to speak to Blanche Denton again – if she would agree to see me.

28

'It goes on everywhere. I'm not saying it's right, but it's understandable.' Ursula tapped the side of her thick spectacles on the jewelled table. She must have noticed my forlorn expression because she added, 'You feel guilty for reporting this woman to the police?'

In need of some advice before I saw Blanche Denton, I'd decided to take Millicent up on her offer of calling on Ursula. I was already beginning to feel comfortable in this treasure trove of a room.

'Yes and no. I had to stop her from performing any more dangerous operations. But I'm sorry she's in Holloway Prison. I'm going to write to see if she'll allow me to visit.'

'You were right to do what you did, though I sympathise with Blanche. She believed she was helping those unfortunate women. These procedures should be available in hospitals where they can be carried out in hygienic conditions by surgeons.' Ursula propped her glasses on her head, pushing back her mane of grey hair. 'And, of course, there are other solutions.'

'Other solutions?' I stood up to help Millicent through the door with a tray of tea and biscuits.

'Birth control. Stopping conception.' She eyed me shrewdly. 'You're a smart girl. I'm sure you know what I'm talking about.'

I nodded, feeling myself redden.

'Good. I'm glad to hear it. And don't let some man fob you off with any nonsense. I've been told some tall tales by lovers in my time. Claiming I wouldn't get pregnant if they danced three times around a mulberry bush or some such rubbish.' Ursula began to rummage around in her book collection. 'You've heard of Marie Stopes?'

'I went to a talk she gave a couple of years ago,' I replied, reeling from this talk of lovers and mulberry bushes.

'I don't agree with all her views. She's against the sheath, but I think this new latex invention sounds promising. It's a step up from boiling sheep's intestines.'

I choked on my tea. Millicent seemed unperturbed by her great aunt's talk of contraception.

Ursula retrieved the book she was looking for and handed it to me. 'If you see Blanche Denton, give her this. It might help her change her way of thinking. In the past, some gruesome methods were used to try to stop conception. Glass caps that shattered inside a woman, disinfectant squirted into the vagina...' She saw me wince. 'When you've had fourteen children, you'll try anything. Fortunately, there are now safer, more reliable methods.'

I thumbed through the book. 'I'm not sure she'll read it. She was so disillusioned when I spoke to her. About everything. She was a suffragette and once shared a prison cell with my mother. Now she's wondering what it was all for. Did they achieve anything?' Blanche's pessimism had rubbed off on me.

'Of course they did. At least some women have the vote, although not enough. And look at Mrs Siddons. She has a seat in

Parliament, and we need to make sure she keeps it.' She banged her fist on the table.

'We're holding a meeting for her supporters here on Tuesday evening if you'd like to join us,' Millicent said. 'We plan to put up more posters and leaflet the outlying villages.'

I nodded. Recent events had distracted me, but with a general election looming, it was time to get campaigning again.

* * *

I'd visited Holloway Prison a few times in my life and it was never a pleasant experience. The worst had been when my mother was on hunger strike.

A warder led me down the familiar corridors to the visiting room. I'd often tried to analyse the distinct smell of Holloway. Carbolic soap combined with boiled cabbage was the best I could come up with.

I'd written to Blanche Denton and been surprised by the warmth of her reply. I was responsible for putting her in a prison cell, yet she didn't seem to bear me any ill will.

As soon as I spotted her in the visitors' room, I could tell she'd lost weight since our confrontation in the squalid house on Dolphin Street.

'Funny I've ended up back in Holloway.' She didn't smile, and we both knew there was nothing funny about her situation. 'I remember being in here with your mother. Of course, we didn't want to be here, but it felt good to be part of something. We belonged. Your mother said it made her feel more alive.'

This was precisely what I didn't want to hear. All the old pain resurfaced. What Blanche said was true. Mother had loved being part of the WSPU. Loved being part of the gang. Father and I hadn't been enough for her. She'd wanted the vote at any cost.

That cost turned out to be her life. When we'd moved from Walden to London in 1913, Mother had said she was going to find work as a writer. Instead, she'd become more involved with the cause and taken part in more protests. It had been an obsession. A year later, she was dead.

Had she lived, would she have been as disillusioned as Blanche? I relegated these thoughts of my mother to the back of my mind to be re-examined later.

'I'm sorry you're here.' I sat on a hard wooden chair across from Blanche. 'I don't believe you killed Rosie.'

'I did in my way.' There was an air of resignation about her.

'Did you smother her?' I was aware of the warder standing by the door, listening to every word.

This roused Blanche as I'd hoped it might. 'No.'

'Do you know who did?'

She shook her head. 'She was fine when she left me. There was a little blood loss, that wasn't unusual.' Her hands trembled. 'I didn't mean to hurt her. I promise I don't know what happened to Rosie after she left that evening.'

'Was it Luke's baby?'

'No.' Her reply was instant. 'He says not, and I believe him.'

We both knew Luke might be too ashamed to reveal the truth to his mother. Was she terrified she'd aborted her own grandchild?

'If they charge you with murder, they'll imply Luke helped you. They know you couldn't have moved Rosie's body on your own.'

'Luke's not involved in any of this.' She seemed to be trying to convince herself. 'He didn't know what I'd done. I kept it a secret.'

'Didn't he ever see you going to Dolphin Street?'

She shook her head. 'I only took appointments when he wasn't around. Luke joined up when he was eighteen and was away fighting for the last nine months of the war. That's when it began. When he came back, he took a job on the barges and was away a lot. I wanted to give it up after he started working in the factory. I couldn't risk him finding out. You must believe me; he knew nothing about it.'

'Then you need to defend yourself to protect him. Did Rosie tell you how she came to be pregnant?'

'She said someone had been nice to her and things went too far. It sounded like it only happened the once and she wished she'd never done it.' Blanche sighed. 'Unfortunately, once is all it takes.'

'Was anyone with her when she came to you? They might have been waiting outside.'

'I didn't see anyone.'

'How did you know what to—' I hesitated. 'Who taught you how to undertake the procedure?'

She shrugged but looked wary. 'Some nurses showed me during the war. A lot of young women fell pregnant then.'

The way she lowered her gaze made me suspect she wasn't telling the whole truth. Probably because she didn't want to be the cause of someone else ending up in a prison cell. I handed Blanche the book Ursula had given me, noticing the warder craning her neck to see what it was.

'What's this?' Blanche asked.

'It's a book about birth control. Clinics are opening around the country, trialling free methods of contraception. They offer advice to married women. They're looking for volunteers to help.'

Blanche turned the pages without interest. 'Most women don't have a choice over whether they get pregnant. Their husbands aren't going to give the time of day to these methods.' She tossed the book back at me. 'Mine wouldn't have.'

'Are you divorced?'

She gave a bitter laugh. 'Working women don't get divorced. They can't afford it. And I had no grounds. A man can beat his wife black and blue, in a court of law that's not a good enough reason to get divorced. I left my husband and joined the suffragettes. I wasn't going to take another beating, and I wasn't going to let him start on Luke. I wanted a different life for us.'

'You wanted to change things. You still do. These birth control clinics are looking for women to help out.' I pushed the book back toward her. 'Read it. This could be a way for you to do something practical about an issue you feel strongly about.'

'You seem to think I'll be getting out of this place.' She picked up the book. 'I'll read it.'

'May I come and see you again?'

'I'd like that.' She managed a faint smile.

I had the niggling feeling Blanche had more to tell. She may not be willing to confide in me yet, but perhaps over subsequent visits, I could build her trust.

29

Mrs Siddons was resplendent in a full-length purple silk gown with an amethyst necklace and matching drop earrings. Elaborately made-up eyelashes fluttered beneath perfectly curled dark hair and her complexion was an unblemished ivory. She wouldn't have looked out of place on the stage, and she greeted her guests with the assurance of an actress.

A large marquee stood in front of Crookham Hall. The weather was fine, and Tolfree & Timpson staff chose to mingle on the immaculate lawns, enjoying the Timpsons' hospitality. The relaxed setting was a contrast to the tense security that had surrounded Constance's speech in Deptford.

I almost didn't recognise Nora Fox without her white cap and overalls. Her chestnut hair was set in waves, and she wore a simple cotton pinafore dress. In the fresh air, her skin appeared healthier and she looked much younger than she had in the biscuit factory. Redvers Tolfree was making a great show of affability; Jack Osmond stuck to his side like a faithful dog.

There was a call for quiet as Mrs Siddons took her place behind a lectern on the lawn. She gave an informal speech and managed to raise some laughs from her generally receptive audience. Even the few members of the press who'd been invited seemed less hostile than usual. I saw Redvers Tolfree watching her with a fixed smile.

Standing guard at Mrs Siddons' side was Ben. He'd swapped his usual police tunic for a flannel jacket with a shirt and tie. I could see why. It was a warm October afternoon and the workers were in their Sunday best. A uniformed policeman wandering among them would have put a dampener on the holiday atmosphere.

I waited until the formalities were over and Mrs Siddons was mingling with her guests before I approached him. 'I didn't expect to see you here today.'

'Detective Inspector Yates told me to come down and keep an eye on things. Constance asked me not to wear my uniform.' His tone was still frosty.

It was a very smart jacket, and it crossed my mind that Constance might have bought it for him.

I tried an apology. 'I'm sorry for what I did. I should have spoken to you about it.'

'You shouldn't have gone to Hopkins Tobacconist, and you shouldn't have gone into that house on Dolphin Street.' He sighed. 'Do you think I want to lose someone else I care about?'

I swallowed hard and stared at the ground, unable to speak.

He was silent for a moment, then asked, 'I heard you visited Blanche Denton in prison. Did she tell you anything?'

I lifted my head and almost smiled. I felt like pointing out that by asking me this question, he was acknowledging that I might uncover things that the police couldn't. But I didn't want to push my luck.

'Not much. She said Rosie made it sound as if she'd only had one encounter with whoever made her pregnant. There is something, though. I think Blanche might tell me more about how she got involved in carrying out those procedures. I'm going to visit her again. I'll let you know if I find out anything.'

'Please do,' he said dryly.

'Nicholas, Rosie's brother, admitted that he gave her the money for the abortion. He thought her boyfriend might have been local. He says she came home with a couple of pheasants and some rabbits. Though I suppose she could have stolen them from someone.' I remembered the conversation I'd overhead at the factory and smiled as I pictured the older woman hiding a gammon under her skirts. 'Perhaps she caught the train home to Walden and ran into someone who was angry with her?'

'Hardly a reason to murder someone, stealing a few pheasants. But Rosie must have got caught up in something,' he acknowledged. 'It wasn't some random attack. She must have been killed by someone who knew her.'

'Redvers Tolfree has a car. I've seen it at the factory. He and Jack Osmond could have been waiting for her, ready to take her back to Walden.'

'You said Nicholas Robson gave his sister the money for the abortion. If Tolfree or Osmond had arranged it, surely they would have paid for it?'

'I suppose so. Have you found out any more about what they got up to that night?'

He smiled grimly. 'Freda Bray was right. Detective Inspector Yates asked around his contacts. Tolfree and Osmond were spotted out drinking and visiting a brothel.'

I grimaced. 'Could they have encountered Rosie at some point in the evening? She became ill in the car, and they panicked.'

Ben shook his head. 'We spoke to Mr Tolfree's chauffeur. He was happy to tell us where he took them that night. He seemed embarrassed by their behaviour. Apparently, they weren't exactly discreet. Detective Inspector Yates' contacts back up what he said about where they were drinking and the prostitutes they saw.'

'Maybe they were celebrating?'

'What do you mean?'

'Celebrating scaring Constance Timpson. They may not be involved in Rosie's murder, but they could be responsible for the shooting.'

'Where would they have hidden the rifle?'

'Anywhere in London from what you've told me. They could have disposed of it in one of the clubs they were in that night. Paid someone to get rid of it for them.'

'I think the chauffeur would have seen it. And he was more than willing to tell us everything we wanted to know. Osmond is supposed to have poor eyesight, although that appears to be in doubt.'

'Ben.' Elijah came over, Horace Laffaye at his side. 'Good to see you again, lad.'

'And you.' Ben gripped Elijah's hand.

'Are you seeing your parents while you're here?' Elijah asked.

'I'm staying with them tonight, then heading back to London tomorrow.'

Horace patted Ben's arm. 'If you'd like to return to Walden, I'm sure it can be arranged.' He winked. 'Just say the word.'

Ben grinned. 'Thank you, Mr Laffaye.'

It went without saying Horace would use his influence with Superintendent Cobbe to arrange the matter.

Over Horace's shoulder, I saw Constance gesturing to me and realised she wanted me to make introductions. She wasn't well acquainted with my father, although they'd met briefly in the past. I darted over to her.

Percy was sticking as close to Constance's side as Jack Osmond was to Redvers Tolfree's. Unlike Osmond and Tolfree, Percy and

Constance made a handsome couple. Both were fashionably dressed, Constance in a deceptively simple calf-length white linen coat and matching dress delicately embroidered with blue silk thread, while Percy had on grey flannel trousers and a checked sports jacket.

'You already know my father, and this is Mrs Katherine Keats, his fiancée.'

Percy's eyes widened. 'Fiancée? Are you sure?'

Constance jabbed her elbow into his ribs. My father raised his eyebrows, and Katherine bit her lip.

'Quite sure.' I was torn between wanting to laugh and kick him in the shin.

'May I offer you my congratulations. Iris told me of your engagement.' Constance exuded effortless charm while Percy and I shuffled awkwardly.

'Oh yes, congratulations and all that.' Percy seemed to gather himself. 'Lovely to meet you, Mrs Keats. Iris has...' He trailed off. It was obvious I'd never mentioned Katherine to him.

I racked my brain, trying to find something to say. 'Mrs Keats is from Exeter.' It was all I could manage.

'Beautiful part of the world.' Percy beamed. 'I love the south coast of Devon.'

Conversation continued smoothly after that, mainly thanks to Constance's expert guidance.

The rest of the afternoon passed uneventfully. I spoke to the factory workers and got their views on the forthcoming election. It was a pleasant surprise to discover Mrs Siddons was viewed favourably by both male and female staff.

The guests gradually departed, and I took the opportunity to stroll around the grounds. Near the edge of the gardens was a mausoleum that had always fascinated me. It was a gothic building decorated with ornate statues and biblical quotations. Inside were the remains of generations of Timpsons. Outside, grey stone angels with eerily lifelike outstretched wings reached out as though they wanted to gather you to them.

Percy strolled over, looking sheepish. 'Sorry. Didn't mean to put my foot in it with your father and Mrs Keats.'

I smiled. 'It's my fault. I should have mentioned Katherine.'

'Why didn't you? There was a time when you'd tell me things like that. And how you were feeling about it.' He leant back into the wings of an angel. 'How long have you known her?'

Reluctantly, I told him about my first encounter with her in Paris, aware I was bringing up the spectre of George. I didn't want Percy to go cold on me again.

'Gosh. That must have been awkward. Is she going to move in with you?'

I nodded.

He contemplated me. 'You can tell me stuff, you know. I mean, we're still friends, like we used to be.'

'I don't want to live with them,' I blurted out. 'It would feel odd. I don't need a mother. I had a mother. She's gone. And I'm too old to have a stepmother.' For so long, it had been me, Father and Lizzy. And Father had been absent for much of the war. To fit into a domestic routine with two parental figures would be strange.

'What are you going to do?' He rested his elbow against the tombstone.

'Millicent may have come up with a solution.' I told him about her suggestion.

He pulled a face. 'I know old Ursula can be a bit eccentric. But they're a reputable family. Millicent's father is a clergyman, you know.'

I gasped at the implication of this. 'You seem to be suggesting that I'm unworthy of being seen in decent company?'

'I'm just saying that you've sullied your reputation. Millicent's a schoolteacher. You ought to consider her standing in the town. Daniel's really keen on her, and there are enough obstacles in their way as it is.'

'I'm sure Millicent and her great aunt can make up their own minds as to whether I'm respectable enough to take lodgings with them,' I said through gritted teeth. I couldn't believe what he'd said. Just as we were beginning to get along again. 'I have a feeling they're not as close-minded and hypocritical as you are.'

'What do you mean, hypocritical?' He waved his hand in protest. 'You ran away with a man.'

'And how many women have you been with?'

He flushed. 'That's different. There are repercussions for females.'

'What about Katherine? Do you disapprove of her spending the night with my father?'

'That's different too. She's older. And engaged. You're young, and you're too...'

'Too what?' I demanded.

'I'm only thinking of you.' His eyes flickered and he couldn't hold my gaze.

'Are you? Or are you still angry with me for going away with George?'

He looked directly at me. 'You're too reckless sometimes. You know you are. Alright, maybe I was angry. I needed you, and you weren't here.'

I could see the hurt in his eyes and felt a pang of guilt. For the first time, I understood: he'd seen my leaving as a desertion of him at a difficult time. I didn't know how to respond, so I stomped toward the hall. Percy ambled across the lawn after me with his hands sunk into his pockets.

It was nearly five o'clock and most of the guests had left. My father and Katherine had gone, and I realised I didn't know how I was going to get home. Four cars remained on the driveway: two Daimlers, one belonging to the Timpsons and the other to Horace; Mrs Siddons little sportscar; and Percy's Ford Model T Roadster.

Mrs Siddons was waving to Horace and Elijah as she walked towards her car. Unlike Horace, Mrs Siddons insisted on driving herself and did so with a confidence that didn't match her ability behind the wheel. Despite the terror I always felt when I was a passenger in her car, I knew I'd have to ask her for a ride home unless Horace offered me a lift.

I was about to walk over to her when I heard a strange pinging noise that sounded like metal hitting metal.

'Get down,' Elijah shouted, waving his hands.

Everyone looked at him in astonishment. Except Ben, who dived in front of Mrs Siddons, pushing her to the ground. As he did, his shoulder gave a strange jolt, and he staggered sideways.

Mrs Siddons took the weight of his body. Gasping for breath, she reached out to cradle him, her eyes widening in horror at the sight of blood seeping through his shirt.

30

'Ben!' Constance yelped.

'Get behind the cars,' Elijah shouted. 'Now. All of you. That was rifle fire.'

Percy grabbed me and we stumbled to the ground behind his Ford.

The shots had come from across the lawn and our only cover was the line of four cars parked behind each other, snaking down one side of the drive.

Daniel and Constance crouched low on the driver's side of their Daimler, which was closest to the hall. Parked behind it was Horace's car. He'd been standing by the rear passenger door when Elijah pushed him to the ground.

'This gravel will ruin the knees of my trousers,' Horace protested.

Mrs Siddons was still in the line of fire, slumped by the front passenger door of her sportscar, holding Ben in her arms. She was parked between Horace's Daimler and Percy's Ford.

Elijah crawled out from the cover of the cars and went over to where Mrs Siddons was cradling Ben. Gently, he placed Ben's head on the ground, and taking Mrs Siddons' hand, he dragged her to where Horace was kneeling. Her gown was ripped, her curled hair had come loose on one side, and she had a dazed expression on her face. For once, she was speechless.

She collapsed onto the gravel next to Horace, who took a small hip flask from his pocket and put it to her lips. She took a sip and then spluttered.

Constance was attempting to crawl towards Ben, but Daniel grabbed her arm. 'Don't be silly.' He held her close to him. 'Which side did the shots come from?' he hissed at Elijah.

'The right. From behind the mausoleum, I think,' Elijah replied in a low voice. 'Do you think you can stay low and run inside to telephone the police?'

'Yes, sir.' Daniel sounded like he was back on the battlefield. He sprinted nimbly from behind his car towards the hall.

I watched him, holding my breath. No more shots rang out and I started to breathe again.

'I need to tend to Ben.' Elijah opened the rear door of Horace's Daimler and manoeuvred himself awkwardly onto the back seat. He then opened the door on the other side and wriggled out to where Ben was lying.

'Be careful,' Horace whispered.

Elijah tucked himself behind the open door, which afforded him a degree of protection. 'I need towels. And bandages.'

Constance went to move, but Percy crawled over to her. 'Stay here. I'll get them.'

He dashed towards the hall and I held my breath again. There were no more shots.

A few minutes later, Daniel and Percy sprinted back.

'The police are on their way,' Daniel reported. 'I've told the servants to stay in the house away from the windows.'

Percy pushed the towels and bandages through the open rear

door of the Daimler towards Elijah. We heard a ripping sound and then a groan from Ben.

'Stay still,' Elijah ordered.

'How is he?' I peered underneath the Ford and could see Elijah tentatively examining the wound.

'Difficult to tell.' Elijah peered at the hole in Ben's jacket. 'I need to staunch the blood, then we can move him into the back of the car out of harm's way.'

'How bad is it?' Mrs Siddons seemed to have revived.

'He's been hit in his upper arm. We need to get him to the hospital. Daniel, get in the car and be ready to lift Ben by the shoulders,' he commanded. 'Percy, are you willing to join me around here? I need you to lift Ben's legs and manoeuvre him into the back of the car towards Daniel while I keep hold of the wound.'

'Yes, sir,' Percy and Daniel said in unison. For a moment, I thought they were going to salute.

'Gently,' I heard Elijah say when they were both in position. I craned to watch, but all I could see was Daniel Timpson's backside as he knelt low in the rear of the car, preparing to pull Ben in.

We heard a low groan and I winced. Between the three of them, they managed to move Ben onto the back seat. Elijah and Percy then joined Horace and Mrs Siddons behind the protection of the car.

'Keep your hand where it is over the wound,' Elijah told Daniel. 'And stay low.'

I crawled over to the Daimler and was relieved to see Ben's eyes were open, though his face was scarily white.

'What do we do now?' I asked.

'Wait,' Elijah said. 'I think whoever fired has gone. But they could still be lurking out there. If we try to drive away, they may decide to have another shot.'

'I'm willing to risk it,' Percy said.

'Me too.' Daniel was still in the back of the car, holding Ben's wound. 'We can get him to the cottage hospital in Walden in ten minutes.'

Constance and I exchanged a glance, knowing we shared the same emotional turmoil, desperate to get Ben to hospital but not if it meant putting Daniel and Percy in danger.

'Let's give it a few minutes to be on the safe side. Are you alright, lad?' Elijah asked.

Ben managed to nod.

Fortunately, we didn't have to wait long before we heard the clanging sound of police cars, followed by an ambulance. Three Black Marias drove over the lawn, pulling up in a row, effectively shielding us from where the shots were fired. The ambulance pulled up next to the Daimlers, and a medic scrambled out of the back.

* * *

'Our arrival will have scared off our would-be assassin if he hadn't already scarpered.' Standing by the mantelpiece, Superintendent Cobbe addressed the room. 'Did anyone see who fired the gun?'

'I didn't see the person. I think the shots came from over by the mausoleum,' Elijah replied.

'I agree.' Horace nodded. He was looking at Elijah with a mixture of tenderness and pride, the disastrous effect of the gravel on his pale grey wool trousers forgotten.

In the safety of Crookham Hall, I sank into the velvet upholstered sofa. We were in a green reception room I'd become well acquainted with several years earlier.

Mrs Siddons had regained some of her composure, though her hair had collapsed from its elaborate structure and fell wildly around her shoulders. Her dress was torn, and there were grazes on her hands. She sipped her tea in her usual regal manner as if her appearance was nothing out of the ordinary.

Constance was staring out of the tall windows that offered a panoramic view of the estate. Her white coat and dress were smeared with dirt. She'd wanted to go with Ben to the hospital but Daniel had stopped her. Instead, he'd accompanied Ben in the ambulance and Percy had followed in his car.

PC Sid King and a team of officers were searching the grounds along with a hastily gathered bunch of estate workers.

'Who was here when the shots were fired?' Superintendent Cobbe asked.

Constance roused herself from her reverie. 'All of the factory workers had left. The staff had finished clearing up outside and were mostly in the kitchen. Mr Laffaye's chauffeur was with them. Outside, it was all of us.' She gestured around the room. 'And my brother and Mr Baverstock. And PC Gilbert, of course.'

'I'd like a complete list of everyone who was here this afternoon.'

'My secretary can provide that,' Constance replied.

'Redvers Tolfree and Jack Osmond were here earlier. They'd left by the time the shooting started. One or both of them could have been hiding nearby.' I mentioned my suspicion that they could have used Miss Bray's typewriter in her absence without being noticed and left the threatening letter on Constance's desk.

'It's possible, though I've found nothing in my investigations so far that would suggest their involvement.' The superintendent leant against the mantelpiece. 'Have you had any more threatening letters?' he asked Constance.

She shook her head.

'What about you, Mrs Siddons?'

'No more than usual.' Although she sounded composed, I noticed a slight tremor in her hand when she lifted her teacup.

Superintendent Cobbe tried to offer some reassurance. 'I'm not sure if this will be of any consolation, but if someone had intended to kill you, this wouldn't have been the ideal way to go about it. I think their intention is to try to scare you into taking a less radical approach in your politics.'

'Well, they've failed miserably,' Mrs Siddons declared. 'I have no intention of being any less vocal. Or any less radical.'

'In which case, I think you and Miss Timpson need more protection, at least until after the election. I'm going to see what men I can rustle up.'

'I can't think of anything worse than having a policeman with me all day.' Mrs Siddons placed her teacup back on the table.

'I'm sure my men have better things to do with their time, too,' Superintendent Cobbe said dryly. 'However, until the election's over, let's try to work together to avoid any disasters.'

'I think Superintendent Cobbe has a point.' Horace patted Mrs Siddons' arm.

'Me too,' I said, knowing what Mrs Siddons was like. She wouldn't hold back on any activities. But this was the second time the sniper had struck. Who knew when they'd try again.

She gave a conciliatory nod. 'Very well, although I'm appalled that a young man is lying in hospital because of what someone tried to do to me. And I should hate for anyone else to get hurt. I'm grateful to PC Gilbert, and I think he should receive a commendation.'

'Hear, hear,' Horace agreed.

I thought of Ben diving in front of Mrs Siddons. The image of his body jolting as the bullet hit him would stay with me for a long time.

Mrs Siddons regarded her grazed hands. 'Why do you think they waited until then to fire at me?'

'Probably the first time they could get a clear shot.' Elijah's fingers twitched as he spoke. Constance saw the gesture and picked up a silver cigarette box and took it over to him. I realised it must have been hours since he'd last had a smoke.

Elijah was right. There would have been too many people obscuring the view of Mrs Siddons. When Constance had given her speech, she'd been raised up on a stage. Mrs Siddons had been at ground level with a lectern in front of her.

'If you have no further questions, perhaps Miss Timpson could ring for my chauffeur?' Horace turned to Mrs Siddons. 'I think it would be prudent if we take you and Miss Woodmore home. I can arrange for your car to be collected and returned to you later.'

'Thank you, Mr Laffaye. That's most kind.' Mrs Siddons inclined her head. 'Mr Whittle, I'd like to thank you for all you did this afternoon. You showed great courage in tending to PC Gilbert.'

'You were magnificent.' Constance gazed at him in admiration and Elijah blushed.

Horace stood up. 'I shall insist my brave editor joins me for a slap-up meal and a decent bottle of wine this evening.' From the look on his face, his brave editor was in for more than just a good dinner that night.

Steady on, Horace, I thought. *There's a policeman present.*

I actually had the temerity to raise my eyebrows at him. He must have taken my meaning because he immediately became more business-like.

'And tomorrow, I expect you and Miss Woodmore to write a dramatic first-hand account of today's events for the front page of *The Walden Herald*.'

Elijah smiled. 'Of course.'

31

'Did you and Mr Laffaye have a pleasant evening?' I placed the coffeepot and two cups on Elijah's desk. I could detect the spicy aroma of cigar smoke on his suit. The smell would soon be overwhelmed by his usual brand of tobacco.

'Very nice, thank you,' he replied with the hint of a smile. 'Have you seen Ben?'

'Not yet. I called at the hospital but he was sleeping. I spoke to his mother and she told me the bullet was removed yesterday, and he's doing well. He'll be in hospital for a while. I'll go back later.' I poured the coffee and took up my notepad. 'Shall we go over what happened yesterday?'

He was obviously as keen as I was to chew over the previous day's events and had already started to make notes on a fresh layer of blotter paper. He didn't bother asking why I was in the office on a Saturday morning.

'Whoever it was had probably been lurking in the grounds for some time. And was familiar with the layout of the estate.' He scribbled in spidery black ink.

'Percy and I were chatting by the statues only minutes before.

They must have seen us from the woods, and as we were walking back to the driveway, run over to hide behind the mausoleum.'

'They picked their moment carefully. Not too many people left around. An easy target.'

'Did they mean to kill?' I pictured Mrs Siddons cradling Ben in her arms. Would she have been lying dead on the ground if he hadn't thrown himself in front of her?

'I'm not certain. Only one shot was fired in the attack on Constance. This time, they fired twice, but I'm not sure they meant to kill. If anyone had seriously wanted Sybil Siddons or Constance Timpson dead, they could have achieved it by now.'

It was a horrible thought. 'Ben has been protecting Constance. His presence might have put them off.'

'She appears to have grown rather fond of him?' He posed this as a tentative question.

'She's smitten with him. And Percy's smitten with her.'

He searched for his matches under the mess of paperwork on his desk. 'What about Ben? Does he have any feelings for Constance?'

I shook my head. 'Not in that way.'

He sighed and lit a cigarette. 'What tangled lives. Anyway, I digress. Let's concentrate on the facts. We have two shootings, probably by the same person. I'm still not convinced the intention of either was to hit the target. It was unfortunate Ben leapt in the way. And we have one murder. Are the Timpsons the link between them?'

'All designed to scare Constance into giving in to the unions, stopping equal pay, cutting her female workforce and employing more men?'

'Possibly. Although I can't help thinking that Rosie Robson was just in the wrong place at the wrong time,' Elijah mused as he puffed on his cigarette.

'Why leave her on the *Sugar Mary* if not to send a message to the Timpsons?'

'True,' he conceded. 'This person has to have some knowledge of the Timpsons' activities.'

I nodded. 'Whoever killed Rosie had to have known when the *Sugar Mary* would be docked at Carnival Bridge. And whoever left the anonymous note on Constance's desk had to have access to the factory. That would have needed inside information.'

'But it was public knowledge Constance was giving a speech at the factory that day, as was the fact she was holding a party for Mrs Siddons at Crookham Hall. The gunman could have easily found out when these events were taking place.' He sipped his coffee. 'Anyone could have entered St Mary's Church. And anyone could have gained access to the Crookham estate on foot. The possibilities are endless. The only concrete fact we have is the identity of the person who hurt Rosie by performing an unsafe and illegal operation.'

'Blanche Denton.' I couldn't help feeling Blanche was another victim. 'I'm planning to go and see her again. We know she can't have been involved in what happened yesterday.'

'Unless Luke Denton was? He's familiar with the estate.'

'Blanche told me he joined the army when he was eighteen and fought for the last nine months of the war. So presumably, he would have been taught how to handle a rifle. What motive could he have?' I chewed the end of my pen. 'I had the feeling Blanche wanted to tell me something more. I thought it was about how she got into doing what she did, but it might be something she found out at the factory.'

He nodded. 'It's worth talking to her again. Apart from Luke, is there anyone else she would protect?'

I hesitated. 'She's close to Reverend Powell. She cleans for him and does the flowers in the church.'

He stubbed out his cigarette. 'You think there might be a romantic involvement?'

'Nothing like that. If anything, she mothers him.'

'Many women fuss over their vicars. I can't see a man of the cloth being involved. What's he like, this Reverend Powell?'

I struggled to find appropriate words to describe Archie. I was saved from this dilemma by the sound of footsteps on the stairs.

PC Sid King's boyish face peered around the door of the main office. 'Thought I might find you both here.' He ambled in and dragged a chair over from the corner. 'The bullet they pulled out of Ben came from the same rifle that fired at Constance Timpson.'

'No surprise there.' Elijah scribbled this down.

'How do you know?' I asked.

'Gun barrels have imperfections. Each barrel is different and it leaves markings on the bullets it fires. Superintendent Cobbe took the bullets fired at Crookham Hall over to the ballistics expert who still had the bullet found at the factory in Deptford. The same markings are on all of them.' Sid took the coffee I handed him. 'We think whoever fired those shots hid in a cottage on the estate.'

'Which one?' Elijah asked.

'Lockkeeper's Cottage.'

'Where Luke Denton stayed after bringing the *Sugar Mary* down?'

Sid nodded. 'We've searched it but haven't found anything significant.'

'Why do you think someone was there?' I prised open the window, suddenly needing air. My palms felt clammy.

'One of the estate workers saw a man going towards the cottage earlier in the afternoon. He didn't think anything of it.' Sid referred to his notebook. 'Reverend Powell, a friend of Daniel's, often stays there at the weekends to get away from London and paint. He wasn't there on the day of the shooting.'

'It would make sense to hide there,' I said, ignoring the heat rising in me as I recalled my visit to the cottage. 'Some paths lead to the hall, and it's close to the canal towpath and the main road from Crookham to Walden.'

'You've been to Lockkeeper's Cottage?' Elijah asked.

I tried to sound casual. 'I wanted to see how far it was from Carnival Bridge. I wondered if anyone might have seen Luke Denton there. But it's a quiet part of the estate, especially now the warehouses are closed, and there aren't many boats on the canal.'

'What did the man going towards the cottage look like?' Elijah asked. 'And more to the point, was he carrying a rifle?'

'Tall,' Sid replied. 'He was some distance away and wearing a cloth cap. They said it didn't look like there was anything in his hands.'

Archie was tall. Sid said he hadn't been at the cottage that afternoon, but I had to find out for myself, even though I was embarrassed to face him again after our interrupted kiss.

* * *

I pushed open the heavy oak door to St Mary's. At first, I thought the church was empty. Then, to my embarrassment, I saw Archie kneeling before the altar in silent prayer. I hesitated and turned to leave. I couldn't bring myself to interrupt his reverie.

'Iris.' He'd heard me.

'I'm sorry. I didn't mean to interrupt.'

He dismissed my words with a wave of the hand and beckoned me to come in. 'How's Ben Gilbert? The police told me what happened.'

'He's doing well. They've taken the bullet out, and his wound is healing. He'll be back on his rounds soon.'

'I'm relieved to hear it.' He walked toward me. 'You look in need of comfort. And I guess praying doesn't feature much in your life?'

'I, er, no, not really.' I wondered what sort of comfort he was planning to offer.

He put his arm around me. 'Come through to the vestry.'

Once inside, he went over to the worktop. Instead of putting the kettle on to boil, he fished out the brandy from the cupboard and poured us both a measure. I took it gratefully.

'I've seen Blanche,' he said. 'Luke's concerned about her health. She didn't look well, so I've asked Mathers to visit. She told me you'd been to see her. That was kind of you.'

I didn't like to admit I'd gone there to see if I could discover more about Rosie Robson rather than to check on Blanche's health. 'I got the impression something's weighing on her mind. Something she's not saying.'

He sipped his brandy. 'I think she'd have sense enough to tell the police everything she knows.'

'She might be protecting someone.'

'Luke's the only one she'd protect.'

'Or you,' I said to provoke him.

He looked startled, then gave a short laugh. 'You're right. She probably would protect me. I can assure you she's not. I had nothing to do with Rosie's death.'

'I'm going to visit her again. She's in danger of being charged with murder. Detective Inspector Yates wants to blame everything on her and, by extension, Luke. Though he can't link her to the shootings now. At least, not the one at Crookham Hall.'

'I doubt it was a woman. A Lee Enfield is a hefty rifle. I don't mean to belittle the abilities of the fairer sex, but a man would be more capable of handling that sort of weapon.'

'Have you ever fired one?'

He nodded. 'I bore arms on occasion during the war. I'm considered to be a pretty good shot.'

I thought of the figure seen at the cottage and felt a flicker of fear. Would Archie calmly admit to being such a good marksman if he'd been involved?

'You said the police told you about Ben?' It was a veiled attempt to find out if he'd been questioned. And by the flicker of his eyelids, he knew it.

'Detective Inspector Yates' sergeant came here wanting to know when I was last at Lockkeeper's Cottage. Does it have something to do with the shooting? He wouldn't tell me why he was asking.'

I nodded slowly. 'They think the gunman hid there. The police searched the cottage, I don't think they found anything.'

He scowled. 'I hope they didn't disturb my paintings.'

I thought this was an odd thing to say, given the circumstances. 'You didn't go there at the weekend then?' I tried to make it sound like a casual enquiry.

'No, though I had wanted to go to the party at Crookham Hall and stay at the cottage afterwards.' His lips curled into that familiar smile. 'I admit, I hoped to see you and lure you back to there.'

'Why didn't you?' The brandy was making me bolder.

He scrutinised me. 'Because Walden is your home, and I guessed that at the party you'd be surrounded by people you know. I didn't want to make you feel uncomfortable. Who was there? The Timpsons, Mrs Siddons, Percy, your boss? That ass, Redvers Tolfree, and his creepy foreman, Osmond? Those two would be high on my list of suspects,' he added.

I nodded. 'Mine too.' He was right. His presence probably would have made me feel uncomfortable. 'My father and his fiancée were at the party too.'

'Fiancée? Is that a new development?'

I nodded. 'I hope they'll be happy together. I think they will if I'm not around.'

He laughed. 'How does your father feel about that?'

'He'd like us all to be one happy family.'

'I have come across happy families. But I've found many of my parishioners achieve greater familial harmony when they're not living under the same roof.'

'That's how I feel. I'd rather be happy for them from a distance.'

'Perhaps I can hide you away in the cottage.' His fingers reached out to touch mine.

'Or I could take lodgings with Millicent Nightingale.' I flushed, remembering the occasion they'd met.

'Ah, the respectable Miss Nightingale.' His eyes were teasing.

'Perhaps, like Percy, you think I'll sully her good reputation?' I felt a flash of irritation, probably born of embarrassment.

'You've been rowing with Percy again,' he laughed.

'He was being an idiot.'

He took my hand. 'My offer stands. If you want to escape from the happy couple, you're welcome to take refuge with me.' The invitation was blatant. 'I plan to stay at Lockkeeper's Cottage this weekend.'

My brain unsuccessfully tried to come up with a casual non-committal reply. All I could mumble was, 'Maybe.'

I felt myself blushing and was relieved when the vestry door swung open. Archie quickly let go of my hands.

'Reverend Powell. I...' Luke Denton appeared looking ashen faced. He stumbled in and stopped when he saw me.

'I should go.' I stood up, glad to escape, but Luke continued.

'It's mother. She's dead.'

32

'No.' I breathed the word before I could stop myself. A peculiar sensation in the pit of my stomach caused me to sink back into my chair. It took me a few moments to understand why Luke's words had affected me so much. After all, I hadn't known Blanche Denton well. I wasn't feeling grief. Then I realised it was guilt. My actions had put her in prison. And now she was dead.

'How did she die?' Archie guided Luke into a chair. 'I thought Mathers was going to see her?'

'He went in with some of her tonic, I'm not sure she took it. The senior medical officer assumed she had dysentery and moved her into the hospital wing. She didn't get any better. She seemed to give up.' Luke's cheeks were wet.

Archie took his hand. 'I'm so sorry.'

'You visited her in prison, didn't you?' Luke gazed at me with wide bewildered eyes.

'Yes, I did.' I braced myself, expecting him to blame me for her death.

'That was kind of you.' He wiped his face with his sleeve. 'She hated it when she thought she'd let you down.'

'Let me down?' I said in astonishment.

'She knew you were disappointed in her. She thought you hated her for what she did. She was relieved when she got your letter saying you wanted to see her.'

My guilt increased. 'I wish I could have got to know her better.'

'Can she be buried here at St Mary's?' Luke gripped Archie's hand. 'I know it's what she would have wanted. I'll feel she's still close to me if she's here.'

'Of course. Your mother was always welcome here. Don't worry about that.'

Luke appealed to me. 'Will you come to her funeral?'

His request took me by surprise. 'If you'd like me to.'

'She talked about you a lot. And your mother. She said you were proof that it had been worthwhile.' Tears flowed down his flushed cheeks.

His words touched me. I wondered whether Blanche would have confided in me if I'd been able to speak to her again. But she'd taken her secrets to the grave.

Archie wiped the tears from Luke's face, and I knew it was time I left them.

Luke looked at me as I stood up. 'Would you mind telling Miss Timpson what's happened? I can't face going into the factory today. They all talk about my mother as if she was an evil person. She was a good woman.'

I touched his shoulder and nodded.

Outside, the road was deserted and grey clouds threatened rain. I walked over to where WPC Jones was standing by the factory gate.

'How's Ben?' Her despondent voice matched her downcast expression.

'On the mend, thank goodness.'

'I'm pleased to hear it.' She gave a faint smile. 'Was that Luke Denton I saw going into the church?'

I nodded. 'His mother died in prison.'

She gave a sharp intake of breath.

'Hadn't you heard?' I'd expected the prison to have informed the police.

She gave a bitter laugh. 'I'm always the last to know anything. Detective Inspector Yates told me to keep an eye on Luke. He wants to charge him with murder. Things are about to get even worse for that young man.'

I was dismayed. 'Is there enough evidence?'

'Probably not. But Yates wants a conviction. The other officers will follow his lead. Ben was the only one that questioned the lack of evidence. Yates listened to him, he won't listen to me.'

'It must be difficult being the only woman at the station.'

'I didn't think it would be easy.' She looked defeated; her shoulders slumped. 'It's even harder than I imagined. They expect me to make tea and clean up after them. They don't think I'm capable of much else. I wouldn't mind, but most of them are so stupid, they couldn't spot a criminal if they tripped over one.'

I gave her a sympathetic smile and left her to the unenviable task of standing at the factory gate for hours.

Constance was alone in her office. She groaned when I told her about Blanche.

'Every day, one more thing to deal with.' The energy she'd gained following Freda Bray's revelations seemed to have diminished. Her red-rimmed eyes and pale skin showed the pressure she was under.

'You can't give up.' I knew that was easy for me to say. I wasn't the one being shot at.

'Maybe they've got what they wanted. If Mrs Siddons loses her seat in the election, it will be even harder for me to continue with my plans.' She sighed. 'I knew it wouldn't be easy, I just never realised how tough it would get.'

'WPC Jones just said something similar.'

Constance gave a rueful smile. 'That doesn't surprise me. This is still a man's world, and perhaps it always will be. Every victory comes at such a high price.'

I was glad I wasn't responsible for people's livelihoods. Constance's elevated position was a lonely one. 'You must miss Ben.'

She looked at me sharply. 'I trust WPC Jones to look after me.'

'I meant it must have been nice to have him to talk to. Not that Ben knows much about business.'

She softened. 'He's a good listener. But I have Daniel. Archie's been encouraging him to venture away from the estate and become more involved here and at Creek House. Now we know Blanche Denton won't be coming back, I can offer a job to another one of their occupants.'

'Another one?' I queried.

'We've given Rosie Robson's job to Micky Swann.'

I didn't say anything. The thought of Micky Swann taking Rosie's job was unsettling.

I left the factory and, on impulse, walked towards Hopkins Tobacconist. Unable to stop myself, I sat on a bench a little way up the road and watched as customers came and went. None struck me as particularly suspicious.

Then I spotted a young woman who seemed hesitant. She was clutching a handbag and glanced around before entering. I waited. A few minutes later, she came out carrying a bag of sweets.

Without any particular plan, I followed her. Would Hopkins be that brazen? Could someone have taken Blanche's place as Mrs Quentin? My breath quickened as the young woman turned into Dolphin Street. I dawdled, keeping a reasonable distance between us. She walked at a steady pace and showed no sign of slowing when she neared number twenty-six. Instead, she carried on to the end of the road and turned right onto the High Street. I sped up and hurried after her, cautiously turning the corner just in time to catch a glimpse of her entering a hair salon.

I followed her and stopped outside the salon, pretending to look at the pricelist in the window. The young woman had already been given a seat and was chatting in a familiar way with the hairdresser. I hovered a while, but it was clear the only thing about to happen was a haircut.

I turned and retraced my route back along Dolphin Street. I thought about Rosie Robson being here alone. Where would she have gone? As far as I knew, she didn't know anyone in the city.

Would she have sought solace in the church? Had Rosie thought of going to St Mary's? The presence of the police might have scared her. Did she know the house next door was a home run by the church? Could she have knocked on the door of Creek House and asked for help?

I wandered along Creek Road, debating whether to catch the tram to the station or do more investigating, when I spotted Archie going into Creek House. Curiosity getting the better of me, I crossed the road and found the front door open. Archie was leaning against the desk in the office, scribbling a note. He looked up and smiled when he saw it was me.

'Constance told me that Micky Swann has taken Rosie Robson's old job,' I said.

He nodded. 'That's the delicate matter Daniel wanted to talk to me about when he interrupted us at the cottage.' His eyes twinkled, then his smile turned to a frown. 'Please don't concoct some theory involving him in Rosie Robson's death. It was Daniel's idea. He's been looking for a job for Micky that's not too strenuous for someone with a weak chest and damaged arm. He decided Rosie's role would be fitting.'

'And with Blanche gone, there's another vacancy that might be suitable for one of your men.'

He put down his pen. 'I haven't thought that far ahead. My main concern at present is looking after Luke and making sure Blanche gets the funeral she deserves.'

'I didn't mean to imply anything.' In truth, I was still suspicious of Micky. I could imagine a vulnerable Rosie walking along Creek Road and encountering his strange amber eyes.

'The funeral will be on Tuesday. Will you attend?'

'Of course. I told Luke I would.'

'There will be prayers. And readings. I know it's not your sort of thing.' His voice held a hard edge. 'Most people treat the church as a convenience. Only bothering to attend when they need it and ignoring it the rest of the time.'

'Perhaps I shouldn't come then.' I felt we'd entered into some kind of battle. I knew the tension was because Archie was angry at Blanche's death.

He raised himself from where he'd been perched on the edge of the desk. 'I'm sorry. It's just sinking in that I won't see her again.' His voice softened. 'You should come to her funeral. She was fascinated by you.'

'I can't think why.'

'Because you represented what she wanted. A new generation of women living a more rewarding life than she had.'

I didn't reply. I wasn't sure how rewarding my life was at this present time, but it was undoubtedly a step up from what Blanche had endured.

He moved closer to me. 'I can see why Blanche was fascinated by you. With your modern clothes and fancy haircut.' He reached out and touched the curve of my bobbed hair, letting his finger run down my cheek and across my lips. 'And your rebellious nature.'

The next moment, he'd kicked the office door closed and pushed me against it. His hands rested on my waist and I wrapped my arms around his broad shoulders. We kissed long and hard before a noise from the lounge brought us back to our senses.

'I won't get to the cottage this weekend,' he murmured into my neck. 'I have to stay here with Luke.'

'It's probably just as well.' I pushed him away. 'This isn't a good idea.'

He grinned. 'Ten o'clock. Tuesday.'

For a second, I wondered what he meant.

'Blanche's funeral.'

I nodded, wriggled free of his grasp, and slipped out of the office. To my relief, there was no one in the hallway, but as I reached the front door, Micky Swann appeared as if from nowhere. I wondered where he'd been lurking. He hadn't come out of the lounge. Had he been listening to my conversation with Archie?

Glancing back at the office, he took a step toward me and said in a whisper, 'You don't listen, do you?'

33

Mrs Siddons was holding court when Millicent Nightingale showed me into the parlour. About a dozen women had squeezed in and were sitting on every available surface.

'Less than half of you in this room tonight have the right to vote. And until we have the same voting rights as men, it's going to be a struggle for any woman to be elected to Parliament. What upsets me most is when my young supporters say they feel powerless. If I'm elected, I can promise you I will push for equal franchise at every opportunity.'

Mrs Siddons showed no signs of being affected by the attempt on her life. My conversations with WPC Jones and Constance Timpson had made it feel like we were fighting a losing battle. But one thing you could say about Sybil Siddons was that she never gave up.

Ursula was on fine form too, and tea was soon replaced by sherry. Millicent and I smiled at the contrast of Mrs Siddons in her usual silk finery and perfect curls with the wizened and wild-haired Ursula.

'The pair of them should team up and scare the opposition into surrender,' I said.

'Ursula would have stood for Parliament if it had been possible in her day. Can you imagine her in the debating chamber?' Millicent poured me a glass of sherry. It wasn't my usual tipple, but I had a feeling I'd be drinking a lot more of it if I became part of the Nightingale household.

'I'd have demanded a front row seat every time she made an appearance. Especially if there was a debate on family planning.'

Millicent laughed and took a sip from her glass. 'I can picture it. "The honourable gentlemen may think a boiled sheep's bladder is a suitable form of contraception, I beg to differ."'

We snorted with laughter. I couldn't remember the last time I'd spent the evening with a group of female companions. It made me think of the camaraderie that my mother and Blanche must have shared when they were on the frontline of the suffragette protests in 1914.

Mrs Siddons appeared at my elbow and indicated for me to join her on the small sofa in the corner of the room. 'I'm sorry I've neglected you recently. I haven't had a chance to talk to you privately since your return.'

'There's been a lot going on.' I sat down next to her. 'I'm fine. Happy to be back at the paper with Elijah.'

'Good. I'll be honest, I've been more worried about Constance.'

'Me too. She looked drained when I saw her a few days ago. Archie – I mean, Reverend Powell – is trying to get Daniel more involved.'

'Archie?' She scrutinised me for a moment. 'Hmm, well, hopefully you can't get into too much trouble with a vicar, however dashing he is.'

I didn't think this was entirely true. I took a gulp of sherry and tried to look innocent.

'I think Reverend Powell is right,' she continued. 'It would be good for both of them if Daniel could take some of the weight from Constance's shoulders. She has far too much responsibility for her age. Enough about the Timpsons, I want to talk about you. How are you getting on with Mrs Keats?'

'She seems nice.' I peered into my sherry glass, wondering how it could suddenly be empty.

Mrs Siddons waved a heavily ringed hand dismissively. 'That's not an answer. Have you spent any time with her?'

'Not really. I think we'll get along. She said she won't attempt to be a stepmother to me.'

'Sensible woman.' She smiled. 'Hopefully, you'll become friends.'

'I want to move out. I mean, I do want to be friends. Just not under the same roof.'

She looked dismayed. 'You intend to go back to your grand-mother's house?'

'Millicent has said I might be able to take lodgings here.'

Mrs Siddons let out a cackle of laughter, causing a few heads to turn in our direction. 'Oh, my goodness, what a coven of witches. That would be magnificent.'

I smiled. 'I didn't think of it quite like that.'

Mrs Siddons took a swig of sherry and continued to cackle. 'I can't decide if Millicent will be a good influence on you or if you'll be a bad influence on her.'

'I'm not planning to get into any mischief if that's what you mean. I've learnt the error of my ways.' I pushed thoughts of Archie from my mind. The kiss at the cottage had been a one-off. Apart from the kiss in the office. But that was all.

'Have you?' She smiled at me quizzically. 'You seem to be spending a lot of time in Deptford?'

'I want to find out what happened to Rosie Robson.'

Her smile faded. 'Don't we all. I heard about Blanche Denton's death.'

'Luke Denton has asked me to attend her funeral. I'll see if I can speak to WPC Jones while I'm there. She told me that Detective Inspector Yates was determined to pin the murder on Blanche. She thinks he'll switch his attention to Luke now.'

'Is WPC Jones still stuck on the factory gate?'

I nodded. 'Yates gives her all the menial jobs. She was feeling miserable when I spoke to her. If things don't improve, I think she might leave the force.'

'I hope she doesn't. The WPCs are crucial in helping prevent crimes against girls and women in vulnerable situations. Sadly, the Home Secretary takes the view that WPCs were only employed for welfare work and not proper police work. He'd like to see them removed from the force. I worry that all the gains we made during the war are in danger of being lost.'

'It's starting to feel like that, isn't it?' I tried not to sound despondent, but for all the talk of a progressive new era, 1922 hadn't evolved in the way I'd hoped.

When Millicent appeared with the sherry bottle, we both held out our glasses for a top-up.

* * *

I pulled my wool coat tighter around me against the November chill.

Apart from a few friends from the factory, Luke Denton, Dr Mathers, Constance Timpson and I were the only mourners in the small cemetery of St Mary's Church.

Archie said a prayer, and under a grey sky, we watched Blanche Denton's coffin being lowered into the ground. Luke stared numbly into the grave.

Afterwards, Constance told Luke to take some time off, assuring him his job at the factory was safe. He mumbled his thanks.

Dr Mathers put a hand on Luke's shoulder. 'If you need anything, let me know. Something to help you sleep?'

Luke nodded. Shivering with cold, or perhaps shock, he let Archie guide him back to his home. I followed them into the house, which felt cold and neglected.

In the kitchen, I put the kettle on the stove. While I waited for it to boil, I washed up the dirty cups and plates piled in the sink.

I took the tea into the front parlour, where Archie was sweeping the grate and attempting to light a fire.

Luke sat in an armchair in a daze. 'I'm sorry, I should be doing that. I can't seem to get myself together.'

'Don't worry, I know how you feel.' I put a cup of tea on the table next to him. 'I didn't know what to do with myself for a long time after my mother died.'

'Did your mother believe the same things that my mother did?'

'They both believed that women should have the right to vote.' I didn't think this was what he was asking, but I needed to tread carefully. He was in a fragile state.

'I don't mean that. I mean... would your mother have been shocked by what my mother did? Would she have thought it was wrong?'

'I don't know.' It was a truthful answer. 'I was only fourteen when she died. We'd never had a conversation about that sort of thing. She would have recognised the truth of what your mother said, how unwanted pregnancies pushed women further into poverty and despair.'

'She showed me the book you lent her and told me about the, er, the birth control clinics. She realised that it was a better way.' He added apologetically, 'I haven't collected her belongings yet. I couldn't face it. Dr Mathers said he'd do it for me. I'll return it to you when he does.'

I could sense Archie watching me and felt myself blushing. 'There are no simple solutions to the problem,' I said gently. 'Your mother believed what she was doing was helping others have a better life. But that sort of procedure should be carried out in a hospital.'

Luke turned his large mournful eyes on Archie. 'She knew she was wrong to do what she did. She shouldn't have performed those operations. I think someone talked her into it. Will God forgive her?'

'She was a good woman who was mistaken in her beliefs. And maybe she was influenced by others to act the way she did. We will never know, but God does.'

'She didn't kill Rosie. I know that,' Luke said vehemently.

'So do I.' Archie had brought the fire to life, and the smell of burning coal filled the room.

Luke picked up a tin box from the table beside him and opened it. 'The first time she came out of Holloway, they gave her medals. This time, she came out in a coffin.'

When I saw the contents of the box I smiled sadly. 'I have a similar collection of medals at home.'

'I'm not sure what they all mean.' He handed me the box.

I took out a silver and enamel brooch of a portcullis shot through with an arrow. 'This one would have been awarded to her for the time she spent in Holloway Prison. These are the dates of her incarceration. And this one...' My voice choked as I picked up a tarnished medal that hung from green, white and purple striped fabric. 'This was awarded to suffragettes who went on hunger strike. They were protesting against being jailed as criminals rather than political prisoners.' To my embarrassment, tears filled my eyes. I quickly wiped them away with my handkerchief. I felt

Archie's hand on my shoulder and suppressed the desire to lean back into him.

'I'm sorry,' Luke said. 'I didn't mean to upset you.'

I cleared my throat. 'I was angry with my mother for a long time after she died. I felt she'd chosen the cause over me. Chosen to die rather than be with me. It took a long time for me to be proud of her. But it does come, with time.'

Luke took the tin back. 'Thank you. If I ever have children, I'll tell them all about their grandmother.'

'You should.'

The three of us jumped at the sound of thumping on the front door.

Archie squeezed my shoulder. 'You stay here. I'll see who it is.'

A moment later, we heard raised voices in the hallway, and I saw a flicker of fear in Luke's eyes. Archie returned with a broad man in a tan coloured overcoat. Behind him were two police constables.

'I'm Detective Inspector Yates. Luke Denton, I'm arresting you on suspicion of the murder of Miss Rosie Robson.'

Archie paced up and down the Dentons' small kitchen while I washed up the teacups.

When Detective Inspector Yates had told him he couldn't go with Luke to the police station, I'd been afraid Archie was going to punch him. The inspector had evidently thought that too and had taken a step back while a burly constable had taken a step forward.

I'd placed a warning hand on Archie's shoulder, and the inspector had settled for giving us a curious look before ushering a frightened Luke out of the door to the waiting police car.

'Luke didn't do it,' Archie growled as he paced.

'I know.' I laid the dishcloth to one side and stepped into his path, holding a hand to his chest to stop him.

He bowed his head. 'I failed that family. They looked after me, and I let them down.'

'No, you didn't.' I put my arms around him and tried to guide him back into the parlour. He resisted.

Instead, he wrapped his arms around my waist and held me close. 'It was kind of you to say what you did to Luke. About your mother. I can see why you would have been angry with her. For putting the cause before looking after her family.'

It wasn't quite what I'd said, but in truth, it was what I'd felt at the time.

He bent to caress my lips with his. Unlike our previous kisses, which had been hot and hungry, this was gentle, almost tender, and gradually turned into something deeper.

When I'd untangled myself from Archie's arms, I suggested he talk to Constance Timpson about finding Luke some legal representation. He'd leapt into action in typical Archie fashion and immediately strode from the house over to the factory.

I didn't know if he expected me to follow him, but I needed to place some distance between us. I left the Dentons' house and wandered back to the bench near Hopkins Tobacconist. I half-heartedly attempted to keep watch, in reality, I was lost in my thoughts. Why did I keep telling myself it wouldn't happen again with Archie, then lose all resolve when I was with him? Admittedly, it had been an emotional morning. But that was no excuse.

I picked up my bag and was about to head to the tram stop when I spotted a young woman walking toward the tobacconist. She had red hair pulled back tightly from her face and wore a neat blue suit. There was something purposeful about the way she moved, then, when she reached the door of the tobacconist, she seemed to freeze for a second. Then she gave a slight toss of her head and pushed open the door.

In less than two minutes, she was back on the pavement. Watching as she walked away, I was unable to resist the urge to follow. She moved quickly, and I had to hurry to catch up.

She turned into Dolphin Street, and I slowed in anticipation of her stopping at number twenty-six. She kept going. I told myself I should stop being silly and turn around and head to the tram stop, as my feet kept walking in the same direction as her.

She turned into a road I was unfamiliar with. It was even more rundown than Dolphin Street. About halfway along, she stopped. I slowed my pace and watched as she knocked on the front door of one of the terraced houses. Then she disappeared inside.

I was some distance away, and by the time I reached the terraced row, I was uncertain of which house she'd entered. It could have been one of three.

On the opposite side of the road was a small public garden. It was nothing more than a square patch of grass with a bench on each side, surrounded by tall railings. A sign on an iron gate read Fair View Square. There was nothing fair about the view; it was grey and dismal.

I walked through the gate and sat on the bench nearest the terraced houses. I checked my watch. It was nearly two o'clock. Forty minutes passed, and I began to shiver. For all I knew, the red-haired woman lived there. Or was visiting a friend. I decided to wait until a full hour passed, then I'd give up.

A few minutes later, the door to one of the houses opened, and the woman reappeared. I guessed she'd been crying as her translucent skin was covered in pink blotches. Her gait was now slow and awkward with none of the speed and purpose she'd shown earlier. She kept pulling at the sides of her skirt.

I stayed on the bench and watched her walk away. It would be unkind to try to talk to her.

I peered over at the house, but I couldn't make out the number on the front door. I wasn't sure of the name of the street either, though I guessed it was called either Fair View Road or Fair View Street, after the garden. I decided to walk up the road, find out the house number and street name and then head home.

As I crossed the road, the front door opened again. A large woman emerged, carrying an ominous-looking black leather bag.

The new Mrs Quentin, I presumed. I carried on walking at the same steady pace.

When I reached the pavement, the door of the house was still open, so I couldn't see the number. The large woman was talking over her shoulder to someone inside.

As I passed, she left the house, slammed the door shut and marched off in the opposite direction to the way I was heading.

Before the front door had closed, I'd caught a glimpse of a figure inside. In disbelief, I stopped and stared back at the house.

I'd seen a tall man with grey hair, a neatly trimmed beard and wire-rimmed spectacles. I was sure it had been Dr Mathers.

35

I realised I'd been holding my breath, and my body had gone rigid. I exhaled and let my shoulders relax. Had that really been Dr Mathers?

I glanced up and down the road. There was no sign of his car parked nearby. I noted the house number and walked to the end of the street. A sign on the corner said Fair View Road. I crossed and went back to my bench in the square. Taking out my notebook, I wrote down the address.

Had the doctor seen me, I wondered? I thought it unlikely. He'd been standing sideways in a doorway halfway along the hall.

I began to shiver. I couldn't sit there for much longer, but I needed to know for certain if it was Dr Mathers.

It was another fifteen minutes before the door opened again. I pulled my felt hat down low and peered from under the brim.

It was Mathers.

He glanced up and down the deserted road. Then he strode away from the house back towards Dolphin Street, carrying his black medical bag. I waited for a moment or two and then followed.

I kept a considerable distance between us, not wanting to risk him seeing me. He took the route I expected and returned to his home at the end of Creek Road.

Dr Mathers. Kindly Dr Mathers. It didn't make sense. But, of course, it did. I looked across at the factory and considered my next move. WPC Jones might still be on the gate. I could tell her what I'd seen. However, as a woman police officer, she had no powers of arrest. And from what she'd told me, she wasn't taken seriously by her colleagues.

I wished Ben was around and not in hospital. He'd go straight to Detective Inspector Yates with the information.

Archie would be at the church. He and Mathers weren't exactly friends, but they respected each other. Also, Archie had a hot temper. I wasn't sure how he'd react towards the doctor or me. I decided to head home and talk to Elijah the following day.

* * *

'Good morning, Miss Woodmore.' Miss Vale peered at me from over the top of her glasses.

'Good morning, Miss Vale.'

'What are we going to be discussing today?' Elijah's hand hovered on the doorknob.

'The usual. Abortions and murder.'

Miss Vale tutted. Elijah sighed, closed the door, and ambled over to his desk. 'Miss Vale will be moving to an office downstairs soon. You can have your desk back when she does.'

I gave him time to light a cigarette before telling him what I'd seen the previous day.

'Dr Mathers? From what you've told me of the chap, it doesn't seem likely he'd be involved in anything illegal.'

'When I visited Blanche in prison, she was vague about who

had taught her to perform a procedure to bring about miscarriage. I thought she was protecting someone. And she was. The trusted doctor.'

'You can't know that for certain,' he protested.

'And who would Rosie Robson turn to if that procedure went wrong? Who has a car?'

Elijah sucked in a breath. 'You're trying to pin the murder on him as well as the illegal operations? Why? Why would a doctor switch from saving lives to taking them?'

'Money. Dr Mathers doesn't have much of it. He talks about retiring to Devon and buying a boat, yet he's living in a house owned by the Timpsons. I hate to say it, but abortion is a lucrative business. The tobacconist is in on it. And it hasn't taken Mathers long to find another woman to take Blanche's place.'

He took a long drag of his cigarette. 'Why kill Rosie Robson?'

'The pathologist said that Rosie would have been bleeding shortly after the procedure and in pain. She was alone in Deptford. The factory was closed. I think she would have gone to the church or the doctor's house. The police were with Reverend Powell and a police car was parked outside St Mary's. Perhaps Rosie saw Dr Mathers' car outside his house and decided to try there?'

Elijah considered this. 'Why would he kill her?'

'The only other option would have been to take her to hospital where it would be apparent to anyone examining her that an attempt at abortion had been made.'

'But Mathers didn't perform the procedure. Blanche did. Rosie wouldn't have known he was behind it.'

'Telling her story would have been enough to shut the business down. The police would want to know where she went to have the abortion. And if the women in the factories found out what happened to Rosie, it would stop anyone else seeking out "Mrs

Quentin's" services. Mathers relies on word of mouth from the factory workers to keep him in business.'

Elijah nodded slowly. 'It would be difficult to prove. Blanche Denton rented that room on Dolphin Street. It would be risky to use the same place again. Presumably whoever has taken her place, the woman you saw with the medical bag, has rented this room on Fair View Road. She's unlikely to admit to anything. And if the police question the occupants of the house, they'll probably say someone was taken ill and they called the doctor.'

'I saw Mathers speak to the woman with the medical bag. It can't be a coincidence that he was there, though I know it will be difficult to prove he's behind it.'

'I'm beginning to agree he could be involved in this sordid abortion business. But when it comes to Rosie's murder, there's no evidence. And why would he dump her body on the *Sugar Mary*?'

'To draw attention away from his illegal operation in Deptford and implicate Luke Denton. He knew Luke was taking the *Sugar Mary* to Walden.' I thought back to the day of the shooting. 'When Rosie was sick that afternoon, Dr Mathers made a joke about her looking pretty in the hope of meeting Luke. Mathers would have assumed Luke got Rosie pregnant and would therefore be the main suspect for her murder. And I think he realised that if there wasn't enough evidence against Luke, the police would link Rosie's death to the threats against Constance Timpson.'

'I'm still not convinced.' But he seemed less sceptical than he had before.

'Mathers couldn't risk taking Rosie to hospital. If the police had questioned her and she'd told them about the house on Dolphin Street, it would have led them to Blanche Denton. Blanche was a fragile woman, and I think she'd begun to have doubts about what she was doing. If she realised she'd hurt Rosie, it wouldn't have taken much pressure from the police for her to reveal everything.'

Elijah was quiet for a moment. 'Talk to Cobbe. The murder was in his area, even though the illegal abortions weren't. He can decide how to handle Detective Inspector Yates.'

'Superintendent Cobbe thinks I'm a nosy parker who should mind my own business.'

'Why would he think that?' he said sarcastically. 'Don't get your hopes up. They might be able to implicate Mathers in the abortion racket, but I doubt there's enough evidence against him for Rosie's murder.'

'Not now Blanche is dead.' As I said it, a horrible thought entered my mind. One that I wasn't willing to voice just yet.

* * *

Before I talked to Superintendent Cobbe, I decided to get Ben's advice.

To my surprise, he was sitting up, chatting animatedly to a pretty nurse who was perched on the edge of his bed and seemed to be hanging on to his every word.

I coughed. 'Sorry to interrupt.'

The nurse jumped up. 'I should be getting on. Call me if you need anything.' With a last smile at Ben, she strode off.

Ben greeted me cheerfully.

I pulled up a chair and peered at him. 'Why are you looking so well?'

'Thanks. Would you rather I was at death's door?'

'No, of course not. But you've just been shot.' Something about him puzzled me. I scrutinised him and realised what it was. He looked like his old self. The Ben I hadn't seen since his heart had been broken and he'd left Walden for London.

He grinned. 'Being shot has made me feel much better.'

I felt a dull thud of emotion but tried to appear light-hearted. 'That's the type of daft thing Percy would say.'

He laughed. 'It is, isn't it?'

'Why has being shot made you feel better?' I felt a weight in my chest as I anticipated his answer.

'Because...' He swallowed. 'Because it's made me realise I want to live. There have been times recently when I haven't felt like that. I miss her.'

My throat constricted, and I couldn't speak for a few minutes. Although I'd guessed he felt that way at times, hearing him say it still caused a painful shard of grief to pierce me. I nodded. 'So do I.'

Ben leant forward to squeeze my hand and winced in pain. 'I survived the war without getting shot. Then I take a bullet at a garden party,' he joked, but I saw him brush away a tear.

I managed a weak smile.

He propped himself higher on his pillows. 'Come on then. What have you found out?'

'Am I that predictable?'

'Yes.' Rather than showing his usual exasperation, he regarded me with affection.

I gave a mock scowl. At that moment, I didn't care about the case. All I wanted was to hug him tightly. But as he'd just had a bullet taken out of him, this probably wasn't a good idea. Instead, I told him about Dr Mathers.

He sank back. 'You should tell the super. Though Elijah is right, there's probably not much he can do.'

'I'm intrigued to know what I won't be able to do much about,' said a low voice from the doorway.

We both jumped, and Ben winced again, clutching his shoulder. I stood up as Superintendent Cobbe came over to the bed.

'Sit down, Miss Woodmore. I'm always interested to hear what you have to say. Even though I don't always approve of the manner in which you obtain your information.'

I sat down and tried to explain my actions of the previous day in a way that would circumnavigate his disapproval. He lowered himself onto the end of Ben's bed and took out his pocket book. He asked me to repeat the Fair View Road address.

'What do you think?' I asked.

'It's an interesting theory. I'll discuss the matter with Detective Inspector Yates. He already has Luke Denton in custody. This will need careful handling.' He stood up. 'Can I ask you to keep your thoughts to yourself and out of the newspaper?'

'Of course.' I knew Elijah would never print anything that speculative anyway.

He nodded. 'You're looking well, PC Gilbert.'

'On the mend, sir.'

'Good. Once you're out of here, we'll have another chat about your future.'

'Yes, sir.'

I waited for the superintendent to leave before saying, 'He wants you back, doesn't he?'

Ben nodded. 'I haven't decided what to do yet.'

'Won't you miss my gran and Aunt Maud?' I grinned. 'Their cooking is better than Sid's.'

'They've been very kind to me,' he answered diplomatically. I could tell by the glint in his eye that the thought of being back with Sid in the station house was appealing to him.

36

I didn't think I'd convinced Superintendent Cobbe of Dr Granville Mathers' guilt and Luke Denton's innocence. And if he wasn't sure, it was unlikely he'd persuade Detective Inspector Yates to release Luke.

I wanted to speak to someone who knew Dr Mathers and had access to his car.

'Can't keep away?' Archie gave that familiar teasing smile.

I'd been relieved to find him in the church. I hadn't wanted to look for him in Creek House and risk another encounter with Micky Swann.

'I want to talk to you about something. And I don't think you're going to like it.'

I followed him into the vestry and, sitting at the wooden table, told him what I'd seen.

Archie's eyes narrowed. 'He was probably calling on someone who was sick.'

'Maybe.'

He considered me. 'Are you serious about this?'

'Yes.'

'Why? Why would he harm Rosie Robson?'

'To protect his business. And his retirement fund.'

He growled in disgust. 'It's against the law. Not to mention morally repugnant. And not something Mathers would contemplate.'

'It's a sensible measure for some women to take if a doctor performs the procedure safely.' I got up. This wasn't an argument worth having. Archie wasn't going to believe me.

'Sit down,' he barked. 'What is it you want from me?'

I remained standing. 'Tell me more about Dr Mathers. Convince me I'm wrong.'

He nodded slowly, and I sat back down.

'He's a good doctor. He helps anyone in need, whether they can afford to pay him or not. As a result, he's not a rich man.'

'Does he live alone?'

'Yes. He has a housekeeper who cooks and cleans for him, but she doesn't live in. He's employed by the hospital, and Constance Timpson pays for his time at the surgeries.'

'He lives in a house owned by the Timpsons. Why doesn't he have his own house?'

He shrugged. 'I've heard rumours. His wife used to take care of the money side of things. They were comfortably off. Apparently, after she died, he made some bad investments and lost his home.'

'How does he intend to retire to the south coast then?'

He was silent for a moment, then said, 'I suppose he might have some money tucked away somewhere. It's not something I've ever asked him about.'

'I'd be interested to know what money he has tucked away. And where it comes from.'

'Why? Why would he kill Rosie Robson?'

I told him why I thought Rosie would have gone to Dr Mathers house.

'If that were the case, Mathers would have taken her straight to the hospital.'

'When the duty doctor or nurse examined her, they'd soon guess what sort of procedure she'd undergone. Rosie would probably have been scared enough to tell them. Mathers didn't want to risk it. Although he may not be directly implicated, it would jeopardise his business.'

'I don't believe it.'

We fell into silence, the only sound the ticking of the wall clock.

I decided to persevere. 'Luke said he thought someone had talked Blanche into performing those operations. It had to have been someone she trusted. But perhaps she'd started to question what she was doing? Mathers knew how much it would distress Blanche if she discovered she'd harmed Rosie. That would make her a liability.' I stared at him, trying to convince him of what I was about to say. 'Do you know what I think sealed Rosie's fate? Mathers presumed Luke was the father of the unborn baby. How would Blanche react if she believed she'd aborted her grandchild? She would struggle to keep something like that to herself. I think she would have turned to you for guidance.'

He made a low guttural sound. 'I knew there was something wrong. Blanche had been troubled for some time. It started before Rosie's death.' He closed his eyes as if remembering. 'But she was worse after. I was forever finding her sitting by the altar. I assumed she'd confide in me eventually. I didn't want to rush her.'

I didn't say anything. I couldn't help thinking Blanche would have been safer if she had confided in someone. By the deepening crease of his brow, I could tell he was considering the evidence against Mathers.

'Do you think Blanche knew Rosie had gone to Mathers for help?' he asked.

I shook my head. 'Blanche told me she had no idea where Rosie went after leaving the house on Dolphin Street. I believed her.'

Archie stretched out his long fingers. 'You're suggesting Mathers drove to Walden and left Rosie on the *Sugar Mary* to implicate Luke?'

I could see flashes of rage in his eyes and knew I had to tread carefully. 'You've driven the car he uses. Could he have hidden Rosie's body in the boot? Is it big enough?'

He shook his head. 'It would be a tight squeeze. But I can get a fifty-inch roll of canvas on the back seat. He could have manoeuvred a small body like Rosie's across the seats and hidden her with a blanket.'

'I'd like to look in the back of the car. It would have been too risky to move Rosie on Friday night with all the police around. He would have had to wait until Saturday. I think by then, he'd come up with the plan to take her to Walden. He could have driven down there, dumped the body and been back home in a few hours.'

'Have you told the police this?' Archie's usually curling lips were now set into a hard line.

'I've told Superintendent Cobbe. He's going to speak to Detective Inspector Yates. But I get the impression Yates won't be persuaded to give up Luke as his main suspect.'

Archie's lips tightened further. 'What are you expecting to find in the car?'

'Maybe a few blonde hairs. I don't know. Probably nothing that will prove my theory, I just want to see for myself if it's feasible.'

'I use the car as well. Not just Mathers.'

'Do you have a key?'

'Yes.' He contemplated me, seeming to weigh up what to do next. 'I'm still not sure about this. But I don't see any harm in you looking at it.'

'It's not on the road outside. Dr Mathers has probably driven it to the hospital.'

'He's holding a surgery over in the factory. It's parked in the yard.'

I thought of the yard at the back of the Timpson Foods factory. It was the ideal place to search the car without being seen. I'd attract attention if I poked around while it was parked on Creek Road.

Archie leapt up. 'Come on then.'

He strode out of the door before I had time to get out of my chair. I hurried after him through the church.

We found WPC Jones in her usual position at the factory gate.

'Mathers still inside?' Archie asked.

She nodded, watching us curiously as we walked around to the back of the factory buildings.

In the yard, Dr Mathers' Ford was parked alongside Constance Timpson's Daimler and Mrs Siddons' sportscar.

Archie fished a key from his pocket and opened the doors and boot. 'I've used the car since Rosie went missing, and I didn't notice anything out of the ordinary.'

I peered into the boot. It was tiny and smelt of petrol and grease. Apart from an oil can, some tools and a few rags, it was empty. The back of the car was more spacious. I leant inside and examined the leather seats. It was feasible a body could have been laid across them, covered by a blanket. I searched the whole car but found nothing of interest.

'Satisfied?' Archie closed and locked the doors.

'I'm satisfied he could have hidden Rosie's body in the back.'

'I'm not sure.' He rubbed his chin, his doubt showing. 'Let's go. I don't want to have to explain to Mathers why we're poking around.'

I went to swing the boot lid closed when the stitching on one of the oily rags caught my eye. I touched it gently with my finger.

It was embroidered with the initial I. The second letter was more difficult to make out as the rag was smeared with grease. But I recognised my grandmother's needlework immediately.

'What's that?' Archie peered over my shoulder.

'It's my handkerchief. I gave it to Rosie when she was sick in Constance's office. On the afternoon she went missing.'

37

Archie's mouth fell open. 'Are you sure?'

'My grandmother embroiders my handkerchiefs with my initials.' I pointed. 'There's the I, and that's a W.'

He whistled. 'The evil bastard.'

'Who's an evil bastard?' WPC Helen Jones was standing behind us.

'Dr Granville Mathers.' Archie rasped the words.

I touched the oily fabric. 'Rosie had this handkerchief on her the afternoon she went missing.'

WPC Jones stared at it and then at me. 'Are you sure?'

I nodded. 'It's mine. I gave it to her when she was sick.'

'Does Dr Mathers own this car?' she asked.

'It belongs to the Timpsons.' Archie's face was grim. 'The doctor and I both use it.'

She gave him a searching look. 'Have you seen this handkerchief before?'

'I don't know. I've never noticed it. But...' Archie ran his fingers through his hair. 'I suppose I'd have just thought it was a rag.'

WPC Jones scrutinised the oil can and other rags. 'I saw Dr

Mathers putting oil in this car the day after Rosie Robson went missing. On the afternoon of Saturday the sixteenth.'

'Did he drive away in it?' I asked.

She shook her head. 'When he finished putting the oil in, he went back inside his house. The car was still there when I finished my shift that evening at five o'clock.'

'He would have waited until after dark to move the body.' I remembered the way he'd rubbed his back when I'd spoken to him. Lugging Rosie into the rear of the car and hauling her out again at the bridge can't have been easy. But it was only a short distance from his consulting room at the front of his house to the car outside. And he would have been able to park on Carnival Bridge, just yards from where the *Sugar Mary* was moored.

WPC Jones slammed the boot lid closed and held out her hand. 'Could you give me the key, please?'

Archie handed it to her without a word.

'I'm going to telephone Detective Inspector Yates from Miss Timpson's office.' She regarded Archie. 'I don't want either you or Dr Mathers to leave the factory. Can I trust that you'll stay here? If Dr Mathers tries to leave, please make an excuse to keep him here until my colleagues arrive. I don't have the power of arrest.'

'That man's not going anywhere,' Archie growled.

WPC Jones turned to me. 'Please come with me and explain to Miss Timpson what you've found.'

I scurried after her, giving a backwards glance at Archie. His face was stone.

When we reached Constance's office, WPC Jones pushed open the door without knocking and marched over to the desk.

Mrs Siddons looked up, startled. Constance was standing by the window and swung around.

'May I use your telephone, Miss Timpson? It's an emergency.'

'Of course.' Constance gestured towards the telephone on her desk. While WPC Jones asked to be put through to Deptford police station, she turned to me. 'What's going on?'

I explained as briefly as I could.

'Dr Mathers?' Constance raised her hand to her mouth. 'I don't believe it. Not Dr Mathers.'

WPC Jones replaced the earpiece on the cradle. 'Detective Inspector Yates is on his way.'

'Do we know where Dr Mathers was at the time of the shootings?' Mrs Siddons asked. 'He was certainly around on the afternoon Constance was targeted.'

'Good God.' Constance sank into her chair. 'You can't think...? Why would he?'

WPC Jones frowned. 'He must have run here quickly if he did fire that shot from the church tower.'

I'd been so intent on proving Mathers was responsible for Rosie's murder that it hadn't occurred to me he might have been involved in the sniper attacks. 'Could he have been at Crookham on the afternoon of the party?' I wondered aloud. 'But what reason would he have?'

'I don't think we should speculate.' WPC Jones glanced at her watch. 'I need to get back down to the yard. Please stay here until Detective Inspector Yates arrives.' She left the office, and Constance, Mrs Siddons and I stared at the clock.

I hoped Detective Inspector Yates had taken WPC Jones seriously. Deptford police station was only five minutes away by car. But all was silent. The minutes crawled by before we heard the clanging sound of the police car we'd been waiting for. In unison, the three of us rose from our seats.

We dashed downstairs to find Archie engaged in conversation with Dr Mathers. A Black Maria swung into the yard. We stood back and watched as Detective Inspector Yates and his sergeant got out of the car.

Yates lumbered over to WPC Jones. 'Where's this handkerchief then?'

WPC Jones went over to Dr Mathers' car and opened the boot. Yates followed and inspected the oily fabric.

He turned to address me. 'Miss Woodmore. You claim this handkerchief belongs to you and that you gave it to Miss Robson on the afternoon of the day she went missing?'

'Yes. We were in Miss Timpson's office.' I nodded towards Constance. 'Miss Robson had been sick. I gave her my handkerchief to wipe her mouth. When she offered it back, I suggested she keep it.'

'Are there any witnesses to this?'

'Mr Percy Baverstock and I saw Miss Woodmore give Rosie Robson the handkerchief.' Constance Timpson addressed the Detective Inspector. 'Dr Mathers was also present.'

Yates turned to the doctor. 'Dr Mathers, could you tell me how this handkerchief came to be in your car?'

Mathers raised his hands in a gesture of bewilderment. 'I have no idea. I must have picked it up at some point. Or my friend, Reverend Powell, may have done so.' He nodded towards Archie. 'We both use this car.'

It was said in the mildest of tones, but it was clear to me Dr Mathers was implicating Archie.

'Reverend Powell will also be accompanying us to the police station,' Detective Inspector Yates said. 'I'd like to interview you both.'

'The police station?' Dr Mathers blinked rapidly. 'You can't think either one of us had anything to do with what happened to poor Miss Robson?'

'That's what I intend to find out. Reverend Powell, if you'd be so kind as to go with my colleague.' Yates gestured towards the front of the Black Maria. His sergeant opened the passenger door of the car, and Archie got in. 'Dr Mathers, if you'd sit in the back with me.'

The doctor hesitated. 'Of course.' He followed Detective Inspector Yates.

Constance, Mrs Siddons and I watched in silence. As they drove away, Archie stared at me through the window, an unreadable look on his face.

38

A few days later, Mrs Siddons and I were back in Constance Timpson's Deptford office, this time with the addition of Percy. He hadn't been in attendance as much recently, but Constance had told him of Mathers' arrest, and he wanted to hear the latest news.

'We have enough evidence to charge Dr Mathers with organising and profiting from the abortion racket. The last woman to take the role of Mrs Quentin, real name Edna Figgis, confessed to everything.' WPC Jones faced Constance and Mrs Siddons across the rosewood desk. Percy and I were perched on the windowsill.

Constance had asked Detective Inspector Yates if WPC Jones could keep her informed of any developments. He'd agreed, and for once, the policewoman wasn't being kept out of the investigation.

'Good grief.' Percy shook his head in disbelief. 'How many Mrs Quentins have there been?'

'Difficult to say. Probably a few over the years. Dr Mathers isn't confessing to anything, and it's doubtful anyone else will come forward and admit to being involved.'

'What about Rosie Robson's murder?' This mattered to me more.

'It's not going to be easy to find enough evidence to ensure a conviction. But Luke Denton has been released, so I think Yates is going to try.'

'I'm pleased to hear it. Surely my handkerchief proves Mathers' guilt?'

'He could have picked it up anywhere. And he isn't the only person to use the car. Reverend Powell has driven it. Luke Denton can't drive, although he has been in the car.'

'First a doctor and now a vicar,' Percy mused. 'You can't trust anyone these days.'

I noticed that Mrs Siddons and Constance didn't offer any words of defence. They'd been taken in by Dr Mathers. Were they now suspicious of Archie too?

WPC Jones continued. 'Kevin, one of the men at Creek House, saw the doctor drive off in the car shortly after midnight on Saturday the sixteenth. He presumed he was going to the hospital or visiting a patient at home. He didn't see him return, but the car was back the next morning.'

'Did he see him putting anything in the car?' Mrs Siddons asked.

'No. He heard the car start and went to the window and saw it was the doctor in the driver's seat.'

'He's sure it was the doctor?' I peered out at the road. From an upstairs bedroom of Creek House, you would have a clear view of the car.

'Yes.'

'Has Dr Mathers said where he was going?' I asked.

WPC Jones referred to her notebook. 'He says he sees so many patients; he can't remember if he went out that night or not. We found his diaries in his consulting room – he keeps meticulous records – and there's no entry for that night.'

'That's incriminating.' But in reality, the evidence against Mathers was insubstantial.

WPC Jones clearly knew it too. 'Mathers is arguing that it was dark and the man in Creek House could have been mistaken, and it might have been Reverend Powell he saw. The vicar was at home alone, and no one can vouch for him.'

'What motive would Reverend Powell have for killing Rosie?' It suddenly occurred to me that I didn't even know if Archie had ever met Rosie Robson. 'And when could he have done it? The pathologist estimates she was killed not long after she went missing, which would mean sometime on Friday night. Archie, I mean, Reverend Powell, has an alibi for that time.'

Percy regarded me curiously.

'Detective Inspector Yates isn't taking it seriously. The problem is, if the case goes to court, Mathers' defence will argue that it could have been Reverend Powell driving the car.' WPC Jones closed her notebook. 'One final matter. Dr Mathers is in the clear for the sniper attacks. Eyewitnesses place him in the crowd when Miss Timpson was on stage, and on the afternoon of the party at Crookham Hall, he was on duty at the hospital.'

Constance rubbed her temples. If Dr Mathers wasn't responsible for the shootings, the threat hadn't gone away. Percy and I left her and Mrs Siddons discussing security issues with WPC Jones.

At the factory gate, I saw Archie heading over to the Dentons' house.

'Luke's home,' he called. 'Come and see him.'

I smiled and nodded.

Percy glanced at me. 'You have remarkably diverse taste in men.'

'And you're so consistent?' I retorted.

'Fair point. Still, I don't see the appeal myself.' He nodded towards the church. 'Religion and all that.'

'Perhaps he doesn't judge me.' I hadn't forgiven Percy for his insulting comments at Crookham Hall.

I caught up with Archie at the front door of Luke Denton's house.

He paused before knocking. 'Have you heard any more about Mathers?'

I nodded. 'He'll be charged with offences related to procuring an abortion. Yates is trying to find more evidence linking him to Rosie Robson's murder. Mathers keeps saying he isn't the only one to have access to the car, but he was seen driving off in it on the night of Saturday the sixteenth.'

Archie drew in a sharp breath. 'Bastard. Now I know he must be guilty. Because I didn't use the car that night.'

'Did you know Rosie Robson?'

Archie seemed surprised by the question. 'Not well. I knew who she was. I was in Walden for the carnival. Reverend Childs asked me to give out some of the prizes in the decorated float competition. And she came by once when Luke and I were at Lock-keeper's Cottage. I don't think by accident. She knew he'd been on one of the barges that came down that week.'

'Did they go off together?'

He shook his head. 'They chatted for a while, then Mathers arrived. He'd been holding one of his surgeries at the biscuit factory. He came to the cottage to pick us up and drive us back.'

'So Mathers knew where the cottage was?'

Archie nodded. 'Whenever he holds a surgery in Walden, he'll ask if I want a lift to Crookham. If I stay for a day or two, I'll get the train back. Occasionally, I've driven myself. Having the car enables me to take my painting supplies to the cottage, but I don't like to keep the car down there too long in case it's needed here.'

I sighed. 'I wish I'd had the chance to talk to Blanche again. I think she would have revealed more about Mathers.'

'Possibly. We'll never know now.' He rapped on the door of Luke's house.

I glanced over to Creek House and saw Micky Swann on the pavement outside, watching us. 'WPC Jones said Mathers couldn't have done the shootings.'

Archie's eyes followed mine, and he frowned. 'Perhaps you should look closer to home. The first one may have been in Deptford, but the second was in Walden. Aren't you suspicious of old Tolfree and his lackey, Osmond?'

Before I could reply, Luke answered the door, bleary-eyed and unshaven. 'Is it true what they're saying about Dr Mathers? That he hurt Rosie? And that he taught mother how to—'

'It's beginning to look that way,' Archie replied.

We followed Luke into the front parlour. The fire had been lit, and the room smelt of woodsmoke. Kindling cracked on top of the coal.

'I can't believe it. He was always kind to us.' Luke removed a cushion embroidered with daisies from an armchair before sinking into it. He placed the cushion on his stomach, hugging it to himself.

On the mantelpiece was a pair of china dogs. Next to them was the tin box containing Blanche's medals. I guessed every homely touch in this room would remind Luke of his mother.

I sat next to Archie on a sofa covered in similarly embroidered cushions. 'Dr Mathers visited your mother when she was in prison, didn't he?'

'He was concerned about her health. She wasn't eating properly. He took her some of the tonic he's given her before.' Luke seemed in a daze. I got the impression the full extent of Dr Mathers' deceit was yet to sink in.

'Did you ever pick up your mother's belongings from the prison?' I ran my fingers over the frayed fabric of the sofa. It felt unbearably sad that Blanche would never be coming back to her home.

'Dr Mathers was going to do it for me.' He hugged the cushion tighter as he spoke. 'I suppose I'd better go myself, hadn't I?'

'Why don't I do it for you?' I suggested. 'I'm familiar with Holloway.'

'Thank you, that's kind of you. I'll admit, I don't want to go there ever again.'

Archie contemplated me, his eyes searching mine. He knew me well enough by now to suspect I had my own reasons for wanting to retrieve Blanche's possessions.

39

When I left the Dentons' house, Percy was still hanging around by the factory gates, smoking a cigarette.

'Still here?'

'I was waiting for you.' He threw his cigarette to the ground. 'I wanted to say sorry for all the things I've said to upset you.'

'I'm not upset.'

'I didn't mean to judge you.' He waved his arms in a hopeless gesture. 'I know everything I say is wrong. I just want us to be friends again.'

I was tempted to say that he'd been puritanical as well as judgemental. But what was the point? I wanted us to be friends again too, so I took his arm. 'Shall we forget our squabbles and start again?'

'Thank you.' He beamed at me. 'Let's go out like we used to. Dancing or the pictures? Where would you like to go?'

I smiled. I couldn't help wondering if Percy had noticed Constance's feelings for Ben and was being fickle with his emotions once more. And was he possibly jealous of Archie? He'd never warmed to George. Still, why look a gift horse in the mouth?

'Would you drive me to Holloway Prison?' I asked.

'It's not a place I've ever been. Given my fondness for the fairer sex, perhaps that's been remiss of me. Do they serve the gin cold?'

I laughed. 'I need to pick up Blanche Denton's belongings. I'm not sure how much stuff there will be. I could do with a ride in your car.'

'Holloway Prison it is then.' He squeezed my arm. 'You're nothing if not unusual.'

* * *

'I'm here to collect the possessions of Mrs Blanche Denton.' I could see Percy wrinkling his nose at the odour of carbolic soap and boiled cabbage. Prison warders weren't known for their sense of humour, and I hoped he wouldn't make any idiotic comments.

The warder nodded. 'About time. That's been sitting there for weeks.' She gestured to a large box. 'Are you going to carry it yourself?'

'That's why I'm here.' Percy gave a slight bow. She appeared unimpressed.

'Sign here.'

Percy carried the box out and incurred the wrath of a warder at the gate, who was scowling at his car. 'You can't park there.'

'We're just leaving.' He did another of his little bows and opened the car door. He placed the box on the back seat. 'Not the most welcoming establishment I've frequented. I presume you want me to take you back to Creek Road?'

'No. Do you know somewhere quiet we can go?'

'Are you making improper suggestions?' He gave me a lecherous wink.

'And if I was, what would your response be?'

'I refuse to answer any questions that might incriminate me.'

The warder was coming towards us, so we hopped into the car and he sped off, waving cheerily at her.

'The improper thing I *want* to do is search that box,' I said.

'That doesn't surprise me.' He pulled into a side street and turned off the engine.

'Let's get in the back,' I suggested.

'Words to gladden any man's heart,' he quipped.

Sitting on either side of the box, we began to poke around in Blanche's belongings.

I found the book that I'd lent her. 'I wonder if she read it.'

Percy chuckled at the title. 'One of yours?'

'Ursula's, actually. You should ask her about boiled sheep's intestines.'

'I'd be too afraid.' He gave a mock shudder. 'Do you know what you're looking for?'

'Yes.'

'What?' He peered curiously inside.

'This.' I held up a green bottle.

'What is it?'

'It's a preparation that Dr Mathers made up for Blanche.'

'So?'

'It's supposed to be her usual tonic. A pick-me-up to give her strength. It didn't work. Instead, she became ill and died.'

Realisation dawned, and his mouth dropped. 'You don't think...?'

'Yes, I do think.'

Percy squinted at the green bottle. 'You may be surprised to learn that I've never spent any time in prison. However, I imagine a spell inside isn't conducive to good health. You said Blanche was already frail. Maybe prison was just too much for her?'

'You could be right.' But I had an ominous feeling. Admittedly, that's all it was, a feeling, albeit a strong one. Although Blanche hadn't been well when I saw her, she hadn't looked gravely ill. It seemed strange that after Dr Mather's visit, she deteriorated so quickly.

'I'm intrigued to know what you plan to do now?' Percy stretched his long legs out of the car door.

'Could you drive me to Deptford police station? I'm going to try to persuade Detective Inspector Yates to test this for poison.'

'First a prison and now a police station. You know how to show a boy a good time.' He got back into the driver's seat and started the engine. 'Can we go and see a Douglas Fairbanks movie next time?'

* * *

Despite his moaning, I suspected Percy had enjoyed his visit to Deptford police station. It was certainly nothing like the station house at Walden.

It was much bigger than I'd expected and full of serious-faced police officers who scurried around with an urgency that gave you the impression they were in the throes of solving some incredibly audacious crimes. I found it hard to believe Deptford was such a dangerous place. I didn't spot any females amongst their ranks.

Detective Inspector Yates had been more receptive than expected. He'd agreed to see us for a start.

I sat across from him in an office that seemed to have documents on every available surface. Folders were piled on the floor and papers were scattered across his desk and even along the windowsill.

Percy leant against a filing cabinet, examining a series of mug shots pinned to the wall.

'Miss Woodmore.' Yates' narrow eyes scrutinised me. 'First, you infiltrate an abortion racket by pretending to be pregnant, then I find you at a suspect's home when I turn up to arrest him. Your handkerchief is discovered in the boot of a car that may have been used to transport a body. And now you've been to Holloway Prison to collect the belongings of a woman you believe to have been murdered. You seem to make a habit of involving yourself in affairs that are none of your concern.'

'Yes, she does,' Percy agreed.

I glared at him.

'I'm not sure whether to arrest you,' he paused. 'Or ask you to join my team.'

'Oh, I wouldn't do that,' Percy warned. 'You'd have terrible trouble maintaining discipline.'

Yates drummed his fingers on his desk, staring at the green bottle I'd placed in front of him. He had hooded eyes that made it difficult to tell what he was thinking.

Eventually, he nodded. 'Alright. Leave it with me and I'll get it tested.' He jerked his head towards the door, and Percy and I took that as our cue to leave.

* * *

Back in Walden, I decided to pay Nora Fox another visit to find out more about Jack Osmond. Until the sniper was caught, the threat to Constance and Mrs Siddons remained.

Was there really nothing wrong with Jack's eyesight? Or was it just a malicious rumour that had turned into fact after being repeated so many times? Some people clearly resented him for avoiding conscription and staying in a comfortable job at the factory.

I avoided the main gate of Tolfree & Timpson's and went around to the yard at the back. I peered through the window onto the factory floor and spotted Nora. She was concentrating on her work and I wasn't sure how to get a message to her. But then the young woman standing beside her noticed me and whispered something to her.

I waved, then stepped back and hid behind a stack of pallets when I saw Jack Osmond and Redvers Tolfree coming down the stairs from the offices.

A few minutes later, Nora joined me in my hiding place.

'Everyone's talking about Dr Mathers. Is it true?' A light sheen of sweat covered her face, and she smelt of sugar.

I told her what I could.

'I can't believe it.' Her shoulders drooped. 'He was such a nice man. He helped me get better.'

I could understand her despondence. Dr Mathers had undoubtedly helped a great many people. It was chilling to think someone so good could also be so evil.

'Nora. I remember you saying there was nothing wrong with Jack Osmond's eyesight. How do you know?'

'Because he has no trouble bagging himself a pheasant or rabbit when he chooses. He can see fine when he's hungry.' Nora saw my expression but misread it. 'Don't look so shocked. Most folk around here do a bit of poaching now and again. We wouldn't have got through the war without the odd bird here and there.'

'He's been seen poaching?'

'He denies it, but he's been spotted more than once out in the fields with a shotgun. When he raises the sight to his eye, he lifts his glasses onto his head.' She snorted in contempt. 'Nothing wrong with his eyes. Everyone knows he got himself promoted to foreman here in the absence of all the decent men who were away fighting.'

'Do you think Mr Tolfree knows?'

She nodded. 'They've been out hunting together. Tolfree once took Jack on a grouse shoot.'

My pulse quickened. 'Do you think one of them could have shot at Mrs Siddons?'

Nora's eyes widened in surprise. She shook her head. 'They haven't got the nerve for anything like that. They're a couple of pigs at the trough, alright. But I can't see them going in for anything dangerous.'

I remembered what Nicholas had told me, and asked, 'Did Jack or Mr Tolfree ever give Rosie anything to take home, like rabbits or pheasants?'

'Not that I know of. They could have done, I suppose. Jack's tried offering stuff to the whores. Brace of pheasants in exchange for you know what. I assumed Rosie knew he was trouble and steered clear of him.'

I wasn't so sure that Rosie had steered clear. Sadly, I was beginning to think we would never know the truth behind her pregnancy.

40

'You might want to tell your friend Reverend Powell he's likely to receive a visit from Detective Inspector Yates today,' WPC Jones said to me. 'The tonic Mathers gave Blanche Denton contained arsenic.'

'Arsenic?' Constance drew in a breath.

When she'd contacted me to say Yates had instructed WPC Jones to give her an update on the toxicology findings, I'd caught the first train to London.

'Why does he want to see Reverend Powell?' I was embarrassed by the way she'd described Archie as my 'friend'.

WPC Jones grimaced. 'I'm afraid he wants to exhume Blanche Denton's body. He plans to test her organs for traces of arsenic.'

I groaned. Archie was going to hate this.

'It's the only way to make sure Mathers doesn't get away with it,' WPC Jones insisted. 'Women will be a lot safer with him in prison.'

We were silent. I peered out of the window over to the church-yard of St Mary's. An exhumation was a grim prospect.

'Has Detective Inspector Yates made any progress in finding out who the sniper is?' Constance asked in a tired voice.

WPC Jones shook her head.

'It's common knowledge at the biscuit factory that there's nothing wrong with Jack Osmond's eyesight,' I said. 'He's been seen out poaching with a gun.'

'He didn't shoot at you, Miss Timpson.' WPC Jones chewed the end of her pen.

'How do you know?' she asked.

'Because when the shot was fired, I could see him from where I was standing. He was in the audience next to Redvers Tolfree and the workers from the biscuit factory.'

I frowned. It was still possible Jack Osmond had fired at Mrs Siddons though. No doubt, he would be furious at the police investigation into his and Tolfree's fraudulent scheme. But the same rifle had been used for both shootings. How had it got from Deptford to Walden?

'Was Creek House searched after the rifle was fired from St Mary's?' I asked.

WPC Jones nodded. 'Thoroughly. We found nothing. Also, there are no likely suspects among the current residents. Each one has a physical ailment of one sort or other.'

Dr Mathers and Archie had said Micky Swann was regaining strength in his wounded left arm. I wondered how severe his impediment really was.

* * *

When I entered Creek House, the first thing I noticed was that the door to the second office was ajar. It had always been closed before.

Archie was sitting at the desk in the main office. 'I thought I saw you going into the factory. What's the latest news?'

I flopped down into a chair. This wasn't going to be easy. I explained about my trip to pick up Blanche's belongings. And my subsequent trip to Deptford police station.

'An exhumation?' He stared at me in horror.

'There was arsenic in the tonic Mathers gave to Blanche. WPC Jones said to expect a visit from Detective Inspector Yates. I'm sorry.'

'No. Absolutely not. Let the poor woman rest in peace.' He thumped his fist on the desk. 'What about Luke? To have his mother dug up and cut up. No. It's wrong.'

'I don't think you have a choice.'

He glared. 'He poisoned Blanche?'

'He'd already decided she was a liability,' I explained. 'And once she was in prison, she had nothing to lose by telling the police everything. All Blanche cared about was protecting Luke.'

'But Blanche didn't know Mathers murdered Rosie.'

'It was his retirement fund he was worried about. And the fact that he might end up in prison on the same charges as Blanche. He thought it would be simple. Under the circumstances, no one would be surprised if Blanche's health deteriorated. He'd intended to go and retrieve the tonic but was arrested before he could collect Blanche's belongings.'

Archie shook his head in disgust. 'Even when I got into that police car, I still didn't think it could be true. All that time, I believed he was a decent man. A true doctor who cared for his patients.'

'He was. Unfortunately, there was another side to him. He wanted money to retire, and he saw a way to get it.'

'His bloody boat in Devon.'

'He thought the abortion scheme was safe. He trained the

women and gave them the medical instruments while they rented the rooms and carried out the operations, taking all the risks. They couldn't implicate him without admitting their own guilt. And the women coming to them for procedures were too scared and ashamed to tell anyone what they'd done.'

'But to kill. And to try to blame Luke by putting the body on his boat was wicked.' His rage made his green eyes and sculpted jaw look more wolfish than usual. I couldn't help thinking that at this moment, Dr Mathers was safer in a prison cell than in a room with Archie.

'If he did that to Blanche for fear of what she might say, then he must have been equally worried about what Rosie Robson would do.' I attempted to find something to make him feel better. 'At least it proves you did nothing wrong.'

'If we say we have no sin, we deceive ourselves, and the truth is not in us.'

Few vicars could have made a biblical quotation sound as menacing. I had no idea what he meant by it.

'The *Sugar Mary* fitted the bill in every respect,' I said. 'It implicated Luke and could also have been seen as a threat against Constance. But we still don't know who was responsible for the sniper attacks.'

Archie unclenched his fists and leant back, stretching his arms above his head. I couldn't help admiring the strong lines of his lean torso. 'I think you need to let that one go. I don't believe it will happen again.'

This statement took me by surprise. 'Have you heard something?'

'I hear lots of things in confidence, and that's where they stay.' He glanced towards the lounge. 'I admit, I may have been naïve when it came to trusting some of my protégés.'

By protégés, I assumed he meant one of the men at Creek

House. Or even Luke. 'You would report anything criminal to the police, wouldn't you?'

'I answer to a higher authority,' he replied, avoiding meeting my eye. 'I think this revolt has burnt itself out, and they've seen the error of their ways.'

'They?' Was he implying that more than one person was involved. It would make sense. While Jack Osmond couldn't have fired at Constance, he was familiar with the woods around Crookham Hall. And Micky Swann knew his way around St Mary's Church. 'The same rifle was used for both shootings. How did it get from Deptford to Walden?'

'Let's just say, there may have been some collusion between factories.'

'But...'

'No buts,' he said firmly. 'It won't happen again. I think that's the best we can hope for. We need to let it go.'

I thought Archie would have realised by now that I wasn't one for letting things go. However, I did take some comfort from his words. The sympathetic response in the newspapers to the attacks on Constance and Mrs Siddons may have been enough to persuade the sniper, or snipers, that their threats weren't working.

Archie suddenly got to his feet and crossed to my side of the desk. 'I need to tell Luke before Yates does. Reassure him I'll handle everything respectfully.' He bent down and kissed me hard on the lips. Then, with one long stride, he was out of the door.

Feeling breathless, I followed him into the hallway, only to see him disappear through the front door.

The house was quiet, but I knew some of the men were probably in the lounge. I decided to risk it and gave the door of the second office a slight nudge with my foot. It creaked and opened a fraction more.

I glanced inside the small room. It contained a couple of filing cabinets and a desk. On top of the filing cabinet was a rack of paper. And sitting on the desk was a black typewriter.

I went over to the filing cabinet and looked in the rack. It was filled with Lion Brand paper. The brand used for Constance's anonymous threatening letter.

I swung around when I heard a noise behind me. It didn't surprise me to find Micky Swann standing in the doorway watching me.

'You again.' A cigarette drooped from his lips.

'Me again,' I stated. 'And you again. You have a habit of showing up whenever I'm here.'

He took the cigarette from his mouth and grinned. 'You're going to be seeing more of me. I'm moving to Walden.'

'How do you like your new home? I heard you got a job at the Tolfree & Timpson factory. Do you enjoy the countryside?' I wanted to find out how familiar he was with the area, particularly the Crookham estate.

'Ain't been there yet. First time I'd seen countryside was when I was in France. Only ever left the city when I joined up. It's gonna take a bit of getting used to.' His eyes lit up. 'My wife and kids are coming too.'

'Where are you going to live?'

'They've arranged for me to rent one of those houses on that new estate near Crookham.'

'Congratulations. Thanks to Miss Timpson, you have a job, and thanks to Mrs Siddons, you have a place to live. Well done on your achievements.' I patted the typewriter. 'You must be pleased your threatening letter didn't stop them from continuing with their good works.'

He had the grace to look sheepish. 'I might have said some daft things. Me and the boys got riled up. We've had it rough, you know?'

'Did scaring a young woman make you feel better?' I was furious he was so nonchalant about his behaviour.

'That letter was meant to be a friendly warning, not a threat.' He stared down at his feet. 'I shouldn't have left it on Miss Timpson's desk. Not that she seemed particularly scared by it. She went ahead with her speech anyway.'

'And got shot at,' I snapped.

His eyes darted up. 'That had nothing to do with us. We was all here, and we can vouch for one another.'

'I don't believe you,' I hissed as I swept past him.

41

I marched out of Creek House. I was fed up with Deptford, fed up with men and fed up with being lied to.

As I trudged towards the tram stop, I saw a familiar figure walking toward me. It took me a second to realise it was Millicent Nightingale. I'd never seen her anywhere but Walden before. She looked out of place on the streets of Deptford in her long skirt and straw hat.

'What are you doing here?' I asked.

'Snooping. Curiosity got the better of me. Sid's been telling me all sorts of tales about what's been going on up here, and I wanted to see it all for myself. Ursula would have liked to have come too, but she wasn't up to it. I promised I'd investigate and report back.'

I smiled. 'Would you like a tour of all the relevant locations?'

'Yes, please.'

I guided her into the factory yard. 'Here's where it started.'

I described where the stage had been, and the chain of events that occurred after the shot was fired. I told her about the scene in Constance's office when Rosie was sick.

We strolled along Creek Road and turned the corner to go to

Hopkins Tobacconist. Then we went to 26 Dolphin Street and 15 Fair View Road. She wrinkled her nose at the combined smell of exhaust fumes and manure emanating from the streets.

'Which is Dr Mathers' house?' she asked when we were back on Creek Road.

I gestured to the end of the small terrace.

She nodded. 'Poor Rosie. In theory, she took a sensible course of action. She wasn't worldly and had no experience of the city. She knocked at the door of a doctor. The one person she thought she could trust.' She glanced up the road. 'It's a shame she didn't go to the church instead.'

'A police car was parked outside St Mary's. Detective Inspector Yates' team were still examining the tower. All the action was happening at that end of the road. This end would have been quieter.' I sighed. 'Rosie must have been too frightened to go to the police. And I suspect knowing so many policemen were close by made Dr Mathers panic and act the way he did.'

'And he killed Blanche Denton? Where did she live?'

I pointed towards the Dentons' house. 'There's going to be an exhumation. The tonic he gave Blanche to put in her tea contained arsenic.'

Millicent nodded. 'Arsenic is tasteless and odourless. It dissolves easily in a hot fluid like tea or cocoa. The doctor knew what he was doing. Is there enough evidence to convict him?'

'If the exhumation shows arsenic in Blanche's body.' I glanced at her in surprise. 'How do you know so much about arsenic poisoning?'

She smiled. 'Ursula and I share a passion for crime novels. Can we have a look at the church tower?'

We headed over to St Mary's. As usual, it was unlocked, and I was relieved to find the church was empty. We climbed the winding staircase to the top of the tower.

Millicent gazed over to the factory. 'What a view.'

'A shell casing was found down here. Whoever was up here didn't bother to hide it. I guess they knew the police would realise where the rifle fire came from.'

'And you suspect one of the men from Creek House?'

'The threatening letter came from there. But the current residents all have physical ailments.'

'What sort of ailments?'

'One is blind. One is missing a hand, and another had his leg amputated. The person I suspect has a weak left arm.'

'None of them sound like promising candidates.' She peered back at the steps we'd just climbed. 'It would be hard to get away quickly with a rifle down those stairs if you have any sort of disability.'

'I did think it could have been Jack Osmond until WPC Jones told me she saw him at the time the shot was fired at Constance.'

'He could have fired at Mrs Siddons?'

'But the same weapon was used in both cases.' I felt like I was going around in circles. Nothing made sense.

'Shall we take a look at Lockkeeper's Cottage tomorrow to see if that gives us any ideas? I can get a key from Daniel.'

I cheered up at this. 'It's worth a try.'

'In the meantime...' She paused.

'What?'

'Perhaps you should stay away from here. The church and Reverend Powell, I mean.'

'What do you suspect him of?' I was fed up with people commenting on my friendship with Archie and it came out more belligerently than intended.

'Nothing criminal.' She gave me a shrewd glance. 'But perhaps he has appetites that would be considered inappropriate for a man of the cloth?'

* * *

Millicent and I met outside Crookham Hall the next day. We started at the mausoleum, and I showed her where I'd been standing with Percy.

'I think the shooter hid in the trees over there and was watching to see who was around. Then, when Percy and I walked back towards the cars, they ran over and hid behind the mausoleum. When Mrs Siddons was in view, they fired. We all hid behind the cars, and they ran back under cover of the trees and possibly went to Lockkeeper's Cottage.'

We walked over to the copse of trees and took the most direct route to the cottage. This meant scrambling through a stretch of undergrowth.

'Lots of areas have been trampled,' Millicent observed as we followed the route we guessed the sniper would have taken.

'The police searched the estate after it happened.'

She pushed through the bracken. 'There's certainly plenty of cover. Whoever it was could have stayed hidden until they came to the path that leads to the cottage.'

When we reached the front door, Millicent fished a key from her pocket and let us in. It felt strange to be poking around, but I reasoned that the police had already searched the place, so we weren't doing any harm.

Everything appeared as it had when I'd been there before. I climbed the stairs, curious to see where Archie slept. There were two small bedrooms, each containing a bed, wardrobe and chest of drawers with a washbasin on top. I didn't come across anything of interest in my quick examination. Downstairs, Millicent searched the parlour and kitchen and even went into the toilet out back.

The parlour consisted of two armchairs next to the fireplace. Archie's paintings were still leaning against one wall, and there was a wooden crate tucked in a corner containing paints and rolls of canvas. In the kitchen was a larder, cooking range and a rickety wooden table and chairs.

Millicent stood by the mantelpiece brandishing a timetable of trains from Walden to Waterloo and a map of the Crookham estate that showed the surrounding countryside, the railway line, canal and Waldenmere lake. She held up the map. 'They could have used this to help them navigate the area.'

'Possibly. It would show you how to get to the main road and into Walden. But you'd still need to know how much tree cover is near the hall if you were planning to shoot at someone.' I ran my hand along the mantelpiece.

She nodded. 'Plenty of places to hide a rifle in the woods around here, though.'

At the end of the mantelpiece was a blue ceramic pot containing matches, pieces of string and a few scraps of paper. I tipped out the contents and examined the bits of paper. I gave a sudden start.

'What is it?' Millicent asked.

'The stub of a third-class train ticket from Waterloo. For the day of the party.'

42

'Did you search inside the cottage?' I asked.

'Yes, of course, we did.' Sid was becoming exasperated.

'And you didn't find a train ticket for the date of the garden party?'

'No. Because there wasn't one there.'

Elijah regarded us with mild amusement. Even Miss Vale had stopped typing and was listening with interest.

'It was inside the blue pot on the mantelpiece.'

'It wasn't when I looked.' Sid jutted out his chin.

'You may not have looked inside the pot.'

'I did.' His expression was stubborn. 'And it wasn't there. Someone must have put it there since the day of the party.'

'But why would they?' I was frustrated, desperate to find a logical answer.

'If Sid said he looked in the blue pot, then the train ticket wasn't there when he did.' Elijah held up his hand to indicate this was the last word on the matter. 'I'm more concerned with what Detective Inspector Yates has found. Has he told you anything?'

Sid took his pocket book from his tunic and turned his attention to Elijah, ignoring me. 'He sent a copy of the pathologist's report to Superintendent Cobbe. Grains of arsenic were found in Blanche Denton's body.'

'What does Mathers have to say about that?' Elijah dragged on his cigarette. 'Sounds pretty conclusive to me.'

'He claims that someone in the prison must have put arsenic in the tonic or that Blanche did it herself. He claims she was suicidal. They use arsenic in the gardens as a weedkiller and rat poison. But Yates searched Mathers' house and found a small quantity of arsenic in the kitchen. He also found a blue cushion on an examination couch in the consulting room. He thinks Mathers used it to smother Rosie after getting her to lie down on the couch. It would account for the blue threads found in her mouth. Yates has charged him with the murders of Rosie Robson and Blanche Denton.'

I let out a long sigh.

'That must be enough for a jury to convict.' Elijah puffed hard, looking satisfied.

'Too bloody right,' Sid said, then glanced apologetically at Miss Vale. 'Yates made a public statement saying Mathers has been charged with both murders.'

'Excellent.' Elijah put out his cigarette and picked up his pen. 'Let's get to work.'

Sid left the office with a polite nod at Miss Vale. He didn't look in my direction.

'Come on.' Elijah waved his pen at me. 'Get on with it. I thought you'd be pleased. This is your doing. And it puts your beloved vicar in the clear.'

'He's not my beloved vicar,' I said crossly.

Elijah ignored this. 'Once you've finished the article on Mathers, I want another piece on one of the men from Creek House. Kevin and Frank's stories went down well with readers. One of the other men is coming here to live. He's got a job at Tolfree & Timpson's. Can you talk to him? His name's Micky Swann.'

I groaned.

* * *

Tired of my bad temper, Elijah sent me out that afternoon to track down Micky Swann. We didn't know if he'd moved to Walden yet or was still at Creek House. I didn't relish another trip to Deptford. I was irritated that people kept mentioning my relationship with Archie.

I was still perplexed by the mystery of the shootings and disgruntled about the train ticket. Jack Osmond couldn't have shot at Constance Timpson, though he knew Crookham well enough to have fired at Mrs Siddons. That didn't explain why there was a train ticket from London in the cottage. Unless Jack Osmond had nothing to do with it and Micky Swann was behind both shootings. He could have got the train down to Walden on the day of the party, although he'd have been conspicuous carrying a rifle over his shoulder. But would he have been able to navigate his way around Crookham? Even if he could fire a rifle with his dodgy left arm.

As it turned out, a trip to Deptford wasn't necessary. When I called in at the Tolfree & Timpson factory to find out when Micky was due to start, Nora told me he'd been there that morning.

'He's a smashing bloke,' she enthused. 'Such a gentleman. The ladies have all taken a shine to him, and that's put Osmond's nose out of joint.'

I couldn't believe what I was hearing. Was this the same Micky Swann? 'Do you know where he's staying?'

'He's come down for the day with his wife. It'll be another week before he starts here. You might catch him by the wharf.

He said he wanted to look around before he went back to London.'

I walked along the canal and found Micky at the deserted wharf, gazing at the glistening water. He looked as out of place in rural Walden as Millicent Nightingale had on the grey streets of Deptford.

'Lovely here, ain't it?' He took the cigarette from his mouth and threw it into the canal. I refrained from telling him that his cigarette butt didn't enhance the scenery. 'I used to watch the barges leaving the creek and wondered what it would be like to get on one and see where it ended up.'

'Do you ever pray?' I asked abruptly.

He smiled. 'That's a funny question. Nah. I don't believe in God. Never have. The reverend doesn't hold that against you. He treats us the same whether we're churchgoers or not.'

'Do any of the men at Creek House go to church?'

'We ain't the most religious bunch. But we know right from wrong, and we regret putting that letter on Miss Timpson's desk. That was wrong. Especially with what happened afterwards.'

'When someone tried to *kill* Miss Timpson, you mean?' The casual manner with which he and Archie referred to the shootings infuriated me. Constance and Mrs Siddons weren't on a battlefield. They'd been subjected to a terrifying ordeal in the course of doing their jobs.

'That wasn't us. I swear it. And I didn't like what you said the other day.' He dug his hands in his pockets, and I noticed the tremor in his left arm. 'We had nothing to do with firing those shots. Do you think one of us hopped on the train with a bloody great rifle strapped to our backs and came down here to shoot at Mrs Siddons?'

'Someone in Walden might have helped you. Or carried out

the shooting at Crookham for you.' I was curious to see how he'd react to this.

'Who'd do that?' He screwed up his amber eyes. 'We don't know anyone down here.'

'Jack Osmond.'

He snorted. 'That spineless beggar? He wouldn't have the guts. Your lot would have given him a white feather.'

'My lot?' I feigned ignorance, but I knew what he was getting at. At the start of the war, some suffragettes had taken it upon themselves to hand white feathers to men dressed in civilian clothes who appeared fit to fight. The white feather was a symbol of cowardice. It was an unkind gesture, and I knew my mother would never have done such a thing.

'He deserves one too. Nothing wrong with his eyesight. Too much of a coward to fight for king and country.' Micky glowered. 'Do you think he was the one that fired those shots?'

'No.' I knew I had to retract what I'd said. 'He was in the crowd when Miss Timpson was targeted.'

'Then you ought to be careful who you go around accusing.' He waved a nicotine-stained finger at me. 'You could get an innocent man into trouble. First me and now Osmond.'

'Innocent?' I fumed. 'You seem to make a habit of trying to frighten women.'

'We never did anything after that one letter, I swear it.'

'What about your threats to me? Telling me to stay out of Deptford. What was that about?'

He looked at me in amazement. 'That you should stay away from the vicar.' He held up his hands as if this was obvious. 'I wasn't threatening you.'

I rolled my eyes. 'You think he needs protecting from me, is that it?'

He seemed bewildered. 'Don't be daft. I was trying to look after you. I told you that. He's good to his men, but he can be trouble if you're a woman.'

My mouth dropped.

'I tried to warn you off him. I told you not to keep coming back. He's bad news for a girl like you.'

I wasn't sure what he meant by 'a girl like me'. I decided not to ask. First Millicent and now Micky Swann. Was Archie so bad?

'I'm sorry if I scared you. I was only trying to help you.' His concern seemed genuine, and I was lost for words.

Had I been too quick to interpret his crude warnings as threats? Given the attack on Constance, it was understandable I'd been on my guard. But could I have misjudged him so badly? And perhaps he wasn't the only person I'd misread.

I struggled to find my voice. 'Nora told me your wife came with you today. Could I meet her?'

'Course you can.' Micky appeared surprised but pleased. 'She's waiting for me by the lake. She'd like to get to know someone from around here.'

We left the canal towpath, and I showed him how he could reach Waldenmere via a shortcut through the woods. With an effort, I put aside the mistrust I'd formed from our previous encounters and tried to pretend I was meeting him for the first time.

He seemed delighted by his surroundings. The season was changing, and the lake was framed by autumn colours. Squirrels foraged in the undergrowth for acorns while blackbirds devoured rowan berries. By the time we found his wife at Heron Bay, I had to admit Nora had a point. Micky did possess a certain charm.

I couldn't deny it was his enthusiasm for a place I loved that helped dispel some of my animosity.

Polly Swann was a tiny woman with copper coloured hair and a pretty freckled face. Although she looked to be roughly half the size of her husband, it was clear she didn't take any nonsense from him. It was also clear that he doted on her.

She smiled up at Micky. 'I think this will do very well,' she said in a soft Irish accent.

I chatted with her as we walked around the lake, pleased that she shared her husband's excitement at the prospect of starting a new life in Walden. When we reached the railway station, I still hadn't posed the question that had been my reason for asking Micky to introduce me to her.

I dragged it out as long as possible, even following them onto the platform. But before Mrs Swann got into the carriage, I asked, 'On the day the sniper fired at Miss Timpson, Reverend Powell said he called on you?'

'That's right.' She glanced at Micky, who shrugged.

'What time did he leave you?'

'It would have been about one o'clock. I asked if he wanted to have some lunch with me and the children but he said he had to get to the factory in time for Miss Timpson's speech.'

'How long would it have taken him to get back to Deptford?'

'About half an hour on the tram.'

'You should leave well alone,' Micky said. 'And I'm not threatening you, I'm trying to keep you out of trouble.'

'I know,' I muttered.

I watched their train pull away, hoping the serenity of Waldenmere would offer the Swann family the same comfort and solace it had given me over the years.

These days, every walk I took by the lake conjured up emotions – joy, sorrow and occasionally anger. I'd learnt the hard way how quickly loved ones could be lost, and lives changed forever. I knew it was why I was sometimes impetuous. Why I'd taken off with George. Time was precious and not to be wasted. But I realised my impetuosity had also led me to make mistakes.

I strolled around Waldenmere, then left the lake path and headed into town. Instead of going back to the office, I rapped on Millicent's door. When she opened it, I found my eyes unexpectedly filling with tears.

'Iris.' Millicent put her finger to her lips and gestured for me to come in. I stood in the hallway while she crept into the book room where Ursula was dozing. Silently, she picked up the bottle of sherry by her great aunt's side and pointed to the kitchen.

Seated at the Nightingales' battered kitchen table, I breathed in the sweet scent of the chestnut brown liquid and took a sip. My mind cleared, and I knew how wilfully blind I'd been to what was staring me in the face. 'Do you still have the key to Lockkeeper's Cottage?'

Millicent nodded.

43

Torches lit a corner of the churchyard. Archie was in front of the grave, bible in hand. Luke stood to one side as his mother's coffin was lowered into the ground for the second time.

Archie said a few final words and stood back. Two men emerged from the shadows, picked up shovels embedded in a loose pile of earth and began to fill the grave.

I watched from behind one of the columns at the entrance to the church. Archie and Luke walked carefully along the wet flagstone path out of the churchyard and onto the road. I waited to see if Archie would go home with Luke, but they parted company. Luke began to amble, head down, back to his house.

Archie climbed the steps to the church with none of his usual vigour. When he reached the top, I stepped out from behind the column.

'Iris.' He jumped involuntarily. 'What are you doing here at this time of night?'

'I wanted to talk to you.'

'I'm always here for you.' He wrapped his arm around my shoulder, and we went inside. The church was lit by flickering candlelight. He sank into the nearest pew, taking me with him. 'I'm sorry. I'm exhausted.' He sat so close I could hear his low breathing.

'They've charged Dr Mathers with the murders of Rosie Robson and Blanche Denton,' I said softly, reluctant to disturb the serenity of this holy place with these miserable words.

I felt his breath on my face when he sighed. 'I'm angry with myself. I thought I was a decent judge of character, but he had me fooled.'

'He fooled most people.' I gazed up at his angular jaw. 'Like you do.'

He inclined his head, and our eyes met. He didn't say anything.

'You left that train ticket stub in the pot at the cottage for me to find, didn't you?'

'Why would I do that?' He kissed the top of my head.

I tried to inch away from him but his arm rested heavily across my shoulders. 'Because you like manipulating people. It's a game to you.'

As I'd stood by the canal, realising the truth of Micky Swann's words, everything else had fallen into place. The door of the second office conveniently left ajar with the typewriter on display. The hints about a confession. The sudden appearance of a train ticket in the cottage. Someone was playing games with me. It could only be one person, and there could only be one reason.

Archie's lips curled into that familiar smile. 'You like solving mysteries, and I'm helping you. I'm afraid I can't tell you where I found the ticket.'

'You found it in your own jacket pocket. You just wanted to make it seem like one of the men from Creek House had taken the train to Walden and shot at Mrs Siddons.' I was mesmerised by the glow of the candles and remembered the way Blanche had sat staring dreamily at the altar. There was something hypnotic about the stillness of the church that let you drift off to another place.

'Why would I do that? And why would I assume a nice girl like you would go snooping around someone else's possessions?' he replied with a hint of sarcasm.

'Micky Swann says he never goes to church. Neither do any of the other men at Creek House.'

'Don't they?' He made it sound as though this had never occurred to him.

'It's unlikely any of them told you anything in confession.' The aroma of incense and candle wax floated around, conjuring up visions of repentant sinners. But I knew none of the occupants of Creek House had been there to seek forgiveness.

'I never said they did. I don't hold formal confessionals.'

'You implied it. In the same way you implied they colluded with someone in Walden because you knew I was suspicious of Jack Osmond. You suspected they'd sent Constance that threatening letter, and you wanted to divert attention away from yourself onto them.'

'Why would I want to hurt Constance Timpson? Or Sybil Siddons, come to that.'

'You didn't want to hurt them. You wanted to scare them.'

'Why?'

'Because you're afraid.'

His hollow laugh echoed around the silent chamber. 'Afraid of what?'

'Change,' I said softly. 'Women being in control. You like to be the one in control, don't you?'

'I support what Miss Timpson and Mrs Siddons do, and I appreciate the financial support they provide.'

'Not *everything* they do,' I corrected.

'I admit, I think they're misguided in some ways. I told you, I believe women should give up their jobs when they marry. It's only fair.'

'No. It's not fair. Women have as much right to those jobs as men.'

I could feel the heat from his body and knew his temper was starting to simmer.

'Men who fought for their country, who faced death and watched their comrades die, now have to stand in a queue at the Labour Exchange. They were told they were fighting to make this a land fit for heroes.' He spat the words. 'Instead, they came home to find women had taken their jobs. They're not being treated like heroes. They're being treated like a burden on society. And that's because of the misguided notions of women like Constance Timpson and Sybil Siddons.'

'No one is disputing these men deserve better. But I'd have more respect for you if you voiced your true opinions rather than pretending to support them.' I wanted to provoke him. 'You're a liar.'

I felt his arm tighten around my shoulders. 'When I told you it wouldn't happen again, I meant it.' His voice was a low growl in my ear. 'I don't want to hear any more about it.'

'When I came here after Ben was shot, you asked if Percy and I had been arguing again. You knew we had because you'd seen us by the mausoleum. You'd been hiding nearby for some time, waiting for your moment.'

'You need more evidence than that to convict a man.'

'I spoke to Micky Swann's wife. You were supposed to be with her when Constance was attacked. She told me you left her at about one o'clock that afternoon. That gave you plenty of time to get back to the church and up to the tower for the start of the speech at two o'clock.'

He inclined his head to acknowledge this. 'That means the rifle was here in the church. You're suggesting that on the day of the party at Crookham Hall, I hopped on a train to Walden with a rifle over my shoulder, shot at Mrs Siddons and then hopped back on the train to Waterloo, still armed?'

'The train ticket wasn't all I found at the cottage.' I felt his body stiffen. 'You pointed me in the direction of it. I'm not sure you meant to.'

He ran his tongue over dry lips. 'In the direction of what?'

'You told me you could fit a rolled-up canvas of fifty inches across the back seat of Dr Mathers' car. Just the right size to conceal a Lee Enfield rifle I'd say.'

'Is that what you think I did?' He tried to sound unconcerned, but I detected a note of unease.

'Yes. You moved your rifle between here and the cottage by hiding it in a rolled-up painting canvas.'

'I do keep a rifle at the cottage,' he admitted, 'purely for shooting animals on the estate. It's kept hidden in the canvas out of harm's way.'

'Animals aren't the only things you've been shooting. If the police were to examine your rifle, I think they'd find it was the one fired at Constance and Mrs Siddons.'

'And do you plan to tell the police about this?' He reached up to stroke my hair.

'You fired twice at Mrs Siddons. You could have killed Ben.' I stated it as a fact knowing he probably wouldn't bother to deny it.

'I wouldn't have hit her. I just wanted her to dance to someone else's tune for a change. Ben shouldn't have got in the way. I'm an excellent marksman. If I'd wanted to kill, I'd have hit my target. You know I didn't intend to hurt anyone.' He moved nearer, bending his head so it was close to mine. 'Constance Timpson and Sybil Siddons have been denying jobs to men who've been shot at for their country. I wanted to show them what it felt like. *That's equality.*'

'No, it's not.' I turned to hiss into his face. 'Many women would have gladly joined up and fought for their country if they'd been allowed. Taking a pot-shot at them as they do their jobs is not the same thing.'

His head dropped. 'I don't deny it was irresponsible. And I'm sorry for everything I've done. Believe me, I've prayed for forgiveness.' He looked up and took my hand. 'Can you forgive me?'

I groaned. 'If only that were all there was to forgive.'

His grip on my hand tightened. 'What do you mean?'

'I have a feeling there's something you're more ashamed of than taking aim at innocent women. You say you shoot animals on the estate. Rabbits and pheasants?'

I felt him relax. 'I know Daniel's sensitive about animals. I don't shoot deer. But it doesn't hurt to keep the rabbit and pheasant population down. And it provides welcome food for families who can't afford to buy meat.'

'Poor families like the Robsons? Did you give rabbits and pheasants to Rosie Robson to take home?'

He shifted uncomfortably on the hard wooden pew. 'I knew the family weren't getting enough to eat.'

'The last thing they needed was another mouth to feed.'

He closed his eyes, realising the worst was yet to come.

I pulled my hand away from his. 'Rosie came to the cottage more than once, didn't she? She may have been looking for Luke, but she found you.'

44

Archie was silent.

'Did Rosie like it at the cottage? I know she used to wander along the canal to avoid going home. She wanted time away from her family. To escape from normal life just for a while. Did you become close?'

He removed his arm from around my shoulders and cupped his head in his hands.

'Look at me,' I commanded.

Slowly he raised his eyes to meet mine. 'I am ashamed. But the silly girl pestered me. I usually sent her home with a brace of pheasants or a couple of rabbits. One day, she came, and we... It just happened.'

I gave a derisive laugh. 'Just happened? Like the way things keep happening between us?'

'Just like that,' he sneered. 'Rosie was keen. She was the one who instigated it, not me. I thought she was older than she was. She certainly looked it when she was dressed in that silly costume at the carnival.'

'So it was Rosie's fault?' My voice dripped with scorn.

'I'm not saying that. All I'm saying is that I didn't force myself on her. We both wanted it. It didn't seem wrong at the time.' He stared down into the black folds of his gown. 'Don't look at me like that. Yes, of course, it was wrong. I swear it only happened once, and I never expected it to end so badly.'

'Did you know she was pregnant?'

He shook his head. 'She never told me. I saw her getting off that charabanc and had no idea. But she was the one who made me pick up my rifle.'

I drew back sharply to look at him. 'What do you mean? You're blaming Rosie for the shootings now?' I couldn't hide my incredulity.

'She smiled at me. A silly complicit smile. It made me angry.' His expression became hard. 'I admit I was weak, but do you know who's to blame? Women like Constance Timpson and Sybil Siddons, who encourage young girls to think they can have it all. That they can take men's jobs and behave like men.' His jaw clenched. 'The truth is, they can't, and whether you like it or not, there will always be repercussions for girls like Rosie Robson if they engage in that sort of behaviour. They entice men to act in ways they know they shouldn't.' He moved his head, so his face was directly in front of mine. 'You know exactly what I mean.'

I lifted my hand and slapped him hard across his cheek. His eyes were wild, and I waited for the retaliatory blow. It didn't come.

It was my turn to glare into his face. 'I can see why you think I'm fair game. You found out about me running off with a man. But Rosie? A sixteen-year-old from a poor family who just wanted to escape from an overcrowded home and a mundane job? What are you? Thirty-eight years old and a man of the cloth. Luke is only twenty-three, and he had the decency to know that Rosie was too young and too vulnerable to take advantage of.'

'I told you. I am ashamed,' he muttered. 'It was a moment of madness.'

'Instead of taking responsibility, you got your rifle and went up to the tower and shot at Constance Timpson. Was that another moment of madness?'

'I'm trying to make you understand. I admire much of what Constance Timpson does. That doesn't mean she has the right to make a desperate situation worse.'

'Do you have the right to fire a rifle at someone because you disagree with their politics?'

'I'm trying to restore some of the natural order we lost during the war. Constance Timpson and Sybil Siddons are too radical. Too disruptive. Daniel Timpson should be running those factories. It's God's will that women carry babies, which means their place is in the home. I do God's work.'

'No. You think you are God. I remember you telling me your mother and sisters doted on you when you were growing up. Did you believe them when they told you how wonderful you were? Because they were wrong.'

He gave a short laugh. 'You're probably right. I was arrogant when I was young. Maybe you are too. Maybe when you're older, you'll settle down and marry a nice man like Percy, become a dutiful wife and have lots of bonny babies.'

'Or maybe one day I'll be writing about the first female prime minister, the first female police detective, the first female high court judge. Maybe even the first female priest?'

He shook his head. 'That will never happen.'

'How do you know? The world's changing, and your so-called natural order has already been lost.'

'Not yet, it hasn't.' He bowed his head. 'But I know I need to change. And with your help I can.'

'Why would I help you?'

'Because I'll never do anything like it again. I've already promised you that.' He raised his head and looked towards the altar, closing his eyes as if in prayer. 'Are you going to tell the police?'

'Yes.'

His eyes snapped open, and his hand clasped my arm. 'I'd rather you didn't.'

'Are you going to stop me?'

He released his hold. 'I won't hurt you. You know that. I don't hurt people.'

I sank back into the pew. 'You hurt Ben. And you certainly hurt Rosie Robson. She was already a vulnerable young woman, and you made her situation worse. Rosie's pregnancy led to her murder. You set those events in motion. And in the chaos after the shooting, she was left with no one to turn to except Mathers. You must bear some of the responsibility for her death.'

'I accept that.' He gazed at the altar. 'I repent, and with God's guiding hand, I'll make amends.' He suddenly turned and pulled me towards him. 'I need your help too.'

Without warning, he lowered his mouth to mine. My lips responded, and for a brief moment I gave in to the attraction I'd felt from the first moment of meeting Archie Powell. My desire for him had been ignited the instant I'd seen him talking to Ben on the steps of the church on that fateful afternoon. I hadn't known then that only hours before, he'd been crouched in the church tower, taking aim with his rifle. I no longer had that excuse.

I pulled away.

He ran his finger down my cheek. 'You're not going to tell the police, are you?'

'Why do you think that?' I whispered.

'Because of the connection between us.' He rested his forehead against mine. 'Maybe even the love?'

I laughed involuntarily, and he recoiled. 'I'm not in love with you. You'll be astonished to learn a woman can be physically attracted to a man and despise him at the same time. It's come as a surprise to me too.'

His expression was the same as when I'd slapped him. He replied with a confidence I knew he wasn't feeling. 'You're not planning to go running to your WPC friend again, are you?'

'No.' I was amused to see the relief on his face. I didn't want to play my hand too soon. Then I heard the doors of the church opening. 'I've already done that. I'm just hanging around so I can watch your arrest.'

Disbelief and fury flashed in his eyes. He gripped my wrist and stared at me, trying to guess if I was bluffing. I held his gaze. We both knew I'd played a dangerous game. And neither one of us was certain how it would end.

'Reverend Archibald Powell.' It was the voice of Detective Inspector Yates.

I let out a long breath. I hadn't been sure WPC Jones would have enough clout to persuade Yates to show up again.

Archie gave a slight smile and nodded at me, as if acknowledging defeat. He let go of my wrist and got to his feet.

'Detective Inspector Yates, could this wait until morning?' He adopted the manner of a humble parish priest. 'I've just conducted Blanche Denton's reburial, and there are still some matters I need to attend to.'

'I'm afraid those matters will have to wait.' Detective Inspector Yates' tone and expression were impassive. 'I think Miss Woodmore will have told you why we're here.'

'I hope you haven't been listening to her fanciful tales. I'm sure you're aware she loves to play detective. Perhaps you should recruit her?'

'Perhaps I should,' Yates replied flatly.

'However, I think you'll find there's no evidence against me.'

'A rifle has been found at Lockkeeper's Cottage on the Crookham estate. It was hidden in a rolled-up canvas that I believe belongs to you?'

'Those canvases are mine, yes.'

'We're going to be testing the rifle.'

'Testing it for what?'

'Our ballistics experts will check to see if it's the rifle used in the recent attacks on Miss Timpson and Mrs Siddons. We'll also check to see if there are any fingerprints on it. I'd like you to come with me.'

'Are you arresting me?' Archie smiled, spreading his hands in a gesture of openness. 'I'm a man of God. You can't seriously think I was involved in those attacks.'

'You're not above the law.' Detective Inspector Yates paced down the aisle, pausing to admire the Portland stone columns. 'But you're right. I'm not going to arrest you. I think that honour should go to my colleague.'

'Good evening, Reverend Powell.' PC Ben Gilbert stepped into the church, his footsteps echoing on the stone floor.

'Ben, I...' Archie faltered, his smile fading.

Ben moved towards him. 'I'm not going to arrest you here. You'll accompany me to Deptford police station where I'll interview you and take your fingerprints. An arrest may follow.'

'This way, sir.' Detective Inspector Yates gestured towards the doors.

'Very well.' Archie nodded, but he didn't move. Instead, he turned to scrutinise me, his eyes like granite and his expression unreadable.

I drew back as he lowered his head and kissed me softly on the lips. 'We have unfinished business,' he whispered. 'Until next time.'

45

'Do you think he'll hang?' I asked.

'Probably. I don't think they'll reprieve him. What he did will be seen as too great a betrayal of trust.' Elijah lit a cigarette and rocked back in his seat.

As much as I hated what Dr Mathers had done to Rosie Robson and Blanche Denton, the thought of the hangman's noose revolted me.

'What about Reverend Powell?' Using his formal title was a way of distancing myself from the intimacy we'd shared. I was still trying to untangle the mess of emotions I felt for Archie. 'What do you think will happen to him?'

'He'll probably plead guilty. His fingerprints are all over the rifle used in the sniper attacks. He'd be a fool to try to deny it.' Elijah blew out smoke. 'I have a hunch he won't get a long sentence. His lawyers will cite his commendations during the war and his years of service as a chaplain. He could have left the trenches, instead he chose to stay on the frontline. I've heard on the grapevine that his lawyers are trying to blame "these unfortunate incidents" on shellshock.'

By 'on the grapevine' I guessed he meant that Horace's contacts had been sniffing out information on the case. 'Aiming a rifle at a woman because you disagree with her is hardly an unfortunate incident.'

'His legal team will emphasise that neither Constance Timpson nor Mrs Siddons was hurt. And that he never meant to hit Ben. They'll try to persuade a jury his good deeds outweigh the bad.' Elijah contemplated me. 'He's not your average vicar, that's for sure.'

'He doesn't have shellshock. He knew exactly what he was doing.' I thought of his serene paintings. They weren't the work of a disturbed mind. They were the work of a man who had a clear vision of how he believed the world should be. And if something wasn't conforming to that, he took it into his own hands to change it. 'I don't think he regrets the shootings. He was sorry for his part in what happened to Rosie and for hurting Ben. But mainly, he was sorry for getting caught.'

'You got to know him quite well. I wish I'd had the opportunity to meet him.' Elijah stubbed out his cigarette. He knew better than to say any more. 'Time to get over to the town hall in Aldershot. The results are due in.'

* * *

Millicent and I laughed at the sight of Percy whirling Ursula around Mrs Siddons' drawing room. The rug was rolled up, and the gramophone was playing a jazz tune.

The Liberal Party had suffered heavy losses at the hands of the Labour Party, but Mrs Siddons had managed to keep her seat. The Conservatives won an overall majority.

Constance Timpson had secured sole ownership of Tolfree &

Timpson Biscuits after Tolfree and Osmond had been arrested for embezzlement. I'd been amused to learn that Redvers Tolfree's expensive solicitor was claiming his client had no knowledge of the scam, and that blame lay solely with Jack Osmond. It was possible Tolfree would walk free while Osmond served time for both of them.

These events had afforded *The Walden Herald* a number of exclusives, much to Horace's delight. I'd been kept busy writing up every story to Elijah's exacting standards. The paper had also found room for one of the anonymous cartoons for which it was becoming famous. Redvers Tolfree and Jack Osmond were pictured in the biscuit factory wearing aprons, where they were seen 'cooking the books' by taking money from the ladysfinger biscuits and hiding it in the fig rolls.

I was exhausted and glad to have an evening off to celebrate with the obligatory sherry. Millicent was on her third glass, and I could tell it had made her bolder. I waited for the inevitable question.

'How are you feeling? About Archie, I mean. You'd become close, hadn't you?'

'I managed to resist him,' I replied stiffly.

She gave me a knowing glance. 'But what would have happened if Daniel and I hadn't called at the cottage when we did?'

I felt my cheeks flush, and it wasn't the sherry. 'You knew?'

'You were both rather breathless. And I saw the paint fingerprints on your arm.'

I cringed. 'And you still suggested I become your lodger?'

She laughed. 'I knew you and Ursula would get on like a house on fire. She keeps telling me not to be so well behaved. She thinks I need someone to help me get into mischief.'

'I need someone to help me stay out of mischief.' I topped up my glass. 'And Percy's afraid I'll sully your impeccable reputation.'

She sipped her drink. 'I rather hope you might.'

'What about you and Daniel Timpson? Are you and he courting?' I felt I was entitled to pry as she'd asked me about Archie.

'Oh no, nothing like that.' It was her turn to blush. 'He's the owner of Crookham Hall, and I'm a schoolteacher.'

'I don't think that bothers him.'

'I have no desire to be mistress of a grand estate. I'd rather stay a schoolteacher.'

'Couldn't you do both?'

'No. The local authorities have made it clear I'd have to leave my profession if I were to marry.'

'It's absurd, isn't it?'

'It's the lot of most women. Although I'll do whatever I can to change it. In the meantime, if I can't marry, I might as well have some fun.' Her brow creased. 'Though perhaps not too much fun. There's the board of governors to consider.'

I shrugged. 'My reputation's beyond repair. I'm not even safe around a man of the cloth. I told myself it was just one kiss, and I wouldn't do it again.'

'And did you?'

I grinned. 'Only a few times.'

She gave a peal of laughter. 'He's the strangest vicar I've ever met. Not that he'll be a vicar for much longer. The church won't tolerate it.'

'That's what will hit him hardest, losing his vocation. He'll manage in prison. In fact, I'm sure he'll help other prisoners. When he comes out, I'm not sure what he'll do.'

'It's all over now. You never have to see him again.'

I remembered Archie's last words to me. *We have unfinished business.* I took a swig of sherry.

I had no desire to meet with Archie Powell again. But I knew he'd be true to his word. One day, he'd make sure our paths crossed.

ACKNOWLEDGMENTS

I'd like to thank the following people for their encouragement and support: my parents, Ken and Barbara Salter, with special thanks to Dad for acting as my historical research assistant. Jeanette Quay for walks and talks – and for taking on the job of videographer. Barbara Daniel for her friendship and advice. Thura Win for his unerring eye for detail as an early manuscript reader.

Thanks to the brilliant Boldwood team for being great at what they do, in particular, my lovely editor, Emily Yau.

As ever, I'm indebted to the numerous people, books, libraries, and museums that contributed to my knowledge of this period. The British Newspaper Archive and the Science Museum were especially helpful in the writing of this book. Also, special thanks to Roger Cansdale and the other historians of the Basingstoke Canal Society.

MORE FROM MICHELLE SALTER

We hope you enjoyed reading *The Body at Carnival Bridge*. If you did, please leave a review.

If you'd like to gift a copy, this book is also available as an ebook, hardback, large print, digital audio download and audiobook CD.

Sign up to Michelle Salter's mailing list for news, competitions and updates on future books.

https://bit.ly/MichelleSalterNews

Explore the rest of Michelle Salter's gripping Iris Woodmore series...

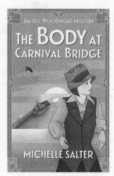

ABOUT THE AUTHOR

Michelle Salter writes historical cosy crime set in Hampshire, where she lives, and inspired by real-life events in 1920s Britain. Her Iris Woodmore series draws on an interest in the aftermath of the Great War and the suffragette movement.

Visit Michelle's Website:

https://www.michellesalter.com

Follow Michelle on social media:

twitter.com/MichelleASalter

facebook.com/MichelleSalterWriter

instagram.com/michellesalter_writer

bookbub.com/authors/michelle-salter

Poison
& Pens

POISON & PENS IS THE HOME OF
COZY MYSTERIES SO POUR YOURSELF
A CUP OF TEA & GET SLEUTHING!

DISCOVER PAGE—TURNING NOVELS FROM
YOUR FAVOURITE AUTHORS &
MEET NEW FRIENDS

Boldwood

Boldwood Books is an award-winning fiction publishing company seeking out the best stories from around the world.

Find out more at www.boldwoodbooks.com

Join our reader community for brilliant books, competitions and offers!

Follow us

@BoldwoodBooks

@BookandTonic

Sign up to our weekly deals newsletter

https://bit.ly/BoldwoodBNewsletter